EVOLUTION

AN ASHWATER NOVEL

MELISSA KOBERLEIN

Parker West Books

Parker West Books
www.parkerwestbooks.com

ISBN- 978-1-7344623-3-3
Parker West Books

Printed in the United States of America

November 2021

Evolution comes with a Spotify playlist!

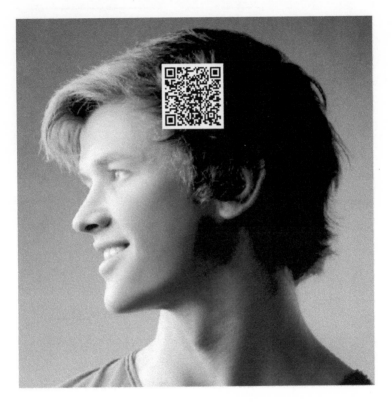

Adam's added some new songs for Evolution. If you'd like to listen to the Ashwater series soundtrack, simply scan the QR code with your device and enjoy the music Adam plays for you.

For Katrina, who is not only my biggest supporter, but a kind and wonderful friend. Your favorite worlds are coming together.

D r. G. drummed her fingers on her desk, her eyes cast out the window of her office at Arcadia Mental Facility. Her visitor was late.

Her desk phone beeped.

"Doctor, your visitor has arrived," her assistant said.

"Send him in." She stood and walked over to the window, crossing her arms.

A quaint town lay before her, fragile at the base of the imposing mountain range towering over it. Above, tall peaks pierced the cloud-filled, cerulean sky. She had many offices across the globe with beautiful views, but there was something about this one that warmed her soul. She chuckled. *If I had one.*

Hello, doctor, a male voice sounded in her head as the door to her office opened.

"You're late, and I'm a busy woman." She didn't turn from the window. Instead, she waited for him to join her.

"Nice view."

"Always has been. Let's cut to the chase. Who are you here for?"

"I've got my eye on someone." He pressed his hand on the glass. "What is it about this place that makes it so…"

"Ripe with options?" She turned to face him, arching a brow.

His expression was solemn, making her wonder if there was more to him than she'd seen in the past. "So strange."

Dr. G shrugged. That was Ashwater—strange and unusual. "You are only approved for one. The last time you took two, we had a hell of a time dealing with the aftermath. We don't want to be the new Roswell."

"Roswell was not my fault." He smirked, his pensive nature dissipating.

"Doesn't matter. Just be discreet please."

"Always." He turned to leave.

"Wait." She grasped his arm. "You never answered my question about who you're here for."

"You're right. I didn't." The boy grinned, his irises lighting up unnaturally.

She rolled her eyes and released him. *Always with the games.*

After he left, she looked back out at the mysterious town she was so fond of.

Good luck, whoever you are.

PART I

1

TEE TIME

Sloan

Sloan Simms paced in front of her house, waiting, the sun high in the sky. The weather was warming nicely for mid-April in the Rockies. A warm breeze swept her long, brown hair off her shoulders, floating in the air like tendrils of smoke. She glanced down at the grass and planted her hands, springing off her feet for a few cartwheels as her golden retriever, Buck, followed, barking with each liftoff.

She smacked off the damp grass that stuck to her hands and pursed her lips at Buck.

"I know, buddy. You don't like when I do that, do you?' She bent down and stroked his ears just the way he liked it. Buck was getting older, and she wasn't sure how much time she had left with him. Which reminded her...

Sloan looked up and down the street again. Her

letter from college should be here by now. Where was the mailman? Like, didn't he have a schedule?

An engine roared somewhere out of sight, quickening her pulse. On the horizon, a jeep swerved around a large pothole that only locals remembered. She sighed and stuck her hands in the back pockets of her jean shorts.

Luke.

He'd finally made enough working at his family's diner to buy a car. It was a rusty piece of shit, but it moved. It wasn't that she wasn't excited to see her best friend, but he wasn't delivering important news. The white jeep pulled up, top down, next to the mailbox. Luke was driving and his twin brother, Derrick, was in the passenger seat, his eyes unreadable. The boys were identical, but she could always tell them apart. Luke wore his dark hair short and had a lopsided grin that smattered of mischief while Derrick's wavy locks swept over his intelligent, thoughtful dark brown eyes. The Smiths played on their radio.

"'Sup, boys?" Sloan swayed her hips to the song, running a hand through her hair as Buck ran toward the jeep, wagging his tail. He loved Luke and Derrick like they were family. They basically were, given the amount of time she spent with them.

"Not much. What are you up to?" Luke leaned over the steering wheel to better see her.

Derrick gave Buck some love. "Good boy, Buck."

She walked over to the jeep and grabbed the frame behind Derrick, leaning across his lap to speak to Luke. "I love this song."

"You and Derrick both." Luke rolled his eyes.

She turned her head toward Derrick and walked her fingers up his arm. "You've got good taste."

He stiffened.

"Touchy?" She grinned up at him.

"No." He swiped at her hand, a smile creeping up on his lips as he looked away. His cheeks deepened a shade.

"What are you doing out here, anyway?" Luke asked.

Sloan stepped back. "Waiting for the mail. What are you guys up to?"

"We're going to check out the renovated disc golf course at Eden's Pass. Wanna come?"

Um, hell yeah. She smiled, her heartbeat quickening. They finally finished the course. It had been shut down since last year. "Let me get my bag."

She turned toward her house, Buck in tow, glancing at the mailbox. It could keep, right? If the letter came, it would be there when she got back. No sense waiting around. She exhaled and headed to her house to get her discs. A game of disc golf was exactly what she needed. Worrying about her future wasn't doing her or anyone else any good. Besides, Derrick and Luke were due for an ass-kicking.

EDEN'S PASS was set about halfway up the mountain peak that overlooked Ashwater. The park was a favorite spot for locals and tourists alike. It boasted a beautiful lake, camping, and of course, one of the best disc golf courses in Colorado. Luke pulled into a spot and turned off the engine. There were only a couple other cars in the parking lot. Good. That meant the new course opening wasn't common knowledge yet. They wouldn't have to wait in a long line. The trio walked to the first tee pad. They'd poured fresh concrete, leveling it, and there was a brand-new example basket with a sign mapping out the course.

Sloan smiled at the brothers. "Guys, this course is going to be badass."

"Yep." Luke reached into the bag strapped around his body and pulled out his driver disc. "A par four to start. I'll go first."

"Of course you will." She pursed her lips at him. She loved him to death, but he was such a freakin' diva. She glanced at Derrick, raising her eyebrows.

"You can go second." He shrugged, flicking his head to shift his hair away from his line of sight.

"Thank you." She glanced at Luke. "At least one of you has some manners."

Luke laughed and stepped up to throw. "Yeah, not me."

He released, and the disc soared through the air low, with pinpoint precision, avoiding the trees to the right. It settled in the grass about halfway between the tee and the grove where the basket was likely hidden.

Luke fist-pumped and stepped off the tee. "That's how it's done."

Sloan reached for her favorite driver and took his place on the pad. She eyed up her trajectory and let it fly.

A streak of yellow veered across the meadow, following the same path as Luke's. It landed ten yards past his. She raised her own fist in the air triumphantly. "Yes!"

"Whatever." Luke crossed his arms and rolled his eyes.

Derrick moved onto the pad. He stood there for a good amount of time, hands on his hips.

"Anytime now," Luke chided.

Derrick ignored him and reached for a disc from his bag. Instead of a backhand, he was going with a forehand throw.

Luke laughed after Derrick released. "What are you doing?"

Derrick's disc cut through the air and rose higher before making its descent.

Sloan smiled as his disc landed a foot past hers. "Well, well. Looks like I've got my work cut out for me today."

"It's all in the wrist." Derrick pursed his lips at Luke.

Luke shook his head and strode off toward his disc. Under his breath, he mocked, "It's all in the wrist."

Sloan joined Derrick to walk to their discs, bumping him with her shoulder. "Great shot."

"Thanks."

They were halfway through the course when they caught up to two boys playing ahead of them. They appeared to be about their age—one dark haired, the other light. Sloan didn't recognize them, but that wasn't all that uncommon, given the touristy nature of their town.

"Sorry to hold you up," the dark-haired boy called to them. He pointed to his friend. "He's still learning."

"I'm learning?" The other kid laughed. He took a few steps and launched his disc with power and sleek technique.

Sloan's lips parted in awe. Then she heard the tell-tale clinking of a disc hitting a basket.

"Holy shit. Did he just throw an ace?"

She arched a brow. The blond had talent, like, pro talent. And he had an accent. British or something.

"Sure sounded like it," Derrick said.

"Know them?" she asked, her eyes not leaving the pair by the tee pad.

"Nope," Luke said.

"Uh uh. Must be tourists," Derrick replied. "Should we go around?"

Sloan put one hand on her hip and ran the other through her hair. Go around and miss an opportunity to meet a pro? She arched an eyebrow and smiled. "We could join them."

"Are you, like, in heat?" Luke asked. Everyone at school assumed there was more to her relationship with Luke, but there wasn't. It was strictly platonic and always had been. But that never stopped them from making crude jokes and sexual innuendos toward each other. They were friends for a reason.

"Why? You offering?" she retorted. She was inter-ested in these new boys but not that way.

"In your dreams." Luke crossed his arms.

"Every night."

Luke laughed. "Are you sure we aren't related?"

"Yes." Derrick frowned, stealing a glance at her. "Can we go around now?"

The dark-haired boy at the tee waved them over.

"So what do you guys want to do?" she asked.

Derrick groaned. "Well, it would be rude not to say hello now."

They walked over to the next tee to meet the new boys.

The dark-haired boy smiled. "What's up? I'm Will, and this is Aiden. You guys go to Ashwater High?"

"Yeah," Luke said. "I'm Luke. That's my brother, Derrick, and that's Sloan."

Will nodded at her but turned his focus back to Luke. Aiden, on the other hand, was transfixed on her, his eyes almost too blue. Was he wearing colored contacts?

Her cheeks warmed. "That was some drive. You play pro?"

"Thanks, love. No, just for fun." He took a step toward her, his eyes sparkling with interest. "But I could teach you some things."

On instinct, she took a step back. While her interest in him landed above the waist, his was clearly below. The next thing she knew, Derrick had his arm around her waist.

She stiffened. *What the…*

He pulled her against his side and smiled knowingly at her. She exhaled. He was being protective. Luke had done this for her dozens of times but never

Derrick. She relaxed against him, thankful for his ruse.

"I think she's good," Derrick said.

Aiden backed up. "Oh, hey, sorry, mate. No offense."

"None taken." Derrick replied, running his fingers up and down her side.

Sloan inhaled sharply, her eyes widening. What was he doing? Luke never did this. She'd hugged Derrick plenty of times, but this was…intimate and pleasant.

Aiden glanced at Will. "You ready? I have an ace to claim."

"Yeah, sure." Will looked back at them. "Maybe I'll see you guys at school? I start next week."

Sloan's head swam with each caress of Derrick's fingertips as she tried to control the flips in her belly. *Oh my God. Luke was right. I am in heat.*

"What grade are you in?" Luke asked.

"I'm a junior. You guys?" Will said.

"Seniors."

"Cool. See ya later." Will and Aiden headed toward their basket.

The boys were out of sight, and Derrick's hand was still rubbing her side. He'd found a rhythm. She closed her eyes, leaning into him.

"What the hell are you two doing?" Luke asked.

The spell broke, and they jumped apart.

"Sorry," Derrick said, color rising on his cheeks.

"Oh, um, it's okay," her voice breathy. Her skin still

tingled from where his hand was on her waist. "Thanks for pretending."

"Any time." Derrick smiled.

Huh. There was something about the way he looked at her, something she'd never seen before, or maybe she'd never noticed. There was a magnetism between them now, and there was much more to Derrick than she thought. He wasn't just her best friend's shy, geeky brother. She wet her lips. He had a sexy side, and that guy's hand knew what it was doing.

Luke walked in between them, interrupting her thoughts. "Let's go."

2

DINER LIFE

Derrick

After dropping off Sloan, Derrick and Luke drove home. Derrick headed up to his room, thankful it was the one thing he didn't have to share with his brother. He quickly changed into his work clothes. He paused by his desk and reached into the front part of his backpack. He held what looked like a clear EpiPen up to the light. The late afternoon sun streamed in through his window. Vibrant green specks floated in a sea of deep red.

He sighed. Three weeks had passed since he'd fished Dr. Rice from the dumpster at the back of his family's diner. Her words still haunted him.

Tell no one.

She hadn't spoken another word to anyone and had been transferred to Arcadia Mental Facility, comatose. What was he supposed to do with the damn thing?

"Derrick, time for work," his dad yelled from downstairs.

"Coming!" He deposited the EpiPen back into his backpack and slung it over his shoulder. He took the steps two at a time and ran out to his dad's truck.

He alternated evening shifts with Luke now that basketball season was over. His dad pulled the truck out of the garage of their two-story house that sat between Main Street and the suburbs, where most of his friends lived. He always thought it was an odd place for a house, but it was close to the diner and school.

Derrick's dad rested his arm on the open window, tapping his hand to "Sunday Bloody Sunday" by U2 playing on the radio. "How was the new golf course?"

"It's really nice. They replaced all the baskets and tees."

"Enjoy it now, son. Next year, you'll be at MIT studying your butt off."

"Uh, yeah, I guess so." Derrick's heart clenched, and he swallowed hard.

The day he found out he got accepted into his dream college, he also learned he didn't get a scholarship. He left that detail out when he shared the news with his parents. They didn't have the money for him to go, and he didn't have the heart to tell them.

Instead, he'd been working on Plan B. Bio-Core offered internships for people who showed potential in bio-medicine or cybernetics. They accepted mostly college grads, but five years ago, a high school student got one. He applied a few weeks ago and had an interview coming up this week. He'd pitched his ideas to Adam, the smartest person he knew. Well, to be fair, he did have a CPU for a brain so smart didn't really cover what Adam could do. But it was a good sign that Adam was impressed with Derrick's ideas about cybernetics and said he had a real shot at landing one of the internships.

"Where'd you go just now?" His dad frowned.

"Nowhere. Why?"

His dad's mouth turned up in a knowing way. "Is it a girl?"

"Dad, no." His cheeks burned as his thoughts drifted to the dark-haired free spirit that had taken up residence in his temporal lobe.

"Why you and Luke don't have girlfriends is beyond me." He glanced in his rearview mirror at himself. "You're good-looking kids."

Derrick rolled his eyes and looked out the window. It didn't matter. Between a potentially dangerous vial of weird blood and figuring out what he was going to do next year, he didn't have time for girlfriend.

THEY PULLED into Dixon's Diner, the high-polish, stainless-steel exterior reflecting the rays of the waning sun. Derrick had worked here from the moment he could carry a fully loaded busboy tub. As much as he hated the hard work and hours, he'd miss the place once he moved on. His dad ambled around the side, to park in the back. The dumpster came into view, and a shiver ran down Derrick's spine. Memories of Dr. Rice still haunted him, and taking out the trash gave him the creeps.

Inside, the diner was filling up with regulars for dinner. Derrick was scheduled to wait tables with Celia Black. He grabbed an apron from the back and headed to his section. To his surprise, his first table was none other than Sloan and her family. He smiled as his stomach flipped, remembering how her smooth waist felt under his fingers a few hours earlier.

Knock it off.

"Golden Brown" by The Stranglers was playing on their table jukebox. Sloan's parents were quintessential hippies. Between owning a head shop on Main, their fashion sense, and their taste in music, they were straight out of a copy of *Rolling Stone* circa 1969.

"Hello, Mr. and Mrs. Simms." He grinned at Sloan. "Long time, no see."

"I"—Sloan's cheeks darkened—"got a hankering for a Dixon burger." She smiled up at him in that way she did, like no one else in the world existed but him. She had the cutest dimple on the one side.

His cheeks warmed.

"How many times have I asked you to call me Charlie?" Sloan's mom beamed at him. "Mrs. Simms is Owen's mother."

She nudged Owen, who finally glanced up from the menu and gave him the 'hang loose' gesture. "Oh, hey man. What are the specials?"

"Dad, you're rude." Sloan rolled her eyes and mouthed *sorry* to Derrick.

Derrick tried his best not to laugh. While Sloan

looked like her mom, she had her dad's attitude in spades. "I'll have to go check. I just got here. Can I take your drink order first?"

"Sure. I'll have a Coke," Owen said. "Charlie, you want one too?"

She nodded.

Derrick glanced at Sloan. "Do you want your usual?"

"Yes, please." She glanced down at the menu.

He felt the same pull toward her that he'd been feeling for a long time. He stared at her parted lips, his mind drifting to things other than drink orders.

Derrick cleared his throat and forced her from his mind. *Get their drinks, douche.*

"I'll be right back."

He headed behind the counter to make Sloan's vanilla malt.

Celia was there cleaning the counters and smirked up at him. "You've got it so bad for her."

"What are you talking about?" Derrick asked.

She nodded toward Sloan. "I have eyes, as does almost everyone else in this place."

Derrick ignored her and set to work getting drinks and finding out the specials. In the meantime, Adam and Evie came in the front door. They'd gotten together last year when Adam first came to town to hide his android-ness. They waved and took a seat at a booth in his section. Sloan got up and joined them. After delivering Cokes to Sloan's parents, he headed to his friends' table.

"What's up, guys?" Derrick asked.

"Not much," Adam replied.

Evie opened her mouth to reply, but the front door opening distracted her. "Hey, Dad. What's up?"

Sherriff Mac Grayson walked over to the table. He came in often, but the set in his jaw meant he wasn't here to eat. "Hey, kids. I hate to be the one to tell you this, but there was another overdose. This time it was a girl from Highmore."

"Oh no. Is she okay?" Evie asked.

"She's alive. I'm more concerned about what we found in her system. Forensics has never seen anything like it." Mac glanced at Derrick. "Can I have a word?"

He cleared his throat. Why did he want to speak to him? He didn't know anything about drugs. He swallowed hard as he remembered what he was hiding in his backpack. "Um, sure."

He glanced at his friends, who mirrored his worried expression.

"Outside for moment?" Mac asked.

"Let me just—" Derrick glanced back at the counter.

"I got it," Celia said, passing them on her way to a table.

"Thanks." Derrick crossed and uncrossed his arms. *Don't act nervous. It's fine.*

He followed Mac out to his truck. Mac turned and leaned against the side, crossing his arms. "I know you were asked by one of my deputies, but I'd feel better asking again. Did Dr. Rice say anything to you when you found her?"

His mouth was bone dry. Dr. Rice's last words had been haunting him ever since the incident. *Keep safe. Tell no one.*

He'd done as she'd asked, but the burden of the secret was getting to him. He thought about telling his brother and friends a million times, but something about the tone of her voice urged him not to. Besides, he'd told the trooper, who was the first to show up, that she was unconscious when he found her. If he told the truth now, wasn't that like a criminal offense or something?

"No, sir," he said.

"Are you certain?" Mac's eyes pinned him in place, making his heart whip up a few paces. Did the man ever blink?

"Yes." Derrick swallowed hard. He didn't enjoy lying.

Mac sighed, tilting his head up to the sky. "Damn. What were you up to?"

Derrick opened his mouth to reply, but Mac wasn't talking about him. He was talking about Dr. Rice, and it was starting to sound like she was somehow involved in the overdoses. Bio-Core did have some unusual pharmaceuticals. He had proof of that in his backpack.

"Has there been any change in her condition?" Derrick asked instead.

"No." Mac frowned, shaking his head. He grabbed the door handle. "I guess that's it. Stay safe."

"Uh, okay. I will." Derrick turned toward the diner, his mind racing.

In the window, Adam, Evie, and Sloan were pressed up against the glass. They'd be full of questions he didn't have answers for. He waved and did his best to smile. He hated the burden he was carrying around.

But his gut told him that the less they knew, the safer they were. Besides, no one knew he had the mysterious vial. Why change that now?

3

QUESTIONS

Sloan

I f there was one thing Sloan loved, it was Saturdays. There was something about waking up around eleven and knowing the rest of the day was hers to do what she pleased.

Too bad it was Monday.

She groaned and sauntered down the hallway of Ashwater High, doing her best to smile at everyone she passed as if she didn't have a care in the world. Inwardly, she was a ball of nervous energy. The source of her unease was burning a hole in the back pocket of her jeans.

"Looking good, Sloan," a girl from English class said, passing her.

"Thanks." She smiled, her eyes shifting to the girl's lips. They'd hooked up a couple months ago. What was her name? Sloan was openly bi and equally terrible with names.

But lips? Those she remembered.

Sloan reached her locker and swore under her breath, her anxiety returning. She pulled out the folded envelope from her pocket, her breath catching. She chucked it on the top shelf.

"Whatcha got there?" Luke asked behind her.

"Jesus." She jumped and shut her locker, reeling around to face him. He was always sneaking up on her at the most inopportune times. The folded-up letter was from Edgewood U—her only shot at getting into college. Luke had gotten his letter from CU a month ago, football scholarship and everything. Too bad she was too scared to open hers. "Nothing. What's up with you?"

Luke narrowed his eyes, glancing between her and her locker. "Okay, sketch."

She looked past him, her pulse quickening in anticipation. She could really use her savior again. "Where's Derrick?"

"He's doing some visit for an internship thing." He shrugged, his eyes wandering down the opposite end of the hall.

Sloan's shoulders sank, and she was glad Luke's attention was focused on some cheerleaders in uniform. Celia Black, their coach, was standing among them with a stack of flyers in her arm.

As if Celia could sense Luke's eyes on her, she glanced up and smiled. He waved.

"Why don't you just tell her you want to smash?" Sloan arched an eyebrow. Those two had been dancing around their attraction to each other for a while. Or at least Luke had.

"Hey, don't talk about her like that. Besides, she's out of my league." He frowned and stared down at his feet.

She couldn't tell if his sullenness was disappointment or sadness. Had he already told Celia, and she'd rejected him? "Come on, mopey, let's go to class."

Sloan hoisted her backpack on her shoulder and walked down the hall with him.

Mazy joined them on Sloan's other side and whispered, "Heard anything yet?"

Mazy was a classic bookworm, class president, and adorable as hell. Unfortunately, Mazy only had eyes for Gage Strickland. The two dated for a while but split up when it was apparent he didn't feel the same way about her. Mazy was also the person Sloan confided in about applying to college. She'd applied so late she didn't really think she had much of a chance to get in, but Mazy insisted otherwise. Always the optimist.

"Nope." She pulled out her phone as a distraction, wondering when she'd get the courage to open the letter.

Mazy smiled and bumped her shoulder into Sloan's. "You'll hear soon. I'm sure."

Walking toward them were Ashwater High's favorite couples, Adam and Evie and Gage and Iris. Sloan had known Gage most of her life and Evie for a couple years. Adam and Iris, on the other hand, were new to Ashwater. They were androids created at Bio-Core, the local bio-medical facility.

As if on cue, "Mony Mony" by Billy Idol started playing on Sloan's phone.

Adam, who'd played the song for her using his internal Bluetooth, grinned. Having an android as a friend had its benefits.

She swayed her hips to the music. "Nice one."

"Hey, guys," Evie said. "What's going on?"

"Not much." Sloan continued to dance. "Derrick's doing an internship thing, and Luke still wants in Celia's pants."

Everyone in the group chuckled except Iris, who slowly shook her head at Sloan.

What? It was the truth.

Luke shoved his hands in his pockets and stormed off.

What was all this broodiness about? She rarely hit a nerve with him. Well, unless he was on his man period. She stopped the music on her phone and called after him, "Hey Luke, you okay?"

Luke raised his middle finger in the air and kept walking.

Sloan's shoulders relaxed. "He's good."

THE REST of the school day played out like it usually did until last period. Sloan set her backpack down on a table in the cafeteria, which did double duty for lunch and study hall. Mr. Garcia was seated at the front with his laptop. He nodded at her. Garcia had a keen interest in Adam, or at least he used to when he was pulling double duty as a Bio-Core scientist and computer science teacher at Ashwater. Now he was supposedly only the latter. Sloan still couldn't believe he was walking around free after he'd threatened Evie's life last year to control Adam. Gage, who'd recently gotten to know Garcia better, swore that he'd changed. But Sloan would always be on guard.

"Is this seat taken?" someone asked from behind her.

She turned. It was the boy from the disc golf course, the non-British one.

"No, go for it," she said.

"Thanks, Sloan." He sat down and smiled knowingly. "It's Will."

"Right." Her cheeks warmed. She was truly terrible with names. "Disc golf." She reached into her backpack for her laptop. She had an essay to write for English and wanted to hang out with her friends at Jack's after school.

"So, have you lived here your whole life?" Will asked.

Sloan groaned inwardly. She had zero desire to chit chat with the new boy. "Yep. I'm one hundred percent townie."

"That's cool."

Was it? Last time she checked, being stuck in a small town in the middle of nowhere wasn't cool.

"I didn't see your boyfriend. Is he sick?"

Boyfriend? Sloan pursed her lips. "Who are you talking about?"

"Derrick, right?"

"Oh." Her mind drifted back to the golf course. Butterflies took flight in her stomach, and she tried her best to steel herself. Derrick didn't like her that way. His attention toward her was a façade, right? "Yeah, no, he's not my boyfriend. He's just protective. His brother, Luke, is my best friend."

"Oh, my bad. I just assumed you two were together."

I wish. Sloan frowned. She wanted to get work done.

He tapped a pencil on the table rhythmically. "So, then, is he sick?"

"No, he had some internship thing." She tilted her head at him. He had the darkest eyes she'd ever seen. They weren't brown—they were black. "Why the interest in Derrick?"

He looked down at the pencil and shrugged. "Just making conversation."

Oh, really? She'd always thought of herself as good at reading people, and her BS meter was off the charts. Well, two could play at that game. "He'll be back tomorrow." She arched a brow. "You can ask him out then. Now, if you don't mind, I've got work to do."

"Oh, I didn't mean..." The color in his cheeks darkened.

"No judgment. I agree—he's cute." Sloan glanced up and caught Mr. Garcia looking back at them. "You'd better get to work. Trust me, you don't want to be on his bad side."

Will chuckled and pulled out his own laptop. "I can handle myself."

"If you say so." She glanced at her desktop, a picture of the mountains she'd taken recently, her mind drifting back to Derrick.

Cute didn't even cut how she was feeling about him. Her breath caught as she remembered his fingers sliding up and down the curve at her side. Would he be at Jack's this afternoon? How long was this internship thing going to take?

She stared at her computer in a trance. Bye-bye, essay.

4

THE INTERVIEW

Derrick

D errick was having some really strange dreams. Most took place at Bio-Core and involved the syringe Dr. Rice gave him. His Aunt Daisy was super into dream interpretation. She'd say it was his subconscious trying to sort out what to do with the syringe combined with his uncertainty about the future. He glanced around the seating area on the top floor of Bio-Core, tugging on his necktie, his hands clammy.

There were three other people there—two guys and a girl. They were a bit older than him, probably college grads or close to it. They were dressed in suits that looked ten times more expensive than his hand-me-down from his dad.

He swallowed hard and tugged again at the snug neck of his stiff, white shirt.

The interim CEO was doing the interviews. Gage, whose family owned the company, warned him that the new head of Bio-Core lacked a sense of humor but was a brilliant scientist. Before serving on the board at Bio-Core, he'd worked for the FBI's science and technology branch. Very prestigious. He was unanimously named interim CEO by the infamous and somewhat anonymous board after Sam Strickland, Gage's grandfather, passed away. Even though it was Sam's wishes for Gage to take over the company, he was much too young and inexperienced.

Derrick cleared his throat and eyed the water cooler by the assistant's desk.

As if sensing him, she looked up. "Thirsty?"

He sat up. He was a little, but he didn't want to be a bother. "Um, no, I'm good."

She smiled and grabbed a paper cup and filled it with water. She walked over to him and handed him the cup. "I'm Dana," she whispered. "Gage told me you were coming in."

He took the cup and smiled. "Thanks."

"If you need anything, let me know." Dana glanced at the door to the office. "It shouldn't be much longer."

He glanced at the others. "But they've been here longer."

She leaned close, out of earshot. "They can wait."

Dana patted him on the shoulder and went back to her desk.

Apparently, Gage had put a good word in for him. That was just fine. He needed all the help he could get to land this job. He took a few sips and assessed his opposition once more. All three were focused on the binders in their laps, paging through their documents. He reached into his pocket for his flash drive, turning it over in his hand. His presentation was good, of that he was sure. But was it good enough to win the internship? That was the question.

The door to the main office opened, and a man with blond hair and piercing blue eyes looked over at Dana. "I'm ready."

The other applicants sat up expectantly. Dana smiled at Derrick. "Mr. Dixon, you're first."

The others frowned, and one of the guys made a snorting sound. Derrick took a deep breath and stood. This was it.

The man held the door for him to enter and extended his hand. "Maxwell Roberts. Please call me Max."

Derrick gripped his hand firmly. "Derrick Dixon, sir."

Max's office was bright with floor-to-ceiling windows. His lips parted. Blue sky dotted with fluffy clouds framed surrounding mountains. As they moved toward the window, the town of Ashwater came into view. Derrick could see Main Street, his parents' diner, even Jack's Arcade. He smiled. From up here, Ashwater looked like one of those miniature towns his mom put out at Christmas. This was some office.

"You have an amazing view," Derrick said.

"Sure is," Max said from a distance behind him.

Derrick turned, his cheeks warming. Max was already seated, indicating a chair in front of his large desk. *Why are you staring out the window like some idiot? Get your head in the game. This is your only chance.*

"Oh, right. Sorry." Derrick bolted over to the chair and sat. "Thank you for seeing me."

"Well, I know there are more applicants waiting, so let's get to it." Max steepled his hands, resting his elbows on his desk. "Why do you want this internship? You're very young. You haven't even been to college yet."

There it was. The question he knew he'd be asked. He'd prepared for all sorts of questions, but this was the one he was most unsure about how to answer. Should he go with the truth or lie? It would be a gamble either way.

He cleared his throat. "Sir, I'm going to be completely honest with you. I did get into college. MIT, in fact. But I didn't get a scholarship, and my family can't afford to send me there. If I told them, they would either mortgage our house or sell our family business. I couldn't bear for them to do either, so I devised a plan B."

"My motivation to go to college is similar to what you are offering for the internship. You see, sir, what I really want to do is develop tech in cybernetics. That's a large part of what you do here. If I were to get the internship, I'd be getting hands-on experience right from the start, working with some of the greatest scientists in the industry." He leaned forward, excitement welling up in his chest. "So, what started as a secondary plan, in all actuality, is really better than my original plan."

Max tilted his head, his piercing blue eyes assessing. "I appreciate your honesty. I also admire your ability to think outside the box. You're a problem solver. That's something very rare for someone your age. Good for you." He leaned back. "Well, then, that leads me to my only other question."

Before Max could ask, Derrick, gaining confidence, interjected, "Why me?"

Max smiled and nodded.

Derrick reached for his flash drive in his pocket and held it up. "May I?"

"Of course." Max pointed to a console behind him.

Derrick had familiarized himself with the Bio-Core system in preparation for his interview, thanks to Gage and Adam. He inserted his flash drive and loaded his presentation with his research proposal. A holographic computer screen hovered over Max's desk.

He turned to face Max. This was it—what Derrick said over the next fifteen minutes would either make or break his future. He exhaled and dove into the deep end of cybernetic research and the theoretical possibilities of the future.

DERRICK CLICKED TO A BLACK SCREEN, signaling the end of his presentation. His heart pounded as adrenaline rushed through his veins.

He'd nailed it.

But Max only nodded slowly, unreadable, stoic

even. Was he impressed? Bored? Annoyed that he'd taken up too much of his time? Hungry for lunch?

Derrick exhaled and sat back down in the seat across from the man that would decide his future. Flashes of waiting tables at Dixon's passed through his mind. He groaned inwardly. *Please say yes...*

Max leaned forward, his eyes focused on Derrick's. "It's ambitious and innovative. Possibly a game changer. How old are you, again?"

"I've just turned eighteen, sir."

"Sorry, it's just so astonishing to hear this kind of proposal from someone so young."

"With all due respect, sir, I may be the youngest applicant, but I'm highly motivated and won't let you down."

"Well, I'll say this—you've got lots of potential." He stood and walked over to Derrick, patting him on the shoulder. "Thanks for coming in. This has been an enlightening experience."

That was it? A pat on the back and an "enlightening experience"?

Derrick opened his mouth to reply but couldn't find the words. Had he screwed up? Did he say something wrong? All he could manage was, "Uh, thanks for the opportunity."

"You bet." Max smiled and opened the door.

As Derrick left the office, his face fell. What the hell just happened? *Did I move too fast through my ideas? Too slow? Were my images not clear?* His limbs moved as if in slow motion. He glanced at the other candidates still in the waiting room. One of the guys and the girl smirked, sensing by Derrick's expression that their chances had increased. The other boy frowned and shrugged at him in sympathy.

Derrick did his best to smile back as reality settled in. He'd failed. He wasn't getting the internship.

He headed toward the elevator as a phone rang behind him. He pressed the button for down as Dana called the next interviewee. His heart sank even further. He stepped inside the elevator and turned.

Dana waved at him with a smile.

Derrick waved back as the doors closed on his future. An ache formed in his heart as his world crashed down around him. What was he going to do now? He couldn't wait tables for the rest of his life. Maybe he could still get into Edgewood? That would be much cheaper than MIT. His mind whirled around his bleak prospects as his lunch threatened to come back to haunt him. *Hold it together. Get out of here before you lose it.*

He took a ragged breath as the doors to the elevator opened into the beautiful atrium at the ground floor of Bio-Core. A massive fountain erupted at the center, the sight both beautiful and painful. This would likely be the last time he was here.

Bile rose at the back of his throat. Time to go. He headed toward the doors, hoping he made outside in time.

"Mr. Dixon!" someone yelled from behind him.

Derrick turned. A woman with short, black hair strode over to him.

"Sorry. Dana called me," she said. "Max has asked

if you would be willing to start your internship early next week."

Derrick swallowed hard, forcing his lunch back down. He studied her face, her words not quite sinking in. "I'm sorry. I don't understand."

The woman smiled and reached for his hand. "The internship? Congrats. It's an honor to be selected out of high school."

"But—" He stared at her hand, still trying to wrap his head around what she was trying to tell him.

"I know. Max takes some getting used to. He's uber hard to read. I'm Payton, by the way."

"Wait." His heart skipped a beat. Suddenly his mind returned, sharp as a tack. Was this Payton Glass? She'd received her PhD when she was twenty. "As in Payton Glass? The only high school student to get an internship at Bio-Core?"

"The one and only. Well, I guess not *only* anymore." She smiled wryly, glancing at her extended hand. "Are you going to leave me hanging?"

"Oh." He shook her hand slowly as her words registered in his brain. "I got it. I got the internship."

"You did."

Derrick howled in victory like Luke always did when he scored a touchdown. His voice was so loud it shadowed the roaring waterfall behind them. Payton laughed as everyone in the lobby stopped what they were doing to stare at him.

He shook Payton's hand a few extra times for good measure. This was everything he'd ever hoped for and more. "You have no idea how excited I am. Thank you. Thank you so much."

"I think I do." She glanced around at the bystanders.

"Sorry about that." He grinned.

"No problem." She smiled and pulled her hand from his. "Well, back to work. Dana will be in touch."

"Great. I can't wait to start."

Derrick turned and strode out of the building, his heart racing, adrenaline coursing through his veins. He'd done it. Once outside, he fist-pumped and hollered into the warm air a few more times, not caring who was around or how deranged he might look.

His future was looking up.

5

GOOD NEWS

Sloan

Sloan swiveled on her stool at the snack bar at Jack's. She picked at the soft pretzel in front of her. Evie, sitting next to her, had her sketchbook out, drawing Adam, Gage, and Luke as they played video games side by side. Mazy and Iris were on her other side, deep in conversation with Daisy about her newest hair color choice—sapphire blue.

Sloan twisted and looked toward the front of Jack's, drawing her bottom lip into her mouth. She wondered about Derrick's internship thingy. How was he going to fit that in with college?

The front door opened, and Sloan's heart leaped and then dropped. Boo. It wasn't Derrick. It was the annoying new kid, Will. He smiled and waved at her.

She nodded and spun back around to frown at the hotdog roller. "The new kid's weird."

Evie glanced his way and back to her subjects. "I

don't know. He seems nice."

"I guess." Sloan popped another bite of pretzel in her mouth and checked her phone. Four-thirty. She hated to admit it to herself, but she was getting down-right grumpy waiting around for Derrick. She didn't even know if he was coming here, so what was the point?

Will was talking to Jack. She spied him leaning over the counter familiarly, like he owned the place. Before she could give it any more thought, the front door swung open again.

This time it was Derrick. Her breath caught. He was wearing a suit, and he was beaming.

Their eyes met, and he grinned even wider, sending butterflies to flight in her stomach.

She hopped off the stool and met him halfway, mirroring his smile. "Someone's in a good mood."

The next thing she knew, he pulled her to him and swung her around. "Yes. I just got the best news."

"Whoa." She held on tight, laughing, his enthusiasm infectious.

He set her back down, his cheeks reddening. "Sorry, I shouldn't have grabbed you like that. I'm just so stoked."

"No worries." She arched her eyebrow, her cheeks warm. Ever since she got a taste for his touch, she welcomed it. "So what's so exciting?"

"I got an internship at Bio-Core."

"I'm sorry, did you just say you got an internship at Crazy-Core?" When? How did this come about?

Derrick shook his head. "Don't call it that. It's a

state-of-the-art facility, you know?"

"With killer androids." Sloan raised her eyebrows and pursed her lips. She wasn't wrong.

"Sloan, be happy for me?" His lips turned down into the cutest pout.

She cracked a smile. "Fine, fine. Congrats. When is it, and how does it fit in with MIT in the fall?"

"I'm not going to MIT. I'm going to be working at Bio-Core instead."

"Oh. Wow. So you'll be staying in Ashwater." She twirled a lock of her hair around her finger as the news sank in.

He was staying, and so was she. A smile crept up on her lips. *Yes.*

"Mom and Dad are not going to be happy to hear that," Luke said, joining them with the rest of their friends.

Gage shook his hand. "Nice going."

Adam added, "I knew you'd get it."

"You two knew about this? That he wasn't going to MIT?" Luke asked.

"Well, yeah. It's going to be my company someday. I have an in," Gage said.

"Oh, right." Luke frowned, his eyes cast down at his Vans.

Adam raised his hands innocently. "I only helped prep for the interview."

Sloan knew Luke's frown. She'd seen it before. He hated when Derrick kept stuff from him. Like making plans without him and lying about his test scores. Derrick was a better test taker than Luke, plain and simple. Luke didn't even really have a problem with it, so why lie?

She side-eyed Derrick. *What other secrets are you keeping?*

"I'm sorry I didn't tell you," Derrick said to Luke. "I wasn't sure it was going to work out, and I didn't want Mom and Dad to worry."

"I just don't get it. I thought you wanted to go to college," Luke said.

"I didn't get a scholarship." Derrick sighed. "Mom and Dad don't have the money to send me."

Ah, that made sense. That was one of the reasons Sloan picked a local college. It was cheap.

She pursed her lips. *Open the damn letter.*

Something in the pit of her stomach twisted. What if she didn't get in? She squashed the thought. Now wasn't the time.

Sloan looped her arm around Luke's. "It's no big deal. It all worked out, right? You're going to your big shot school for football, and he's going to be geeking it out at the android plant."

Evie and Mazy frowned at her.

She glanced at Iris and Adam, who both wore scowls. Jesus. Everyone was so touchy. "Sorry. No offense."

Iris narrowed her eyes. "Offense was already taken, but I accept your apology."

Sloan did her best to smile. *Note to self—don't piss off Iris.* They'd gotten closer since Iris started acting more human, but there still times the android scared the shit out of her.

"Who wants to play some DP?" Adam asked, a smile returning.

"What's that?" Will asked, joining them.

Sloan groaned inwardly.

"It's a competitive dance game in the back," Gage said. "We're going to play. You in?"

Will smiled. "Sure. I love games."

Sloan narrowed her eyes. *Oh, I bet you do.* Why did Gage always have to be a freaking gentleman? Like, now they had an uneven number, which meant no co-op. She glanced at Derrick and pouted.

The group headed to the back of the arcade. Will edged Sloan out and fell in line with Derrick. She glared at the back of his head. *Jerk.*

"How's it going?" Will asked Derrick.

"Great. I just landed the coolest internship," Derrick replied.

"Oh yeah? Where at?"

"Bio-Core. I'll be starting soon."

"Are the rumors true?" Will asked. "I've heard some shady stuff about that place."

"Nah. Don't believe everything you hear." Derrick glanced at Sloan and winked. "Especially in Ashwater."

Her stomach fluttered. *Wink away, sexy pants.*

"Noted," Will replied. "So what will you be doing there?"

"Well, Bio-Core is doing some really cutting-edge stuff," Derrick said. "I'll be working on some cyber-netic research."

"I'm not going to pretend I know the first thing

about what you're talking about, but it sounds cool," Will said.

Sloan chuckled. *You and me both.*

"So does that mean you're sticking around here instead of going to college?" Will asked.

"Yep," Derrick said.

Sloan smiled, balled her hands into fists, and fought the urge to jump up and down. Unlike Luke, she was ecstatic Derrick was staying in town. Regardless of whether she got into Edgewood, she'd be staying local too, and that meant she and Derrick could spend lots of time together. Her mind drifted to all the things she wanted to do alone with him.

Will glanced at Sloan as if sensing her thoughts. "Cool."

Her cheeks flushed, and she stared down at the floor. *Knock it off, perv.*

Derrick

Sloan picked "Rock the Casbah" by The Clash. He made sure to find a spot next to her in the back row. Too bad co-op was out. Her hair was down, and it fanned out in a cascade of silk as she danced. Every time she turned, he caught her scent—something tropical and coconut. She smiled up at him, and his heart clenched.

Celia was right. He had it bad for Sloan, and it had been that way for a long time.

Will was on his other side and holding his own for

his first time playing. For the most part, he liked Will. He seemed cool.

After they finished their last moves, the screen lit up with their scores. As usual, Adam was in first place. Iris, second, Luke third, he'd come in fourth, and Gage fifth. Sloan and Mazy followed, and Will had beaten Evie, who came in last. Poor girl. DP just wasn't her game.

"That was really fun." Will looked at the screen. "But it looks like I need some practice."

"I'll play with you any time you want," Adam said.

"I bet." Will laughed and pointed at the screen. "Nice score. Do you ever lose?"

"Not really." Evie nestled against Adam's side. "It's his game."

"You mean you created this?" Will's eyes widened.

Adam and Evie exchanged glances before Adam replied, "I had some help from Derrick with the programming."

Derrick nodded. Other than their tightly knit group of friends, only Daisy and Jack knew what Adam and Iris were, and for the time being, they wanted to keep it that way. "Yeah, hopefully we can add some new songs? Maybe some nineties?"

Adam shrugged. "I've been working on Jack. We'll see."

"The owner?" Will asked.

"Yeah," Evie said. "He only allows eighties' songs in the arcade."

"I totally get it. The eighties were awesome." Will

nodded knowingly, as if he had a special relationship with that decade.

The group fell silent.

Will glanced around and rubbed his forearm. "The music, I mean."

Okay, that was weird.

Luke clapped Derrick on the back, breaking the awkward silence. "All right, I'm heading over to the diner for my shift." He glanced at Sloan. "Do you need a ride?"

"Um, yeah," she said.

"'Kay." Luke tossed Derrick his keys. "Take her home."

"Sure." Derrick's eyes met Sloan's, and his stomach fluttered at the prospect of being alone with her.

Sloan smiled. "Cool. I'll get my bag."

After she walked away, Will started talking to him, but Derrick wasn't listening. He was too busy watching her say goodbye to the other girls. She had the warmest eyes and inviting smile. She could have anyone she wanted in Ashwater. He was sure of that. He didn't stand a chance with her.

He sighed with longing. He was a straight-up geek, and she was cool, athletic, beautiful, sexy, and so out of his league.

"Okay?" Will asked.

"Sorry." Derrick shook his head, his eyes never leaving Sloan. "What?"

Will chuckled and tapped Derrick on the chest with the back of his hand. "Never mind."

6

RIDE HOME

Sloan

S loan leaned back, allowing the spring air to sweep up her hair as they headed toward her house. "Drive" by The Cars played softly on the radio. She loved Luke's jeep, even if it was a rusting piece of shit that had definite plans to leave him stranded at some point. With any luck, she wouldn't be with him. But for now, she was perfectly happy to be there.

She glanced over at Derrick. She'd never seen him wear a suit before. He wore it well. His dark hair rustled in the open air. Her fingers itched to run her hand through his thick locks.

"What?" he asked, looking between her and the road.

"You look sexy in that suit," she teased.

"Stop." His cheeks reddened.

She stretched her arms, closing her eyes, tilting her

head toward the darkening evening sky. "You're so uptight."

"Compared to you, I guess."

"Truth." Sloan glanced out at the trees passing by. She didn't have a favorite season, but spring in Colorado was beautiful. Everything looked so plush and green. Her mind drifted to something that had been bothering her all day. "What do you think about the new kid?"

Derrick shrugged. "Seems cool. Why?"

"I don't know. He was asking me about you at school. Kinda gave me the creeps."

"Me?" He glanced at her, eyebrows raised.

"Yeah. It was super weird. He asked if you were my boyfriend." As soon as the words left her mouth, she regretted them and laughed to cover up her nervousness. *Be more obvious, why don't you?*

"Your boyfriend? Why would he... Oh. The golf course."

"Yep. The golf course." Sloan rubbed her hands up and down her thighs, trying to cool her jets as memories of his hands on her side surfaced again for like the millionth time.

"Sorry, again, if that made you uncomfortable."

Uncomfortable? That was one way of putting it. She shifted in her seat. Time to change the subject. "So, you're staying here next year. That's a big change."

"Yeah, and based on Luke's reaction, my parents aren't going to be too happy about it." He gripped the steering wheel, his knuckles whitening. She could only imagine how that conversation would go. Luke and

Derrick's parents always seemed pretty cool, but they were dead set on both their kids going to college because they didn't.

"Well, I'm happy about it." Sloan smiled at him. "I was already losing Luke. Now I get to keep you."

"I'm glad too." He smiled back, his eyes lingering on hers for an extra beat.

Her stomach did a few flips. His smile was different from Luke's. Luke had a broad, lighthearted smile. Derrick's turned up on one side with an air of mischief. Oh, the trouble she'd like to get into with him.

"So, what are you doing next year?" he asked. "You haven't said anything."

Sloan sighed. There went her blissful mood. "I don't know."

"Oh, well, that's okay."

"Is it, though?" She turned toward him.

The last thing she felt like was okay. She was overwhelmed about her future. No, that wasn't true. She was stone-cold terrified. What if she didn't get into Edgewood? What then? Work at her family's headshop for the rest of her life? She couldn't do that. She just couldn't. Everyone thought she had the coolest parents and the headshop was so awesome.

Well, it wasn't what she wanted to do for the rest of her life. The butterflies in her stomach turned into daggers, poking at her insides.

A lump formed at the back of her throat. *Don't you dare cry.*

She could feel his eyes on her as she fought back the tears welling up in her eyes.

He slowed down and pulled off to the side of the road. He put the car in park and turned to face her. "What's going on? Are you okay?"

"It's nothing." She shifted in her seat, not sure what to do with her hands. She felt like she could jump out of her skin. She didn't want to talk about this with him. All he'd do is pity her—no one thought she was college material.

"Hey…" He reached for her shoulder.

Before he could finish, she put her hand on his knee and made her way up his thigh.

"Whoa, what are you doing?" He pushed her hand away.

Her cheeks burned. *Oh God.*

Derrick wasn't some piece of ass to help her forget her troubles. He was her friend, and she knew his name, for God's sake.

"I'm sorry," she said. "Just forget it. Can you take me home?"

"You're avoiding."

Sloan stared down at her lap. She hated that he knew that. She hated that he rejected her. She especially hated how that letter was holding her life in check. She inhaled sharply and let the truth fly. "I applied to Edgewood."

He parted his lips in surprise.

She narrowed her eyes at him. Why was it such a surprise that she wanted to go to college? Sure, she was no Mazy, but she had decent grades.

"Sorry, I just thought you were going to say something else." He smiled. "That's great news."

She slouched down in her seat and frowned. *Yeah, great news.*

"Um, it's not good news?" he asked.

"I don't know what it is."

"Wait, I'm so confused. Why are you unhappy?"

"Because I don't know if I got in or not."

"Oh." Derrick ran his hands over the steering wheel and shrugged. "A letter will probably come soon."

"It already did." She picked at one of her cuticles.

"And?"

She let out a loud sigh, rubbing a torn piece of skin at the corner of her nail. "I haven't opened it."

"Where's the letter?" His eyes were on her, almost as if he could read her thoughts. She was scared, and he knew it.

"In my locker at school."

"Hey." He squeezed her hand and waited for her to look up at him. "It's only a letter. You'll get around to it when you're ready."

Sloan looked down at his hand on hers. It was warm and reassuring. She glanced up—there was no judgment in his eyes. She exhaled slowly. "Thanks, Derrick."

He gave her hand one last squeeze and started the jeep. Before he pulled back onto the road, he arched an eyebrow and glanced down at his thigh where her hand tried to set up shop. "For future reference, I'm not that easy."

She laughed, as the tension in her body released. "Noted."

Under his breath, he added, "You're still hot though."

Sloan sucked in her bottom lip, fighting a grin, as her stomach did some gymnastics. She did an internal fist pump instead. All was not lost—he thought she was hot.

Derrick

Derrick watched Sloan walk up her steps, his thoughts drifting to her hand on his thigh. He gritted his teeth. *You stupid loser. The girl of your dreams just fell into your lap, almost literally, and you pushed her away.*

Wasn't that exactly what he'd been hoping for? He sighed as the truth returned to slap his sex-on-the-brain head back to reality. She wasn't really interested in him that way. She was just avoiding a difficult conversation—her defense mechanism. He'd seen her do it tons of times. He'd just never been on the receiving end.

He put the car into first and headed home.

His thoughts drifted to the rest of his day, and his chest lightened. He couldn't wait to start his internship at Bio-Core. The equipment, software, and labs were the stuff MIT grads dreamed about. Also, once he got security clearance, he might be able to figure out what was in that vial Dr. Rice gave him or, at the very least, find out where she got it from. Payton worked in environmental medicine. Maybe she could help?

Derrick pulled up to the stoplight in the middle of town. Iris was sitting on a bench, her arms crossed. He rolled down his window. "Hey Iris, you need a ride?"

She glanced up at him and frowned. "In that piece of shit? No thanks."

His jaw dropped. She could be rude sometimes, but sarcasm? That wasn't really her thing. Besides, she had a vendetta against outdated fashion, not cars.

"Are you okay?" he asked. "Did something happen with Gage?"

"I'm great." She smiled sweetly, which was as much out of character as were her rude words.

"Okay, uh, see you later, I guess?"

She waved without looking up, like he was a pest.

Fine, whatever. He put up the window and stepped on the gas. Was she glitching again? She did have an incident with peanut butter pie not long ago. He'd say something to Gage about it later.

When he pulled into his driveway, all thoughts of Iris left him. He sighed, staring at the light shining through the window from their living room.

It was time to share his good news. Luckily, he only had to tell one of his parents.

When he opened the door, his mom was talking to someone. Mr. Garcia. Derrick exhaled and set his backpack down, shutting the door a little harder than normal. Why was he here?

"Derrick? Is that you?" she asked from the other room.

"Yeah. It's me."

He headed into the living room. Mr. Garcia was making himself comfortable in his dad's chair, and his mom had her feet tucked under herself on the sofa. Mugs of tea sat on the coffee table.

"Mr. Garcia stopped by with receipts," she said.

Sure he did. Derrick eyed Garcia, who was all smiles. Ever since his computer science teacher decided to help his parents with the record keeping at the diner, Derrick had been uneasy. First it was because of his stint at Bio-Core last year when he held Evie Grayson at gunpoint. But now it was because Garcia liked his mom a bit too much for Derrick's liking.

"How was your day?" She tilted her head, surveying his clothes. "Are you wearing your suit?"

"Um, yeah. There's something I want to talk to you about." Derrick looked at Garcia, hoping he would get the clue that it was time for him to leave.

"Athena told me that you are going to MIT in the fall. That's quite impressive," Garcia said.

"Right." Derrick glanced between his mom and Garcia, neither of whom looked like they were going to move.

"Oh, right." Garcia stood up, finally getting the hint. "I'll see you tomorrow, Athena."

His mom smiled up at him. "Sure thing. Thanks for dropping off those receipts." She turned to Derrick. "Walk him out, honey."

Derrick stifled an eye roll and did as she asked. Why did he need walking out? Just go.

As Garcia passed the threshold of the door, he turned to say, "She's really proud of you, you know."

Derrick swallowed hard and nodded. He didn't know how long that would last after he told her about his new life plan. He shut the door and headed back to the living room.

His mom was picking up the cups of tea. "You hungry?"

"No, I'm good."

She returned from the kitchen and sat back down on the couch. "What do you want to talk to me about?"

He sat down next to her and took a deep breath. *Here goes nothing.* "It's about why I'm wearing my suit. I had an interview today for a very prestigious internship. They typically only give it to college graduates."

His mom sat up straighter. "That's fantastic, but why am I only hearing about this now?"

"Because I wasn't sure if I would get it or not. Turns out, I did." He did his best to smile, but he was a ball of nerves.

"Okay so why don't you look happy?"

"I am. It's the chance of a lifetime. I'll be able to work with some of the greatest minds in cybernetics. I'm really excited."

"Right." His mom narrowed her eyes at him, her suspicious hackles up. "If this is happy, I'd hate to see sad. So, when is it? How does it fit in with MIT?"

And there it was. The thing he'd been dreading.

Well, better to tear the bandage off quickly. "I'm

not going to MIT. I'm going to work at Bio-Core instead."

Her mouth dropped open, and her eyes grew to the size they did when he'd told her that he'd dropped her favorite vase. "I'm sorry. I don't think I heard you right."

"Mom, it's what I want. I'm not going to MIT. I'm staying here."

She shook her head. "Okay, let's just take a deep breath. First of all, college is important. Especially for someone as gifted as you. Second, I don't want you anywhere near that facility. It's dangerous. You do recall finding one of their scientists in the dumpster behind our diner, right?"

How could he forget? He was carrying around a reminder of the incident daily. "I know it's a shock. But it's an even better opportunity than MIT, I promise. It's what I want to do."

"Can you at least tell me what changed?"

Derrick glanced down at his hands. He was fearing this part the most. The last thing he wanted to do is make his parents feel guilty about their financial situation. "You know I got into MIT, but what I didn't tell you was that I didn't get a scholarship."

"Oh." She looked down at her wedding ring and twisted it around with her other hand nervously. When she looked back up, her eyes were glassy.

His stomach churned. Oh no. Please don't cry.

"We can work it out," she said. "Don't worry about the money."

"Mom, no. You don't understand. Not getting the

scholarship was the best thing that could have happened. It led me to an even better opportunity at Bio-Core."

She shook her head, her jaw set with pride. "You should have come to me about this. Your dad and I will work out the money so you can go to college, and that's the end of it."

"No. I don't want to go to college. I want to work at Bio-Core."

"You're only saying that because you were afraid to tell us about the scholarship. You're young. You need to go to college."

Derrick stood and sighed, his frustration mounting. "Why won't you listen to me? I'm going to work at Bio-Core. It's a done deal."

She opened her mouth to respond but closed it as his words sank in. "I'm sorry. You're going to have to give me a moment to wrap my head around this. You don't want to go to college?"

"Nope."

A few tears slipped down her cheeks. "I don't know what to say."

He sat back down and put his arm around her. "Please don't cry. This is good for me. I really am excited about my internship. I swear, it's even better than MIT."

"But that place… I'll worry." She reached for a tissue and dabbed at her eyes.

She wasn't entirely wrong, but that wasn't going to stop him. "I promise I will be perfectly safe there. Did I mention it's a paid internship?"

"It's not about the money, Derrick. I want you to have a good education."

"I will. There's no better way for me to learn than to have the hands-on experience MIT students only dream about."

"There's no talking you out of this, is there?" She frowned.

"It means I'll be staying in Ashwater." He raised his eyebrows for extra emphasis.

She embraced him. "You're so grown up. I don't know where the time went, but here you are."

"I'll always be your son." He hugged her tightly, swallowing the lump in his throat. "The better one."

She chuckled against his shoulder and let him go, brushing his hair off his forehead. "You need a haircut."

"I know."

"And you're telling your father about this."

Damn. He'd hoped she'd do that for him. "But you'll help, right?"

She narrowed her eyes at him.

Derrick swallowed hard. Right. Now wasn't the time to press his luck.

7

THE HEAD SHOP

Sloan

S loan slung her backpack on a chair behind the counter at the front of the store and glanced around. Glass cases of pipes, bongs, and other paraphernalia lined the sides of the store, framing racks of tie-dyed T-shirts, hand-knitted beanies, and jewelry. The walls and ceiling were adorned with peace signs and marijuana leaves. It was late afternoon, so her mom was probably stocking something new that shipped in today.

"Mom? Where you at?" Sloan asked.

"I'm here." Charlie's head popped up from behind a rack of beaded bracelets. They had expanded beyond the basic smoke stuff a year ago when tourists came in looking for gifts and souvenirs. Made sense, considering the store was called Relics. Her dad's idea for the store was born in Europe while backpacking. He came across some cool paraphernalia in an antique shop, and the rest was history. The bonus was that her mom's parents owned the property—no rent.

"Ooh, these are nice." Sloan picked up a dark, beaded bracelet. It oddly reminded her of Will's eyes.

"Yeah, they just came in." Charlie smiled. "Someday, this is all going to be yours."

Sloan swallowed hard. Neither of her parents had ever said it out loud, but it was the unspoken truth. She knew her parents had always envisioned her taking over, but she also never told them it wasn't something she wanted.

"Yep," she said quietly, turning away.

Charlie wrapped her hand around some of Sloan's hair. "How was school?"

"It was okay." She reached for her hair back, picking at the split ends. The letter was still sitting on the top shelf of her locker. She'd chickened out again.

"Cut it, already, Rapunzel."

"Never." She dropped her hair and sighed.

"What's wrong?"

"Nothing. Where do you want me?"

Before Charlie could answer, the door opened, and Adam and Evie walked inside. Evie smiled at Sloan while Adam looked around, his lips parted in awe. This was his first time in the shop. Happened a lot for first timers.

"I guess that's your answer." Charlie squatted back down and picked up some more bracelets to put on the racks.

"Hey, guys." Sloan walked over to them. She glanced at Adam. "It's a lot to take in, I know."

Adam blinked rapidly, indicating he was using his CPU brain to research what he saw.

Evie put her arm around him and squeezed his waist to snap him back to the present. "We were headed to my mom's shop and thought we'd stop in. You'll never guess who's playing at Purgatory next weekend."

Purgatory was a club in the neighboring town of Limbo that was open to teens for concerts. The town was a dead zone, save that club. "Who?"

"Lotus."

"Shut up." Sloan wet her lips. "I thought their tour was set for the next six months."

Evie shrugged, smiling. "I don't know. I guess they're making a detour on their way out west."

Excitement bubbled up inside Sloan. She reached for Evie's arm. "We're going."

"Absolutely."

Adam picked up a sensual-looking pipe and turned it over in his hands.

"Kinky taste, Adam." Sloan arched an eyebrow at him.

"Put that down." Evie blushed.

He did as she asked but soon found another pipe to examine and then another. He bounced around the glass display cabinets like a pinball in a machine at Jack's, his eyes taking in as much merch as possible. Along the way, his eyes blinked rapidly as he researched the items before him.

"Sorry," Evie said to Sloan. "He's still very curious about things."

"It's cool. Lots of people want to test them before they purchase."

Adam raised up a blue, double-chambered bong with dancing Dead bears. The song in the store changed to "Touch of Grey" by The Grateful Dead. "I would like to test this one."

Evie walked over to him and took it out of his hand. "No. For a few reasons. The most important one being that you're not twenty-one."

Sloan swayed her hips to the tune. The Dead played often in the shop, but "Touch of Grey" was banned from the playlists. Her dad said it was too popular and, therefore, cliché. But she still liked it.

Charlie popped her head up. "That's weird."

"Sorry, I added it," Sloan covered for Adam, who'd changed the song with his Bluetooth capability.

"You better not let your dad hear it." She smirked and bobbed her head a few times. "It is a really good song."

Sloan turned back to Adam and Evie. "Evie's right. You have to be twenty-one to smoke." She leaned closer and whispered between the two of them. "In the shop."

"You are a bad influence." Evie frowned.

"Thank you." Sloan grinned.

"Why don't you want me to try it?" Adam asked Evie.

"I don't know. What if it has some weird effect on you? Remember what happened to Iris with the peanut butter pie?"

"Don't be so uptight, Evie." Sloan glanced at

Adam. "If you want to try some, I'll hook you up. Just not here."

Adam glanced between them. Evie narrowed her eyes and pursed her lips.

"No, thanks." He frowned and shoved his hands into his pockets as the song changed again to "Love is a Battlefield" by Pat Benatar.

"What is happening to the playlist?" Charlie asked.

"Sorry, Mom, that was me again." Sloan's voice shook.

"Well, I draw the line at Pat Benatar. We're a head shop," Charlie yelled from the back of the store.

"Sorry. I'll take it off." Sloan turned back to Adam and mouthed, *Thanks a lot.*

"Sorry. Sometimes it just happens." Adam raised his eyebrows.

Evie swatted his middle. "Yeah, he's sorry. Love *is* a battlefield. Let's go." She glanced at Sloan. "Lotus, next week?"

"Definitely."

After they left, Sloan headed to the back to turn off Pat and get the playlist sorted. Her mind drifted to Derrick. Did he like Lotus?

Derrick

He stared at the shop from across the street. He'd been in Relics a bunch of times to see Sloan, but he was always with Luke. Now he was alone, and his palms were clammy. But after the awkward moment from the other night, he wanted her to know that he did genuinely like her. So he was here to ask her out on a real date. Plus, he'd gained some confidence after telling his parents he wasn't going to MIT. So if she said yes, telling Luke would be a breeze?

Derrick cleared his throat. Yeah, right.

He stepped off the curb and stopped mid-stride. Adam and Evie exited the shop. He almost raised his hand to say hello but thought better of it. He was on a mission.

After they were on their way, he wiped his moist hands on his jeans and headed across the street. Just before he reached the door, a shadow cast in front of him on the sidewalk as someone approached him from behind, causing his chest to tighten.

"Hey, got a minute?" the shadow said.

Derrick turned, his heart racing.

The shadow belonged to Will.

"Jeez, don't creep up on me like that," Derrick said.

"Oh, sorry." Will looked at the sidewalk. "I thought you saw me."

"No." Derrick looked back at the door to the shop and sighed. Ashwater was too small of a town. He couldn't cross the street without someone wanting to chat. He turned back to Will. "What's up?"

Will walked up to the front window of the store and cupped his hands around his eyes to peer in. "Is this a head shop?"

"Yeah."

"Do you have a fake ID or something?" Will tilted his head at Derrick with an eyebrow raised.

"No. I'm not here to purchase." Derrick crossed his arms. He was losing his nerve.

"Then why are you here?"

Derrick took a deep breath to keep the impatience from his voice. "Is there something you wanted?"

Will nodded. "Yeah, right. Sorry. Mr. Garcia said that you were in charge of the tech club at school. I'd like to join."

Tech club? That was the last thing he wanted to talk about it. "Um, yeah, sure. I'm not really sure how active I'll be since I'm starting my internship soon."

"That's right. Super cool. When does that start?"

"I go in for orientation tomorrow. I'll be doing half days the rest of the school year."

"You have to be stoked."

"Yep." Derrick glanced around. "Well, I'll email you some stuff for the club."

"Thanks, I appreciate it." Will smiled knowingly and patted him on the shoulder. "Good luck."

Derrick wasn't sure how to respond since he didn't mention why he was at Relics. "Uh, thanks."

Maybe Sloan was right. Will was odd.

After Will strode off, Derrick turned back toward the task at hand, his mind racing. *Hey, Sloan, would you like to go out with me? If you're not doing anything...*

He took a deep breath and opened the door.

8

PROPOSITIONS

Sloan

By the time she finished breaking down boxes in the back of the shop, Sloan had a solid plan on how to use Lotus to figure out if Derrick had any feelings for her.

It was time to ask the boy out.

As if he could read her mind, Derrick was in the shop talking to her mom. Her heart skipped a beat, and she beamed at him. Wow. This was kismet. She sauntered over to him, forcing her legs not to burst into a sprint. *Don't be too anxious.*

He wore jeans and a black T-shirt that accentuated his upper body in all the right places. She glanced at his lips, and her cheeks warmed, remembering her desire to lay one on him the other night right before he turned her down.

"Hey," she said.

Derrick smiled, and her heart melted. That

lopsided grin was so freaking cute. It was driving her nuts.

"Derrick was just telling me that he's staying in town next year," her mom said. "Isn't that nice?"

"Mmhmm." *Yes. It was very nice.*

"Well, I'll leave you two alone." Her mom winked at her before walking away.

Thanks, Mom. She was always so intuitive about who Sloan liked. Too bad she wasn't about her career path.

"I was wondering—" Sloan started.

Derrick spoke at the same time, but she didn't catch what he said.

"Sorry. What?" she asked.

"Oh." He laughed and shoved his hands in his pockets. "What were you saying?"

Stop looking so adorable. Her hands twitched, wanting to slide her arms around his waist. She swung her hair over her shoulder and smiled. Her hands and pits felt like she'd just come out of a sauna, and she wiped her hands on the front of her jeans.

What was wrong with her? She'd asked out lots of people. Why was this so different?

She cleared her throat. Deep down, she knew exactly why—this wasn't about having a good time. This was an entirely new scenario, one she'd never experienced.

Sloan liked him. Like, like-liked him.

"Lotus is playing at Purgatory next weekend," she said.

"Oh, yeah? That's awesome." He moved closer.

She moved toward him on instinct, like a magnet. The hairs on her scalp prickled. "Yeah. Evie told me they're making a detour. They weren't supposed to stop anywhere near here."

He stepped closer, his eyes fixed on hers. "That's lucky."

Sloan leaned against a counter and traced a circle with her finger on the glass.

"Yeah," she said, breathlessly, looking down. *Quit screwing around. Just ask. Do it.*

He followed suit and leaned next to her, placing his hand on the counter next to hers, nudging her index finger. His touch, although the smallest graze, sent shock waves up and down her arm. "We should go together."

Her breath caught. OMG. Was this really happening? *Say it.* "Like a date?"

"Like a date."

Sloan's mind whirred, and her heart pounded. If he kept nudging her finger like that, she would burst into flames. She couldn't think, could barely breathe. The thought of being alone in a dark club, dancing with him was...

She laughed nervously, covering her desire to mold her body to his like clay. *Dude, get your shit together and answer him.* "Sure."

"Cool." He squeezed her hand in his.

Sloan stared at his lips—so soft and supple. The air between them was like static electricity, tangible. Her instinct was to pull him close and lock lips. Unlike the other night, this time she was all desire and zero diversion. She parted her lips.

The doorbell sounded as the front door opened. "Guys, the greatest thing has happened."

Luke.

Sloan and Derrick separated on instinct.

Derrick stared at the floor as the color rose on his cheeks. "What's up?"

"Get ready to experience Lotus up close and personal." Luke gestured with the sign of the horns. "They're coming to Purgatory next weekend."

"Uh…cool." Sloan raised her eyebrows at Derrick. She wasn't surprised Luke knew about Lotus coming. Adam and Evie were probably telling everyone.

"Cool? That's all you have to say about our favorite band?" Luke walked over to her and felt her forehead with the back of his hand. "Are you feeling okay?"

"I know. Chill." Sloan pursed her lips. "Adam and Evie already told us. That's all."

"Listen." Luke grabbed Sloan by the shoulders, staring at her intently. "If you're going to come with me to see a kickass band, I expect a lot more enthusiasm. Whatever this"—he waved his hand in front of her face—"is? I don't want to see it next Friday."

"Uh," she stammered, looking at Derrick. *A little help here?*

Without looking away from Sloan, Luke pointed at Derrick. "And I'm cashing in on the shift you owe me next Friday."

Sloan's stomach clenched in anticipation. *Tell him.*

Derrick opened his mouth to reply, giving Sloan a glimmer of hope he'd say no. But instead, the corners of his mouth turned down, disappointment spreading across his face. "Fine."

Seriously? Her heart sank as any shred of a date with Derrick dissipated.

"This is going to be epic." Luke released Sloan and glanced at the counter next to them. He picked up the same lewd pipe Adam had when he first came into the store. He turned it over a few times, chuckled, and set it back down.

Sloan shifted her weight, her heart heavy. There was so much tension hanging in the air, and she was fresh out of penis pipe jokes.

Derrick cleared his throat.

Luke looked between the two of them. "You guys are acting super weird."

"I'm going to the diner. See ya." Derrick turned and left, Luke and Sloan staring after him.

Wow. So you're just going to leave? Okay. Sloan crossed her arms.

"Uh, okay," Luke said to Derrick's back. When he turned back to Sloan, he shrugged, his smile returning. "Tell me you're excited."

His enthusiasm was palpable. She hated keeping her feelings hidden from him. She could always tell him anything. But in this case, there were no words that would warm him up to her wanting to date his twin brother. She took a deep breath and forced a smile to her lips.

After all, she was excited to see Lotus. "Yes, of

course. What songs do you think they're going to cover?"

Luke rattled off some songs he was hopeful for as she rearranged some glass pipes.

Her thoughts drifted back to Derrick. Was he afraid to tell Luke about asking her out? Hadn't he thought about that before he asked her? Who was she kidding? She was just as scared as he was to tell Luke. Secret relationships could be fun, couldn't they?

She wiped a smudge off the counter. Butterflies took flight in her stomach as she remembered how his fingers sought hers. She smiled. They were a non-starter for now, but when Luke left for school, all bets were off.

Derrick

Derrick pushed open the door to the diner with more force than he intended.

"Whoa." Celia held the door from the other side while balancing a tray with stacked plates. "What'd the door do to you?"

"Sorry." He grabbed the wobbling tray.

"No problem. Just be more careful." She took the tray back from him and headed to the kitchen.

He wasn't scheduled to start for another hour, but work was the only thing that would calm his frayed nerves. His insides were churning. He'd finally worked up the courage to ask out Sloan and she said yes. Then it all went to hell.

Thanks a lot, Luke.

Derrick hoisted his backpack up on his shoulder and glanced at the booths.

Mac Grayson, who was sitting at the closest table, looked up. Derrick nodded and gripped his backpack protectively. The syringe Dr. Rice gave him was in the front pocket.

"Derrick," Mac said, nodding back.

"Sheriff." Derrick didn't like the suspicious look Mac gave him—like he knew he was hiding something. He was either really good at his job or a mind reader. He groaned inwardly. Why did he have to be the one to find a woman in their dumpster?

He headed to the kitchen to put his bag down and grab an apron.

The familiar scent of sautéed onions eased his mind.

His dad was at the grill, flipping some hamburgers. He turned and wiped his brow with his forearm. "Hey, son. Thought you started later today."

"Yeah, thought I'd make a few extra bucks." Derrick tied his apron around his waist.

"Every bit helps."

His dad had taken the news about the internship much better than he expected. He even offered to help him buy a car to go back and forth to Bio-Core as long as he continued to help out at the diner when he could. If he'd known he was going to take his news so well, he would have told him first.

"I'm proud of you." His dad tossed the turner in the air and caught it. "You're going to do great things. I can feel it."

"Thanks, Dad."

His dad whistled and focused back on the burgers while Derrick headed back out front. Sheriff Grayson had left. Celia was bouncing around in her usual efficient manner, handling most of the booths and half the dining room. A new girl she was training took on the other half.

Garcia was at a table next to the register with his laptop out. He glanced up at Derrick and motioned across the table. "Hey, got a minute?"

"What's up?" Derrick slid into the booth.

"I heard you got an internship at Bio-Core." Garcia smiled.

"That's right."

"Congratulations."

"Thanks." Derrick shifted in his seat. He could be working. "Was there something else?"

Garcia put his elbows on the table and leaned forward. "I have a proposal for you."

"A proposal?"

"You and I both know that there are dangerous things going on at the facility."

"Yeah, so?" He couldn't deny that. Bio-Core had multiple lines of androids they were testing out below ground and a drug problem above. He had proof of that in his bag. Still, they were on the cutting edge of cybernetics like no other place in the world. He accepted the risk of working there willingly.

Although, Dr. Rice had accepted the risk too and look what happened to her.

"If you ever need my help with anything. Or if you see something odd, you can come to me."

Derrick narrowed his eyes. This was the man who'd held one of his friends at gunpoint not long ago. "Why would I trust you?"

"Because a long time ago, I was you."

"You were an intern?"

Garcia looked out the window. "Yeah, it seems like forever ago. I was fresh out of grad school. Back then, I felt like the luckiest person in the world. I was going to work with the brightest minds in the industry. I still remember the first time I walked through those doors. It was like my entire future success was right there in front of me, waiting for me to grab it."

Derrick leaned forward, intrigued by the admission. He'd had those same feelings when he went there for his interview.

Garcia looked back at Derrick. "Something tells me you know what I'm talking about."

"What happened? What made you—"

"Turn into a power-hungry deranged lunatic?"

"Oh, I didn't mean—"

"No, it's a fair assessment." He sighed. "I'm not sure. When I first started out, there was a lot of praise for my work. Promises were made that I would move up in the ranks. The dangling carrot was a spot on the coveted board."

Derrick nodded slowly. He'd heard about the board from Gage. They made all the important decisions about the direction and future endeavors for Bio-Core. Most of their identities remained secret from the outside world. Dr. G., Maxwell Roberts, and the late Sam Strickland were the only people he knew were on it. He'd never met Dr. G. but Gage believed she was a decent person.

"So, I picked up the work that Ryssa Strickland had started. The board was so hopeful about her research. I had some great breakthroughs with..." Garcia glanced up at Derrick and swallowed hard.

"Adam?"

"Yeah. Sorry. Anyway, I was making all the right moves. I could feel myself getting closer and closer to an elusive board seat. It was all I could think about. Looking back now, I realize it wasn't ambition—it was obsession. Even Naomi, who was my friend and always kept me grounded, felt like a threat."

Derrick's pulse quickened at the mention of Dr. Rice. He thought about the last time he saw her. She'd risked her life to get that vial out of Bio-Core. Now that he was going to be on the inside, he was even more determined than ever to figure out what it was.

"She was the only person who cared about me in that place, and I sold her out." Garcia looked out the window again.

"Sold her out? Did you—"

"Of course not. I know it's hard to believe, but I've changed. I did my best to make amends with Naomi. I'd hoped that we could be friends again. Then, well, you know what happened."

Derrick eyed him carefully. He seemed to be genuinely sad about Dr. Rice, and there wasn't a motive he could see for hurting her. Maybe Garcia had changed. "I guess there's been no improvement in her condition?"

"None that I'm aware of." Garcia's expression changed, his eyes intense. "Look, just be careful in that place. It has a way of changing people. I did things I never thought I was capable of." He leaned forward. "Your mother is worried about you, and she has good reason to be. I won't tell her what I know because it wouldn't be safe for her, but if I can help you, I will. Be careful about who you trust. If you come in contact with any of the board members, be on guard. Some of them are dangerous."

Derrick looked down at his hands, balled up into fists. He released them, revealing red crescents where his nails had assaulted the tender flesh of his palms.

Garcia grabbed his wrist. "Don't make the same mistake Naomi did."

Before he could say more, the door opened, and Derrick's mom walked inside. She smiled and waved at them.

Garcia's face lit up at the sight of her as he released Derrick's arm and stood. Before he left, he whispered, "If you need anything, call me."

He greeted Derrick's mom with a kiss on the cheek. The act made Derrick's skin crawl. He swore under his breath as a truth emerged in his mind, crystal clear.

Garcia had feelings for his mom.

Ugh. That's why Garcia was offering his help. He saw Derrick as an *in* with his mom.

Derrick groaned and scratched at a crack in the laminate tabletop. Did she have feelings for Garcia too? Did his dad know? Were his parents getting a divorce?

The question hit him hard, like a sucker punch to the stomach. The thought of his parents splitting was unthinkable. They depended on each other so much, and what about the diner? He frowned toward the swinging door that led to the kitchen. He could still hear a faint whistle from his dad as he cooked. His last thought before focusing on work was that Garcia was on the up-and-up for the time—but only because he'd never do anything to hurt his mom.

9

CRIMSON

Sloan

I f there was one girl in Ashwater who knew how to shop, it was Mazy Patterson. Although Iris could give her a run for her money. Word had spread that Lotus was coming to Purgatory, and Ashwater High was humming with talk of the concert. Sloan didn't know anyone besides Derrick who wasn't going, and according to Mazy, an event of this magnitude required new outfits.

Sloan headed to Dalia's dress shop with Mazy and Evie. Iris greeted them at the door in a short skirt and short-sleeve crop sweater. She'd gone from killer android to supermodel in less than three months. Well, part of that killer was still there.

Since Iris started working at the shop she'd made some pretty astonishing changes. It was like the place had gone from mom and pop to Fifth Avenue. Even Dalia, the owner, was sporting new fashion Iris had either made or ordered. Considering it was one of the only places to shop for clothes besides the big box store closer to the city, it was a welcome change.

"We're going to need everything. Outfits, shoes, and accessories," Mazy started.

"I want something that moves." Sloan swayed her hips.

Evie shrugged dismissively and wandered over to a chair to sit down. She grabbed a magazine and perused. Sloan chuckled at her. Shopping was so not her bag.

"For the concert at Purgatory?" Iris asked.

Sloan and Mazy nodded.

Iris looked away, blinking, her brain computing something. "I can't believe I'm saying this, but you might want to follow Evie's trend. T-shirts and jeans seem to be the norm."

"Great." Evie set the magazine down and stood, beaming. "Let's go to my house. I'll have you dressed in no time."

Mazy frowned at Evie. "Not so fast." She looked back at Iris. "We're not going for norm. Lots of kids from school are going, and this isn't an ordinary band. It's Lotus."

"So it's a special concert?" Iris asked.

"Sort of," Sloan said. "I think what Mazy means is that she wants to stand out in the crowd."

Iris's eyes lit up. "Ah. I've got it. Slutty chic."

Mazy's eye grew to saucers, and her lips parted. Sloan covered her mouth to stifle the laugh. No one would ever dare suggest that Mazy do 'slutty chic.'

"I can't believe we're not closer." Sloan linked arms with Iris and smiled demurely. "Lead the way."

Evie walked past them toward the juniors' section. "I'm not doing slutty chic, but I could use a new push up bra."

A half an hour later, all three girls were finishing up in the dressing rooms. Sloan had tried on a few things but no winners. Mazy and Evie had struck gold on the first try—pink and black dresses respectively. No surprise.

Iris slung a deep red tank dress over the top of the door. "Try this."

Sloan stared at it. Red? She never wore red. "Seriously?"

"Give it a try. Trust me," Iris said.

"Okay." The fabric was stretchy and looked comfy. She slipped into the dress and turned around a few times, adjusting the neckline around her cleavage. Not bad. Not bad at all. She emerged from the dressing room to get some second opinions.

"Yes. That's the one." Mazy said. "It looks amazing on you."

Evie, who'd grown bored, was propped up in a large chair, sketching a mannequin. She glanced up, assessed, and gave Sloan a thumbs-up.

Sloan looked in the mirror again. The dress hugged all her best assets and surprisingly, the color did look good with her complexion and hair.

"Red is your color," Iris stated.

"Weird. I never wear red." She turned around a few times.

"Now you do." Iris came up behind her, pinching and pulling at the fabric around her hips. "This fits you perfectly. I recommend you wear your hair down."

Sloan smiled at Iris's reflection in the mirror. "Thanks, Iris. You're the best."

"I'm starving," Mazy said. "Anyone want to grab food at Dixon's?"

"I'm in." Sloan was always up for Dixon's. Especially if Derrick was working.

"Yes." Evie stood. "Iris, do you want to come?"

"No thanks. I'm meeting Gage at Jack's."

A twinge of jealously nagged at Sloan. She wished she could have a slice of what Iris and Gage had with Derrick.

"You know, it's good to spend some time with friends too." Evie eyed Iris. "I'm not with Adam constantly."

Iris tilted her head. "But I prefer to be with Gage over you."

Evie scowled. "Hey. Rude, much?"

"We all know that," Mazy interceded. "But spending all your time with one person isn't healthy. You will be more well-rounded if you spend time with us too."

"Oh." Iris looked away, her eyes blinking rapidly as she researched Mazy's sentiment. When she was done, she frowned. "It seems you're right. I need to play a little hard to get."

"That's not—" Mazy started.

Evie kicked Mazy's shoe. Mazy stared at Evie, who glared right back.

Mazy mouthed, *Fine,* and looked at Iris. "Yep, time to play hard to get."

"Okay. I'll text Gage that I won't be going to Jack's," Iris said.

Evie stared after Iris frowning. Iris's barb still stung.

"You've still got me, girl." Sloan put her arm around Evie and bumped her hip into hers. "And I'm slutty chic."

As the girls walked over to Dixon's, Mazy fell back with Sloan. "Did you open the letter yet?"

Sloan stared straight ahead. "Nope. It's still sitting in my locker."

"If you want me to open it for you, I will."

If only it were that easy. The thought of Mazy's disappointed face if she didn't get in was too much. After all the nights of cramming for SATs and bolstering her last quarter grades, it would be beyond embarrassing.

"I'll get around to it," Sloan said with forced nonchalance.

"Enough already." Mazy stopped. "You can't let fear run your life."

Sloan turned. "That's easy for you to say. You're perfect."

"That's not fair. I'm invested in your future now too. After all that cramming to get you a shot at college, you'd think you would be excited to open that letter." Mazy crossed her arms and started walking again. "And to be clear, nobody's perfect."

She was right. As much as Sloan didn't want to admit it, she was letting fear run her life, and she did owe Mazy for all her help. "I'm sorry, you're right. I'll open it before Lotus."

"Promise?" Mazy arched an eyebrow at her.

Sloan smiled. Mazy would make a fantastic life coach. Was that a real job? "I swear. You can watch me do it."

"Good."

The girls reached the diner and found a booth toward the front. Luke was working the dining area while Celia and Derrick had the booths up front. Sloan's heart fluttered at the sight of him and then sank as she remembered he wouldn't get to see the sexy red dress she bought for the concert.

"Hey guys, what's up?" Derrick approached their table, standing closest to Sloan, who was seated on the outside.

She stared at his waist, which was eye level. All kinds of thoughts entered her mind that had nothing to do with cheeseburgers and french fries. She wanted to lace her fingers with his, kiss those playful lips, and run her hands through his thick, dark hair. The warmth from his body next to hers was driving her crazy. She inhaled sharply, trying to control her urge to touch him.

Screw it. She stood, reaching her arms around his middle so she could maneuver behind him. Her hands lingered on his arm and waist, enjoying the sensation of being this close to him. "Excuse me. I just need to use the restroom."

He turned his head toward her, their faces close. He glanced down at her lips and then back up to her eyes. "Sure, no problem."

Okay, time to move. Her hands weren't listening. *Let go.*

His cheeks flushed. He grabbed her hands and moved her away. "Do you want your usual?"

Her fingers still tingled, and she was in a daze. What did he ask? Her usual? "Oh, yeah, thanks."

She turned and bee-lined it to the restrooms, her cheeks hot as Hades. Before she knew it, she bumped into Luke.

"Are you okay? Your face is all red," he said.

She was rather warm all over. "I'm just hot."

"Why are you out of breath?" Luke looked around her. "Who are you here with?"

"The girls," she squeaked out, pushing past him.

"Hey—" he called after her.

Sloan closed the bathroom door and checked the stalls. Empty. She wrung her hands and stifled the scream at the back of her throat. This was maddening. She couldn't even stand next to him without wanting to throw herself at him. How was she going to control herself around him until Luke left for college?

She looked in the mirror and ran toward it, gripping the sides of the sink. OMFG. She'd never seen her face so flushed. Her cheeks matched her new dress.

Calm down.

Sloan paced, fanning her face, willing her

breathing to return to normal. She had the patience to let a letter sit on the shelf in her locker for weeks, but a boy she likes stands next to her and she can't help but give him a pat down? Christ. She was a hot mess.

The door opened, and Celia came inside. "You okay? Luke said you weren't feeling good."

"I'm fine. Just a little overheated." Sloan went to the sink and washed her hands to avoid eye contact with Celia. She couldn't keep this up. Between her feelings for Derrick and not sharing with Luke, she was losing it.

"Right. Okay, well, if you need anything—"

"I'm fine. Thanks." Sloan glanced in the mirror. Her face was still rosy, but it was dissipating.

"Take it or leave it, but my advice is to be honest. It's like getting into a pool at the beginning of summer —much less painful if you jump."

Celia's words hit the nail on the head. She was absolutely right. Dancing around this whole thing with Luke was ridiculous and not her style at all. She was always upfront and honest, to a fault even. But the middle of dinner shift wasn't the time to broadcast her feelings. Maybe after the concert.

Sloan turned around. "I'm not sure what you mean."

"Yes, you do." Celia turned and left.

10

FIRST DAY

Derrick

It was the first day of Derrick's internship, and "Don't Stop Believin'" by Journey played on the radio in his dad's truck. Appropriate considering that by some miracle he'd landed this opportunity and, if he wasn't mistaken by how she'd grabbed him last night, Sloan was as into him as he was her. His skin still tingled from the memory as he belted out the chorus of the song and tapped on the steering wheel. Not even Garcia's warning could touch his mood today.

After gaining clearance with the security guard, he pulled into the designated spots for employees. Looking up at the building before him, he was struck by how majestic it was, set against the tall peak that overlooked the town. More impressive were the thousands of feet of lab space that lay belowground. He smoothed out his shirt and tie and headed inside.

Payton, as if sensing his arrival, greeted him as he entered the massive atrium lobby, the white noise from the waterfall omnipresent.

"How are you?" She pushed her glasses up on her nose and smiled. Her white lab coat was pristine, and she had a smart tablet in the crook of her arm.

"I'm good." He rocked on the balls of his feet with nervous energy. He was so much more than good—he was ecstatic.

"Great. You've been assigned to Drs. Murray and Burman. But I will be your mentor."

Payton Glass is my freakin' mentor? She studied environmental medicine, an area he had little interest in, but she was famous for her work. She'd traveled all over the world and published numerous articles about water, soil, and even volcanic ash exposure and effects on the human body. As for what she was studying in Ashwater, he didn't have a clue.

"That's great," he said after his split-second internal rave. "I look forward to learning from you."

"I'm here on Mondays, Wednesdays, and Fridays, and I'm at Arcadia on Tuesdays and Thursdays."

"Arcadia? You're doing research at the mental hospital?"

She smiled wryly. "Yep. Top secret stuff."

Derrick didn't know if she was serious or not, but it didn't sound like she was going to elaborate.

"If you would follow me," she said. "I'll show you to your lab."

He tried his best to maintain his composure, but as soon as she turned to lead him to the elevator, he did a few air punches. A few bystanders smiled at him, his enthusiasm palpable.

Once inside the elevator, they headed down. She handed him a card on a lanyard. "Here is your ID. You need to wear it at all times, and you will use it to access your floor and lab."

She pressed her ID to a scanner by the buttons and pressed level -6.

Exiting at their level gave him some déjà vu. He was relatively certain he'd never been to this floor, but he had been to the lower floors last year when he'd helped to rescue Adam. The hall was white and sterile with cool LED lights above and at the base of the walls, illuminating doors on both sides.

"Your lab assignment is down this hall," Payton said. "You will be working with two top-notch scientists. They're working on some innovative prosthetics utilizing cybernetics. There are a couple of patients at Arcadia who are candidates for prosthetics. Your team hopes to have something to test soon. Maybe you can help them along." She smiled and continued down the hall.

Derrick nodded, his pulse quickening with anticipation.

"Here we are." Payton opened a door and motioned him inside.

As he walked through the doorway, he was struck by the size of the place compared to the narrow hallway he'd just left. Consoles lined both sides of the room, which spanned at least thirty feet. The ceiling was a clear twenty feet as well. On the far wall, enormous monitors were linked to operating systems. At the center of the room, some robotic units and 3-D printers were encased in glass. A man and a woman in white lab coats studied the robotic arm inside the glass, one looking perplexed while the other frowned.

"Wow." His heart raced like a horse in its final stretch. "This is—"

"I know. I felt the same way when I started. Completely different field from you but still the same feeling." She nodded toward the scientists. "Come on. I'll introduce you."

The man and woman looked up as they approached. Both appeared to be quite a few years older than him. Probably late thirties. The man was thin with short, dark hair and large glasses. The woman had equally dark hair, but her glasses were much more stylish and she wore the tallest shoes he'd ever seen.

"Dr. Murray, Dr. Burman, this is Derrick Dixon, your new intern," Payton said.

The woman reached her hand out first toward him. "Pleased to meet you, Derrick. I'm Dr. Murray, but since you're joining our team, you can call me Jasmine."

"Pleased to meet you." Derrick took her hand. The bracelets on her wrist jangled. Up close, he was struck by her eyes. They were so light brown, they reminded him of gold.

"And I'm Dr. Burman, but you can call me Raj."

Derrick shook his hand. "Nice to meet you."

"Jasmine and Raj are some of the brightest scientists we have here a Bio-Core. They're known as the dynamic duo." Payton smiled. "It's a tremendous honor that Max placed you with them."

"You're too kind," Raj said, blushing.

"Speak for yourself." Jasmine flipped her hair over her shoulder. "I'm spectacular."

"Well, I'm very excited to work with you. This is like a dream come true for me," Derrick said.

"Then let's get you suited up." Payton walked over to a console and picked up a lab coat draped over a chair. She shook it out and helped Derrick put it on. At the pocket was a blue logo for Bio-Core. She stepped back and assessed. "Looking good."

"Thanks."

Her phone buzzed, and she pulled it out. "I need to take this. Just a minute."

She walked into the hallway, and the automatic door shut behind her.

Derrick turned around, his fingers itching to touch everything. He grinned from ear to ear. *This is really happening.*

"Raj, look at this." Jasmine waved him back over to the encased robotic arm.

"Feel free to look around," Raj said to Derrick before joining her.

Before he could explore, Payton came back in. "Sorry about that. My girlfriend has a really important tennis match this afternoon. I wanted to wish her luck."

"No problem." Now his palms were sweating, and

he felt like he was going to burst if he didn't test some equipment out.

She gave him a once over and laughed. "I'm guessing you're the type who wants to jump right in?"

"If that's all right?" he replied, heading for what was likely the mainframe.

"Sure. No problem." She grabbed his arm before he was out of reach. "I'll be back at noon to take you to lunch. You have a thing."

Now that grabbed his attention. "A thing?"

"Max likes to welcome all new members of the Bio-Core team. That includes interns like you."

"Oh, okay." He wondered if that included any of the other board members.

Payton left, and he flexed his fingers, anxious to get his hands on a keyboard.

This is it. Don't screw up.

He hadn't moved an inch after he sat down at the mainframe. So far, he'd learned the basics of the robotic arm that created 3-D prints, and Jasmine and Raj were both brilliant as Payton indicated. They all gelled nicely, and Jasmine and Raj were open to new ideas. He was just about to highlight some of the ideas that had gotten him the internship when Payton came back.

Had he really been here for four hours already? It felt like half an hour.

Although his stomach disagreed.

"Looks like somebody's keeping busy." Payton stood behind him, assessing his screen. She pointed at a line of code he was especially proud of. "I only dabble in coding, but I know that's impressive."

"Thanks." He stood. "I'm starving."

"Good, because there will be quite the spread."

"Have a nice lunch," Jasmine said, not looking up from her computer. Raj waved in similar fashion.

"You aren't coming?" Derrick asked.

Jasmine glanced up and shook her head. "It's not really our thing."

Derrick frowned. Even though they'd just met, he'd gotten a solid team vibe from them. It would have been nice to walk into whatever this lunch thing was with people he already knew.

After they left the lab, Payton said, "It really isn't their thing. They abhor distractions, and that includes social lunches. But the food's great and this one is in your honor, so you have to go."

"Okay." Derrick had a feeling there was more to it than that but left it alone.

They took the elevator up to the top floor where Derrick had his interview with Max. Dana was at her desk when they entered the waiting area.

She smiled when she saw him. "Hi, Derrick. Settling in okay?"

"Yes, ma'am."

She pointed to the door on the opposite side from Mr. Robert's office. "Help yourself. Mr. Roberts will be over shortly."

Derrick followed Payton into a large board room. It had floor-to-ceiling windows and a buffet set up on the opposite side. Two people chatted by the food.

Derrick inhaled and homed in on the smell of baked goods. He had a sweet tooth, and if he wasn't mistaken, there were brownies.

"Come on, I'll introduce you to an important board member." Payton nudged his shoulder for him to follow.

Derrick pulled at his collar, his tie feeling tighter than it had a moment before.

They approached the pair, who were in deep conversation and almost didn't acknowledge their presence.

"Excuse me, Dr. G., I'd like to introduce you to someone," Payton said.

So this was the infamous Dr. G. that helped Gage get his abilities under control. She was short, slender, and her hair was pulled back into a tight bun.

"This is Derrick, Bio-Core's newest intern. As you know, he's working with Drs. Murray and Burman. Derrick, this is Dr. G. She's currently heading up a special cases ward over at Arcadia and is a member of the board."

Dr. G smiled at him. "Pleasure to meet you. Gage has spoken highly of you."

"Thanks, you too."

Dr. G. glanced at the man next to her. "And this is one of my colleagues from back east, Dr. Martin Arcanas."

The man had round-framed glasses so thick they magnified his bright blue eyes. He pushed them up on his nose and extended his hand. "Hello. Sorry, for the ridiculous-looking glasses. I broke my good pair on the flight here."

"Nice to meet you." Derrick shook his hand.

Payton's eyes lit up. "Dr. Arcanas, I'm so glad you could make it. We've spoken a few times on the phone. I'm Payton Glass."

"Oh yes, of course." Dr. Arcanas beamed at her. "Madi has told me about the wonderful work you've been doing."

Before Derrick could ask about the work and who Madi was, Payton said, "If you don't mind going solo for a bit, I'd like to catch up with Dr. Arcanas."

Did he have a choice? "Uh, sure."

Dr. G. patted Derrick on the back. "I've got him."

After Payton and Dr. Arcanas walked away, Derrick got the distinct feeling he was just thrown to the wolves. Garcia warned him about the board members, and now here he was, alone with one. He hoped Gage's instincts about her were right. He opened his mouth to make some small talk, but she waved away his sentiment. *Okay...*

Dr. G. turned and faced the door. "So what do you think about Bio-Core's interim CEO?"

Direct much? They'd just met. What kind of a loaded question was this? Garcia's advice might actually be helpful—be on guard and careful about who he trusted. "Um, he seems like a good guy."

"A good guy?" She tilted her head and frowned.

What was he supposed to say? He'd only met the man once. Before they could continue their conversation, the man himself came into the room. He wore a very similar suit to the one he wore for Derrick's interview. A stream of scientists in white lab coats filed in behind him.

Max headed straight for Derrick, smiling. He extended his hand. "Derrick, you're settling in okay? You have everything you need?"

"Yes, Mr. Roberts. Thank you."

"It's Max, please."

"Oh, right," Derrick said awkwardly. "Max."

"Dr. G." Max nodded curtly.

"Max," Dr. G. replied in kind.

Derrick sensed there was no love lost between the two. It also occurred to him that Max's entrance was perfectly timed to disrupt their conversation.

"Well," Max said, clasping his hands together, "let's get some food. Our in-house chef makes the best tuna salad sandwiches." He picked up a plate, and Derrick followed his lead.

Max wasn't wrong. The in-house chef was very talented. Derrick sampled a few different mini sandwiches, and of course, he had two brownies. They were delicious. Payton, who'd returned to his side for lunch, was enjoying a cup of soup and her veggie pita.

Once everyone finished their food, Max stood up. "If I could have your attention for a few minutes."

The conversations around the table quieted as everyone turned toward him.

"Thank you for sharing your lunch break with me today. As you know, I like to welcome new recruits with a toast." He glanced at Derrick. "Today, we welcome our newest and almost youngest ever intern?" he raised an eyebrow at Payton.

She smiled and whispered to Derrick, "You're eighteen, right?"

"Yeah."

"Yes, I still hold the title," she said.

Max and a few others around the table chuckled at her quip.

"In any event," Max continued, "I want you all to meet Derrick Dixon and don't let his age fool you. He's got some innovative, brilliant ideas in cybernetics. Based on what he showed me during his interview, I think Bio-Core is lucky to have him. He's joined Drs. Murray and Burman on their prosthetic research team. Please welcome him and"—he raised his glass of iced tea toward Derrick—"if you need anything at all, please don't hesitate to ask. My door is always open. Cheers."

Everyone at the table raised a glass and took a sip. Derrick's cheeks warmed. Was he supposed to say something in return? He'd never been toasted before, let alone the center of attention like this. It was weird and...good.

He cleared his throat. "Thank you, Max, and thanks to everyone else for welcoming me."

Max nodded at him and sat down.

Payton leaned over. "You'll get used to being brilliant. There's a lot of it going around here."

"Thanks, but I'm not that special. I even have a twin brother."

She turned to face him, her eyes growing serious.

"Modesty will get you nowhere. My first piece of advice as your mentor is to own your shit. You got this internship because you're wicked smart. If you don't own that, they'll eat you alive."

Eat him alive? Who was she talking about? He glanced around the table. Quite a few of the people at the table eyed him and whispered with others. He swallowed hard. He might find allies here, but there would also be rivals. He understood why Jasmine and Raj didn't want to attend these kind of luncheons.

Payton noticed him shifting uncomfortably under everyone's gaze. "Not what you expected, huh?"

"Nope."

"Put on a smile anyway. If it helps, think about your new lab and getting to work with our top scientists. Frankly, there's nowhere else in the world you'd be given this opportunity. So why not embrace it?" She arched an eyebrow at him.

He did as she asked and smiled. She was right, after all. This was the chance of a lifetime. Inwardly, he took note—there was bound to be competition in a place like this. Payton had all but said so just now. Best to stay out of the fray. If he kept his head down, performed well, he could learn so much, do so much. Everything else was white noise.

11

A TRAVELER RETURNS

Sloan

By the time Sloan got to Jack's to meet up with Mazy, she'd all but lost her nerve. It was two days away from the concert at Purgatory, and she planned on keeping her promise.

It was time to open the letter from Edgewood.

If she got in, she would celebrate with some fun DP songs. If she didn't, she could drown her sorrows at Daisy's snack bar. Either way, she wouldn't be alone.

When she opened the door to the arcade, Jack was at the front counter bobbing his head to the guitar riff of "I Wanna Rock" by Twisted Sister while paging through a magazine. Sloan had always been fond of Jack. They were both free spirits and spoke their minds, although Jack did so at a much slower pace. He did have good taste in music though. She swayed her hips back and forth and rolled her arms in the air, her long hair sashaying across her back.

Jack peered up at her, smiling. "That's why you're my favorite. Don't tell Evie."

She danced her way over to Jack and high-fived him. "I won't tell."

"How late is Relics open tonight?"

"Mom is there until eight."

"Cool. The gang is in the back room playing DP," he said.

"Is Mazy here?" she asked.

"She's the blonde, right?"

"Yeah, the perfect, serious one. Wears a lot of pink."

"Right. I don't think so."

Before Sloan could give it another thought, the door opened again, and Mazy appeared as though she and Jack had somehow conjured her on demand, although this was a very frazzled version.

Hey, what's wrong?" Sloan asked.

Mazy growled. At least it sounded like a growl. Sloan didn't think Mazy could make that sound.

"The asshat is back." Mazy said.

"Asshat?" Jack asked, looking at Mazy's bottom half. "Do I want to know what that is?"

Sloan shook her head. "Asshat could be used to describe any number of people. Which particular asshat are you talking about?"

Before Mazy could answer, Steel Strickland walked into Jack's. He was the spitting image of Gage, but that was where their similarities ended. Steel was an actual asshat. His rap sheet was long, and he was generally a foul person. Today, he wore a black leather jacket and had sunglasses on even though it was dark outside.

"I'm back." He spread his arms wide to a virtually empty arcade.

Mazy rolled her eyes. "We know."

Steel took off his glasses and arched a brow at Sloan. "Sloan Simms. Still a slut?"

She narrowed her eyes. "You still the yeast infection I can't get rid of?"

Steel frowned, her barb unexpected, but he recovered quickly. "Sounds itchy."

"Annoyingly so," Sloan said, measured.

He shrugged and sauntered over to Mazy. He brushed the back of his hand across her bare shoulder. "Why did you run away? Aren't you happy to see me?"

"Don't touch me." She batted away his hand.

"Oh, Mary Elizabeth." He pouted for added emphasis.

"Look, I don't want any trouble," Jack said.

"Oh, Jacky, I'm not here to cause trouble. I just wanted to make amends with my brother. He's in back, right?"

Jack scratched at his beard. "Uh, yeah. He's back there."

Sloan turned and stared at Jack. Why would he do that? He should have kicked him out! She turned back around. "Don't even think about it. You are not welcome here or anywhere in Ashwater."

"I'll just be a minute. I promise." Before Sloan or

Mazy could protest, he was bolting to the back of the arcade.

"Jack!" Sloan yelled. "He hates Gage. This means trouble."

"Really? He said he wanted to make amends."

"Yeah and he also called me a slut. Now you know what an asshat is."

Sloan turned around to follow Steel. Mazy was already in hot pursuit. She caught him just outside the DP room, grabbing his arm.

He allowed her to turn him around. "Ooh, someone likes it rough."

"If you hurt him, you'll answer to me." Mazy's jaw was set, her eyes ablaze. She and Gage were through as far as Sloan was aware, but one wouldn't know it looking at her now.

"Is that so, kitten?" He reached for a lock of her blond hair. She slapped his hand away.

"And me," Sloan added when she reached them.

Steel rolled his eyes. "Oh my God. It's, like, so overwhelming how protective everyone is of Gagey-poo. He's so special." His tone dripped with acidic malice. He focused on Mazy. "He dumped you, sweetheart. Why are you defending him?"

Mazy loosened her grip, his retort hitting a nerve. Her eyes turned to daggers and Sloan was genuinely concerned for Steel's wellbeing. Did she still have feelings for Gage?

"Okay, bye." In a flash, Steel spun around and disappeared into the DP room.

"I hate him," Mazy fumed. She wrenched open the door.

Sloan had never seen Mazy so angry. Well, that wasn't entirely true. There was that one time she didn't get the highest grade on an English test.

Knock it off. Now wasn't the time to evaluate whether or not Mazy had anger issues.

Sloan followed her inside.

Adam, Gage, Derrick, and Luke were in the middle of a game. Iris and Evie sat with their backs against the wall just inside. "Devil Inside" by INXS was playing.

Steel jumped in the middle of the floor, disrupting their game play, and played air guitar right on cue with the guitar solo. "Gage, why haven't you ever invited me to play? This is so much fun."

In a flash, Adam shut the game down, and Gage stepped up to Steel.

"What the hell are you doing here?" Gage said.

"Oh, you're no fun." Steel frowned. "Mary Elizabeth and Sloan made much better company."

Gage grabbed Steel with one hand and pushed him back toward the door. Gage had discovered that he, along with Steel, had been born with mind control abilities, and he was clearly using them now.

"Everyone stay here." Gage's eyes never left Steel's, but Sloan knew he meant business.

Iris stood and made to go with him. Gage shook his head. "I'm fine. I got this."

Steel laughed, and it made the hairs on Sloan's arms stand on end.

"I'll be back, bitches," he said in a singsong voice.

As soon as they were out the door, Derrick was by her side, his arms around her. "Are you okay?"

Whoa. She hadn't expected this. She melted into him, linking her fingers around his back, and rested her head on his shoulder. She smiled and closed her eyes. He was warm and cozy. She swayed, lulled by his physical presence.

A minute passed.

"Um, Sloan?" Derrick asked.

Girl, get yourself together. He's a human being, not a weighted blanket. She pulled back and nodded. "Sorry, yeah. No big deal."

"No big deal?" Mazy huffed, her eyes flashing. "He called her a slut."

Derrick's eyes grew dark, his jaw set. "If I see that douchebag again, I'm taking his head off."

"No, it's okay. I can take care of myself," Sloan replied.

"She's right," Mazy added. "She called him a yeast infection."

"Wait, what?" Evie asked.

"She did." Mazy smirked at Evie. "If I hadn't been so mad…"

Evie chuckled until it converted into full-blown laughter. "I wish I could have seen his face."

The boys looked at each other, confused. Iris looked the same until she did a quick search. She cringed. "Ew."

Adam frowned. "How does the yeast—"

"Adam, don't." Evie's eyeliner was smudged more

than usual from tears of laughter. "Search, please, or I'm going to lose it."

Luke touched Sloan's shoulder. "Hey, you really okay?"

She looped her arm around him for a quick hug. "I'm good. Thanks."

Luke narrowed his eyes at Derrick, and she recognized the sentiment—she was his bestie, not Derrick's. She looked down at her feet and exhaled.

Thankfully, Gage returned before it got any more awkward. "My brother is such a jerk."

"Are you okay?" Iris asked, putting her arm around his waist. "I was worried."

"I'm okay, I promise." He cupped the back of her neck and kissed her. When they parted, they gazed into each other's eyes like the rest of the world didn't exist.

Sloan rubbed her palms together, the urge to crack a joke absent. There was something about the tenderness between the two of them that struck a chord with her. She stole a glance at Derrick, who also seemed to be caught up in their moment. He side-eyed her and half-smiled.

"Get a room," Luke said, unaffected. "So what's the deal? Is he staying in town?"

"I guess so." Gage frowned. "Sorry, guys."

"Don't be sorry." Mazy crossed her arms. "It's not your fault your brother has narcissistic rage issues."

"It is to him." Gage glanced at the door, and for a split second, Sloan thought he was sad about Steel's hatred for him.

"Who wants nachos?" Adam asked, his singular love for fake cheese always present.

"I could go for some pretzel-chos," Luke said.

The others nodded. Daisy's snack bar concoctions would be a welcomed remedy.

Derrick grazed Sloan's hand covertly. "You coming?"

Sloan glanced over at Mazy, who still looked anxious and upset as she complained to Evie. The thought of opening the letter by herself made her palms sweaty. *Nope. Not doing it alone.*

It looked like she was indeed headed for snackville. "Yep."

The letter would have to wait.

12

ARCADIA

Derrick

Derrick stared at the tiny sparkles floating in the dark fluid in the vial at the base of the pen-like syringe. There were labs at Bio-Core that probably could have tested the contents, but he didn't have access or the know-how to use them. The only way he was going to learn more about what he had was to find someone he could trust who was willing to help him. Payton was at the top of his list.

He glanced up at the building before him from his dad's truck. There was no sign, but it was unmistakably Arcadia Mental Facility It had an old feel to it—brick and mortar with white pillars. The opposite of the Bio-Core facility, with its sterile hallways and labs. He watched the windows lining the upper floors. Two, in particular, caught his eye. Several people peered out, lined up, as if their heads were unattached to their bodies and resting on the windowsill. Their stares were intense and made Derrick uneasy.

He looked around at his surroundings to see what could possibly have their attention. It was a cooler afternoon with cloud cover. The parking lot was relatively empty, and the trees dotting the rows of parking spaces swayed in a light breeze. Nothing out of the ordinary.

A knock on his door caused his heart to jump to his throat. It was Will. In a flash, he had the vial back in the front pocket of his backpack and got out of his dad's truck.

"What are you doing here?" Will asked.

"I was about to ask you the same question." Derrick reached back into the truck and pulled out a box. Inside was the latest prosthetic to test out. Jasmine and Raj pretty much had this one completed when he started, although he did do some of the programming for it. "I have work here."

"But I thought you were interning at Bio-Core." Will shifted his feet and looked down at the ground. Was he nervous about something?

"I do. But we're testing something out here. Why are you here? Aren't you supposed to be in school?"

"I had an appointment."

"Here?"

"Yeah." Will rubbed the back of his neck. "Um, could you do me a favor and not tell anyone? It's private."

Derrick didn't want to pry. It was a mental hospital. He nodded, apologetically. "Of course. It's not my business."

"Thanks. I appreciate it."

"No problem."

"Well, good luck with whatever you've got there." Will glanced at the box. "I'll see you later?"

"Yep, see ya."

Derrick hoped that Will was okay. He made a mental note to be nicer to him. The last time they'd talked to him, Derrick had been a little rude when Will had asked about the club.

He locked his dad's truck and headed inside. The automatic doors opened, and he went up to the counter. A man with a headset was talking on the phone. His name badge said Brad. Brad raised his index finger toward Derrick to indicate he'd be with him shortly. Derrick turned around and assessed the lobby. It had chandeliers, lots of marble, and an abundance of velvety looking chairs and sofas to sit on. It reminded him more of a hotel lobby than a mental facility.

"Sorry about that. Can I help you?" Brad slid the microphone on his headset away from his mouth.

"Derrick Dixon." He showed the man his Bio-Core ID. "I have a package for Dr. G."

Brad took the package from him. "Thank you. I'll make sure she gets it."

Payton had an office here too. Since he was here... "Could you tell me where Payton Glass's office is?"

"Sure thing." Brad pointed to a scanner sitting on top of the counter. "Scan there please. All the doors in the facility will require you to scan. Miss Glass is on the third floor, Room 313. You can take the elevator or the stairs." Brad indicated behind him with a nod.

"Thanks." Derrick did as he asked and took the elevator up to the third floor. As he exited on his floor, he bumped into a tall man who was obviously in a hurry. The man brushed past him into the elevator, almost knocking Derrick down. By the time he looked to see who it was, the doors had closed. Rude much?

He shook it off, found his way to Room 313, and knocked.

Payton answered the door, her face lighting up when she saw him. "What a nice surprise. Come in."

Her office was small but efficient. She had a desk that faced the door. On one wall were shelves of medical devices, and on the other side of the room was a counter with microscopes, racks of test tubes, and two refrigerators. "Welcome to my home away from home. It's smaller than my office at Bio-Core, but this one allows me access to patients."

"It's nice."

"So what brings you here?"

"I dropped off a prosthetic for Dr. G., and since it was a Tuesday, I thought I'd see you."

"Oh, that's great. Are you feeling good about the work?"

"Yeah, I think so," he said.

Truth be told, he didn't think the prosthetic was quite right yet, but he'd just started and didn't want to be negative right off the bat. There were some distinct connections missing to enhance the prosthetic to work seamlessly with the body.

Derrick wandered over to the refrigerators. "What are these for?"

"Beer."

He laughed. "Okay."

"Samples. Occasionally my lunch."

"So what are you working on?"

"Top secret stuff."

"Sounds exciting." He raised his eyebrows at her. Was she going to tell him more?

Payton smiled, assessing him as if deciding on what, or rather how much, to say. "Can I trust you?"

His instinct was to say yes, but she had already told him to be on guard. Instead, he replied, "As much as I can trust you."

She laughed. "Nice. I'm exploring some interesting environmental factors that could potentially impact the human body. Mostly water and air quality."

"Here?" He tilted his head at her. Of all the places in the world where there were interesting and unique environments, Ashwater was dull.

"Yes." She turned away from him. "Ashwater definitely has its secrets."

Well, he couldn't argue with that. He glanced at a microscope. Again, he wondered if he could trust her to help him figure out what was in the vial.

"Did you know Dr. Rice?"

"Yes, of course. Lovely woman." Payton turned back around. "I was so sorry to hear what happened."

"Has she made any improvement?"

"I'm afraid not. You can visit her if you want. She's just down the hall."

Derrick didn't know Dr. Rice very well, yet he wanted to check in on her. Since he was the last person she'd spoken to, he felt some kind of bond to her. Then there was the promise he'd made to keep the syringe secret. "Yes, I think I'd like that."

"She's in the medical wing on this floor. Use your ID to access." Payton looked at the tablet sitting on her desk. Room 340."

"Thanks."

Her phone rang. She answered it and mouthed to Derrick, *See you later.*

He left her office. On his way to Dr. Rice's room, he contemplated telling Payton about the syringe. Chances were pretty good she'd know what the contents were or at least be able to figure it out.

When he reached Dr. Rice's door, he took a deep breath, preparing himself for a variety of tubes, bags of fluid, pumps, and the like. He pushed open the door, and his breath caught.

The bed was empty.

By the window, Dr. Rice, wearing a hospital gown, sat upright in a chair, looking out the window.

"Dr. Rice?" Derrick asked.

She didn't budge. He couldn't see her face clearly. Her hair covered her gaze toward the window. He wavered in the doorway. Should he go get someone?

He went over to her and patted her arm. "Dr. Rice?"

No response. It was like she was frozen or something. He leaned over to look at her eyes. They were hazy. He inhaled sharply as she tilted her head and looked up at him. She mumbled something faintly.

"What is it?" he said. "What are you trying to say?"

Again, she mumbled something incoherent.

Derrick shook his head. "Don't worry. I'll go get someone."

He made to leave, but she grabbed his arm with surprising strength. She pulled him close, and their eyes met.

Her eyes changed, and he saw something in her irises—something bright. Like the vial. He pried himself free and staggered back. He needed to get help, but before he could do anything, all hell broke loose.

Sirens sounded from somewhere down the hall. Someone announced, "Code Violet," on the speaker system.

Derrick looked back at Dr. Rice. He should tell someone she was alert. He went into the hallway. People in scrubs and lab coats headed toward a room down the hall. He looked the other way. Dr. G. headed his way toward the emergency.

He tried to get her attention. "Dr. G."

"Not now, Derrick." She pushed past him.

"Wait. Dr. Rice is awake."

Dr. G. stopped dead in her tracks and turned around. "Excuse me?"

Derrick pointed to her room. "Yeah, she's sitting up by the window."

"That is...good news." She came back to the room and peeked inside at Dr. Rice. She glanced up at him. "You found her that way?"

"Yeah and there's something in her eyes."

Dr. G. walked over to Dr. Rice and tilted her head back, peering down at her. She came back out and shut the door. "Thank you for letting me know. Time for you to go."

"But—"

"I said, thank you. I've got it from here." She stood in front of Dr. Rice's door as if standing guard. Apparently, the emergency was her second priority now.

He didn't have much choice. He turned and headed back down the hall.

Derrick glanced back to see Dr. G. going back in Dr. Rice's room. He hoped she was going to be okay. As he made his way downstairs among the sirens and confusion, he couldn't help but long for the calm solitude of his team's lab back at Bio-Core. This place was chaotic. Most people thought Bio-Core was peculiar, but Arcadia? Yeesh. There was no comparison.

As he strode over to his dad's truck, another thought occurred to him—what the heck was a Code Violet?

13

CONFESSIONS

Sloan

For as long as Sloan could remember, her parents and Mac Grayson were friends. They grew up together. So, it came as a surprise that he was using such a threatening tone with her dad in the store.

"I'm only asking because I need to get to the bottom of this." Mac crossed his arms and pivoted. His impatience was clearly growing.

"I understand that. Believe me, I do. But I can't spy on my customers. That's not only immoral—it's creepy," Owen replied.

"There's a drug out there that's killing our kids. You see tons of potential suspects. I'm just asking for a little good Samaritan help here. If I have to, I'll shut you down."

"On what grounds?" Owen put his hands on his hips. "We've known each other since we were kids, for God's sake."

Sloan pursed her lips as she watched them go back and forth like a tennis match. Her dad would never agree to eavesdrop on customers, and she suspected Mac already knew that. So what was this really about?

Before she could give more thought, the front door opened, and Will came inside. He froze and stared at the sheriff and her dad arguing.

"Sorry, is the store closed?" Will asked.

"It absolutely is not. We're open for ten more minutes." Owen narrowed his eyes at Mac. "Let's go in back to finish this conversation."

Mac nodded.

Sloan headed to the front of the store. "Hey, how's it going?"

"Hi. What was that all about?" He looked past her to where her dad and Mac were arguing.

She sighed. "It's because there's been a bunch of overdoses lately. Something about a new substance the cops haven't seen yet. The sheriff thinks he can figure out who's dealing it by bugging our store."

"Huh." Will nodded slowly. "That's a good idea."

What the actual...

"A good idea?" She tilted her head, her eyebrows knitted together. "What are you, some kind of detective now?"

"Oh, sorry." Will held out his hands apologetically. "That came out wrong. I meant, from the sheriff's perspective. It would not be good for your parents' shop."

"Yeah, we're not going to spy on our customers.

We know most of them, and they would never take or deal a drug that's as lethal as this one."

"Right. Of course." He shoved his hands in the front pockets of his jeans and perused the shelves of paraphernalia on the wall.

"You have to be eighteen," she said, watching him.

"Oh, no, I'm not here for that." He smiled. "Everyone says that you are the Lotus aficionado, and they are playing tomorrow night at Purgatory. Are they worth seeing?"

He came here to talk to her about Lotus? Super weird. On the other hand, it was kinda cool that kids at school recognized her for her taste. She was a devoted fan. "You should definitely go. They usually play some original stuff and then some covers. Totally worth it."

"Oh, cool. Are you going?" he asked.

A record scratching noise sounded in her head. Wait, did he want to ask her out? She shifted her weight nervously. Shut it down. "Uh, yeah. I'm going with Luke."

"Oh." He shook his head, smiling. "I wasn't, I mean…"

"Oh." She grimaced. He wasn't asking her out. "Sorry. I'm a creature of habit."

"No, it's fine. I'm just looking for stuff to do. Ashwater isn't exactly happening, you know?"

"Well, if you were looking for a date, I know for a fact that Shannon Wells would gladly hop into your lap."

Will blushed and grinned. If she wasn't mistaken, he muttered, *I know,* under his breath. Before she could question it, he asked, "Cheerleader, right?"

"Yep. She'll probably be at Purgatory tomorrow." She raised her eyebrows for added emphasis.

He wrinkled up his nose. "I think I might be entering a blond phase. No offense."

Sloan laughed, relaxing. New kid might be all right. She liked when people said what they thought. "None taken. You're not my type either."

She glanced down at his blazer. He wore them to school all the time. *Who wears a freaking blazer?*

He looked down and smirked. "What? I like to look nice."

Sloan shrugged and rearranged a couple pipes some customers had looked at. "Whatever warms your shorts."

He laughed. "Is that like your special talent? Cracking inappropriate jokes?"

"Must be." She arched an eyebrow.

"Derrick said you were funny."

Her cheeks warmed at the sound of his name. She knocked over a pipe, which clanged as glass hit glass. She righted the pipe and looked up at Will. "Wha— Um, Derrick said I was funny?"

Will nodded, a mischievous look in his eyes. "You like him."

"I—what? I don't know what you're talking about." She was stammering and also knew exactly what he was talking about.

"It's not my business." He turned to leave. "So, I guess I'll see you at Purgatory?"

Now that he'd mentioned Derrick, it was all she could think about. How was his internship going? Was he thinking about her as much as she thought about him? Damn, she wished he could go to Purgatory with her tomorrow.

"Sloan?"

"What?"

"See you at Purgatory?"

"Um, yeah. See you there."

After he left, she turned the open sign to closed and grabbed her phone. She wanted to text Derrick in the worst way. When she looked at her phone, her heart leaped into her throat—he'd already texted her.

DERRICK: *Hey, I've had the weirdest day. You busy?*

Was she busy? She screamed and jumped up and down.

SLOAN: *Just closed the shop. What did you have in mind?*

She saw three bubbles and did a little jog in place. *Yes!*

"Christ, Sloan, are you okay?" Her dad rushed out from the back.

Mac had his hand on his gun in its holster, scanning the store.

She shoved her phone in her back pocket. "Oh my God. Sorry. I'm just texting a friend."

"Well, don't scream like that. You almost gave me a heart attack." Owen put his hand over his heart as if checking to make sure it was still beating.

Mac smirked and clapped her dad on the back. "Comes with the territory of having a teenage daughter, Owen. They scream. A lot."

"No kidding," Owen replied.

"Think about what I said." Mac headed to the door. "Sloan, be careful tomorrow night."

"Of course." She stood up straighter.

By the door, he stared at a pipe depicting two people in an interesting embrace and frowned. "Not that I won't be just around the corner."

He shook his head and left.

Sloan pulled her phone back out.

DERRICK: *Meet me at Jack's?*

"Dad, I'm going over to Jack's for a bit. Okay?"

"Okay, tell Jack and Daisy hello."

Sloan headed to the door, texting Derrick back. "Will do."

JACK'S WAS ALWAYS one of her favorite places. She felt at home there. Before she opened the door, Derrick startled her from behind.

"Hey." He slipped his hand around her waist, and she felt his breath on her hair. With his other hand, he pulled her hair to the side and whispered, "Thanks for meeting me."

She inhaled sharply, closed her eyes, and leaned back against him. She found his hand on her waist and interlaced her fingers with his turning to face him. His eyes were dark and smoldering. She wet her lips and did her best to quiet the pant emanating from the back of her throat. "You're welcome."

An older couple headed their way on the sidewalk. Derrick acted first and separated, running his hand through his mussed hair, cheeks reddening.

Sloan grinned and opened the door. "Come on."

It wasn't busy. Daisy was cleaning at the snack bar. Her hair was purple, and her lips matched. Jack was nowhere to be seen.

Daisy looked up, noticing them. "Hey, kids. Want anything before I close up?"

Sloan shook her head. She was hungry but not for tot-chos.

"No thanks, Aunt Daisy," Derrick said.

"How about some music?" Sloan asked, heading to the jukebox.

"Sure," he replied, following her.

She scanned the options. She put a few coins in and played, "Orange Crush" by R.E.M.

"Nice choice. Want to play some Pac-Man?" he asked.

Pac-Man, huh? It was hidden behind a bunch of other games. She said, "Sure."

Sloan followed him to the far side of the arcade where the classic games were located. He set his backpack down and leaned against the game, hiding the controls.

"Do you not want to play?" she asked, arching an eyebrow as her mind went to all kinds of dirty places.

"No. Something weird happened today, and I'm not sure what to think about it."

She propped herself next to him, yanking her mind from the gutter. Too bad. "What? What is it?"

"I was at Arcadia delivering something for work. Since I was there, I went to see how Dr. Rice was doing. It felt like the right thing to do since I found her and all."

Sloan reached for his hand. "Oh jeez. That must have been weird."

"It was. Like, I was prepared for her to be hooked up to all this stuff, but she wasn't." He glanced up at the game console, eyes unfocused, as if conjuring the memory. "She was awake, Sloan. Or at least she was somewhat conscious."

"That's good news, right?"

"I don't know." Derrick tilted his head as if he still hadn't sorted out his feelings about what he'd seen. "She was sitting by the window in a chair. I tried talking to her, but she was, like, incoherent. And her eyes…they weren't right."

"Not right how?" Sloan inched closer and brushed her hand against his.

"It was like there was something in her eyes. It gave me the creeps."

"Did you tell someone?"

"Yeah, Dr. G. was there. She said she'd take care of her." He looked at her, his expression changing from deep-seated concern to warmth. "Afterwards, I only wanted to see you."

A fire lit in her belly, and her heart clenched. She smiled up at him. "I'll take that as a compliment."

"You should. I feel better around you. I always have."

She squeezed his hand. "I'm glad. I feel the same."

"Speaking of which, did you open your letter yet?" He raised his eyebrows.

"No." She frowned and crossed her arms across her chest.

"I could open it for you, if you want?"

She rolled her eyes. "No, I'm going to do it. Mazy's been up my ass about it."

He chuckled. "That's what Mazy does."

"It's just...what if I don't get in? Do I keep working in my parent's shop?" She cringed and sighed loudly.

"You're going to get in." He pushed a lock of her hair behind her ear. "So, stop saying that."

She turned toward him. "How can you be so confident?"

"Because." He leaned forward. "You're Sloan Simms. When have you ever not gotten what you wanted?"

She cracked a smile. "True."

They stood that way for a moment, stealing glances at each other's lips. She wanted to kiss him in the worst way, and she saw the same desire in his eyes.

"Aww, you two are, like, so adorable," someone said near them, making kissing noises for emphasis.

Steel.

Sloan's eyes turned to daggers. "What the hell do you want?"

"Um..." Steel rolled his eyes. "To play Pac-Man, which you two are totally not doing."

"You want to play this game?" Derrick asked suspiciously.

"Yeah. It's a classic." Steel smiled, arching an eyebrow, moving toward them. "So, does the other one know about you two? I forget his name. Duke or something."

"It's Luke." Derrick put his hands on his hips.

"Oh, right." He pointed at Sloan. "The sporty twin is your bestie, right? Super protective. Well, my lips are sealed. This puts a whole new spin on bros before hoes."

"I know you didn't just refer to Sloan as a ho." Derrick stepped up to Steel so that they were toe to toe.

"I mean, if the thong fits..." He shrugged.

Something flashed in Derrick's eyes, and it sent a chill down Sloan's spine. She stepped between them— or at least tried to. *What was this? WWE Saturday night?*

"I'm not afraid of you." Derrick's gaze never left Steel's.

"You should be." Steel's lips turned up into a sneer.

"Stop, he's not worth it," she said to Derrick. She could practically smell the adrenaline rolling off them. This was about to turn ugly. She pushed Derrick out of the way and kneed Steel in the groin. "Back off!"

Steel doubled over, coughing and groaning.

"For your information, I'm a boyshort kind of girl." She grabbed Derrick's hand. "Let's go."

He picked up his backpack, and they headed to the front door.

Daisy yelled, "Hey wait. What—"

Ignoring her, they ran outside and down the street. A few blocks down, her heart pounded, and her head swam. Did she really just knee Steel in the balls?

They came to a stop at an intersection, breathless.

"I can't believe you did that," Derrick said.

"Me either."

"Normally, below the belt is off limits for guys. But not for that asshole." He fist-bumped her. "Props."

"He had it coming." She was still running hot because of his slut comment a while back.

Derrick leaned toward her, a smile spreading across his lips. He arched an eyebrow. "Boyshorts, huh?"

Sloan laughed. "Hey, comfort first."

He put his arm around her. "Come on, I have my dad's truck. I'll drive you home."

"Thanks."

As they walked to his truck, Sloan got a terrible feeling in the pit of her stomach. What would Steel do when he saw her again? She'd connected solidly with his boys. He wouldn't forget.

As if on cue, she heard Steel's voice in her head, *"Payback's a bitch."*

She stiffened and glanced around. "Did you—"

"What?" Derrick asked.

She knew Steel and Gage had the ability to communicate through thought. Or, at least that was what she'd heard.

Had he spoken to her, or was it her consciousness telling her to be on guard?

Sloan wanted to be home under the covers with her dog, Buck, in the worst way. "Never mind. Let's just get out of here."

14

FRUSTRATION

Derrick

Derrick had to see if Dr. Rice was all right. He was tired of carrying around the syringe. He had enough on his plate with Steel's newfound interest in him and Sloan. The guy was a serious douche and held a grudge. With Sloan on his current shit list, he needed to be prepared—Steel was capable of anything.

He skipped his late morning classes and stopped at Arcadia. His grades were impeccable, so his teachers let him slack on attendance. He had a lot of work to do later at Bio-Core and was more than ready to unload the distracting and complicated syringe. As he walked in the front doors, it appeared the hospital had recovered from yesterday's chaos. The hallways were quiet, and nurses walking the halls spoke in low tones. Derrick used his ID at the clearance checkpoints and bee-lined it to Dr. Rice's room. He took a deep breath, knocked, and pushed open the door.

The room was empty. Bed made. Machines turned off. No sign of occupancy. He checked the door again. He was at the right room. He shut the door and looked down the hallway. Where was Dr. Rice?

Derrick headed down the hall to Payton's office and knocked.

"Come in." Payton sat at her desk, typing. She glanced up gazing just above her glasses. "Hi, Derrick. Did I forget that we were meeting?"

"No, I stopped by to see Dr. Rice, but she's not in her room."

"Right." Payton stopped typing. "She was transferred to another facility for rehabilitation."

"What facility?" Derrick advanced toward her desk. He didn't like the sound of this one bit. They had rehab at this hospital.

"Listen, I don't mean to be rude, but I'm kind of in the middle of something here." She looked back down at her laptop.

He considered leaving. He respected Payton and didn't want to do anything to jeopardize their relationship or his internship. On the other hand, that stupid syringe was burning a hole in the front pocket of his backpack. He needed to speak with Dr. Rice. He sat down in the chair opposite Payton. "I'm sorry, but I need to know where Dr. Rice is."

Payton shut her laptop and groaned. "Why do you have such an interest in Dr. Rice? I know you were the one who found her, but this is borderline obsessive, don't you think?"

Derrick weighed his options. He didn't know how much Payton knew about why Dr. Rice was transferred, but she clearly knew more than he did. "I just want to make sure she's all right."

"I can't help you." She stared at her desk, her breathing deliberate and slow. It was almost as if someone or something was forbidding her from talking to him. A knot formed in his belly.

"Can't or won't?" He frowned and crossed his arms.

"I have a lot of work to do," she said, not looking up.

He wasn't going to get anything out of her. His instincts told him to stop pushing. She might be in danger like Dr. Rice was. He stood. "Okay, sorry to bother you."

Payton simply nodded, her eyes focused on a spot on her desk.

As he left her office, he weighed his options. He could ask Dr. G where she was. Or Max, for that matter. But something told him they would be just as evasive as Payton was. The only thing he knew for certain was that Payton knew exactly where Dr. Rice was and what had happened to her. What he didn't know was why she was keeping it a secret from him.

He headed to his dad's truck. Looked like he'd have to keep the syringe for a while longer.

. . .

Each time Derrick entered his lab at Bio-Core, it reminded him what an amazing opportunity this was. He was very thankful. The only problem was that his team was having some major setbacks in their research. He knew their last prototype wasn't going to work. But as Raj told him—they had to produce, or their funding would be pulled, even if the work was sub-par.

"Hey, Derrick," Jasmine said, her eyes on the 3-D printing arm. "I think I may have figured out some of the issues with force sensors."

Derrick sighed. It wasn't that it wasn't good news —it just wasn't enough. The real problem was the ability to fully integrate a prosthetic to a person's skeleton, muscles, and most importantly, nervous system. They'd had no problem with the first two, but the nerves were a whole different thing. Still, he didn't want to be discouraging to his team. "That's good news. What would you like me to work on?"

"Something new." Raj glanced up from his desk. "We're going to have a test subject today."

"Seriously?" His heart rate whipped up. Before they had to take their work to Arcadia. Now subjects would be coming to them? They would be able to test so much more here.

Raj frowned. "Not in the way you're thinking. We're getting a subject from downstairs."

Downstairs? Oh. An android. They were integrating some of that technology into their research, but Derrick wasn't sure how they could help. "Why?"

"You know how the powers that be are." Raj

waved his hand upward. "We haven't had a true breakthrough with our research. Sure, we've worked out the theoretical magnitude of what we want to accomplish, but the reality is we're still pushing basic prosthetics. The board is not happy. So it has come to this."

Jasmine had been listening. "We need to produce. Plain and simple. It's time to get our hands dirty."

Raj chuckled. "Poor choice of words, Dr. Murray."

Derrick swallowed a few times, his mouth dry. "Wait, what exactly are we doing?"

Before either of his team could answer, the door opened, and two men rolled in a gurney with a man in a gray, neoprene bodysuit. His eyes were closed, and there didn't appear to be any sign of life.

One man asked, "Where do you want this?"

"Over here." Raj pointed to a spot next to their 3-D printer.

The men's faces strained as they pushed the cart to Raj's desired location as if the body weighed a ton. They turned and left without a word.

Derrick was frozen in place. His legs wouldn't move, his voice stuck in his throat. This wasn't really happening, was it?

Jasmine walked over to a tall cabinet and pulled out three black, vinyl aprons. She tossed one to Raj and Derrick before donning one herself.

Derrick looked down at the apron in his hands. They were really going to dissect the body on the table. At once, he realized the potential to see the interworking of the skeletal, neural, and muscular systems up close.

But every time he looked at the gurney, he saw Adam's face. Android or not, this was not what he signed up for.

"Raj, I think our intern has a weak stomach." Jasmine put her hand on his shoulder. "Listen, to me. You need to remember what this is. It's a piece of brilliant technology, not a person, and we need a breakthrough. This could be it."

"You took the internship to learn, correct?" Raj asked.

Derrick cleared his throat, willing words to come out, but nothing came. Of course he wanted to learn. Just not by cutting into bodies.

Raj added, "Don't worry. You will only be observing this time. The apron is precautionary."

"If you want to be placed with a different team…" Jasmine narrowed her eyes, her skepticism rising.

"No." Derrick swallowed hard. "I can handle it."

From Jasmine and Raj's point of view, the androids really were just tech. What they didn't realize was that two of Derrick's closest friends were androids, and if he wanted to keep them safe, he planned on keeping it that way. He couldn't explain his feelings without jeopardizing them. No, his only choice was to suck it up.

His hands trembled as he lifted the strap of the apron over his head and tied the loose ends at his back. His heart pounded. He was about to be part of an android autopsy.

As he walked toward the body, he replayed Raj's words in his head over and over—only observing *this time*.

Sloan

After school, Sloan grabbed her dress and her letter and went over to Evie's house. Mazy would be there, and she was going to keep her promise and open it. It was time to put an end to this whole business. Besides, she was in a great mood because of the concert, and even a denial from Edgewood couldn't stop her from having a good time.

Mr. Grayson answered the door and waved her inside. "Hello, Sloan. The girls are upstairs."

"Thanks." Sloan ran up the steps two at a time, the letter burning a hole in the back pocket of her shorts.

Iris was still staying with Evie and was in her bedroom with the door open. She was wearing a strapless dress for the concert, admiring herself in a full-length mirror. She looked hot. But Iris looked gorgeous in everything she wore.

"Nice duds," Sloan said from the doorway. She was wearing a T-shirt, shorts, and Converse.

"Thanks." Iris looked her up and down. "You look...like you."

Sloan laughed. "Gee, thanks, Iris. You really know how to sweet-talk a girl."

"You're welcome." Iris smiled.

Sloan headed down the hall to Evie's room. Mazy

was sitting at the window seat, looking outside. No Evie. Sloan slung her backpack down. "What's up?"

Mazy turned. "Oh, good. You're here. Did you bring it?"

"Yep." Sloan pulled out the folded letter. "Where's Evie?"

"Shower." Mazy got up, her eyes dancing with excitement. This girl loved anything academic. "Open it."

"Okay." Sloan's heart jumped into her throat, and her palms got sweaty. She unfolded the letter, her hands shaking. She looked up at Mazy, who was practically jumping up and down. Sloan exhaled and handed the letter to Mazy. "You do it."

"Really?" Mazy took the letter.

"Yeah. I can't." Sloan sat down on Evie's bed. Among the drawings on the wall, mostly of Adam, there was one of her sitting in a pile of leaves. She remembered that day—fall, junior year. Simpler times. Now her future hung in the balance and in Mazy's anxious hands.

"Okay." Mazy broke the seal on the envelope and pulled out the tri-folded letter. Her eyes scanned the words, her expression unreadable.

"Well?" Sloan thought her heart would burst.

"It's not a rejection." Mazy raised her eyebrows.

"I got in?" Sloan got off the bed, clasping her hands together.

"Um, you didn't *not* get in." Mazy tilted her head as if looking at the letter from a different angle would give her more insight.

"What does that mean? Did I get in or not?" Sloan was woozy from the sheer anxiety. This was no time for guess-what-Mazy's-thinking.

Mazy sighed and handed her the letter. "You got deferred."

"Deferred? What does that mean?" Sloan read the letter for herself.

Yep. Deferred.

"It could mean lots of things. You did apply late. There might be a lot of applicants this year. It also might mean they are waiting to get your final grades before making a decision. They already have your SAT scores, right?"

Sloan couldn't breathe, her throat dry and sticky. She'd only prepared herself for acceptance or rejection. How ridiculous was her life? For weeks, she'd deferred opening a letter that said she was deferred.

She slumped down on Evie's bed. "I can't believe this."

"No, no, no. You're taking this all wrong." Mazy sat down and put her arm around her. "This is going to work out."

"I'm such an idiot to think they would accept me. I applied too late." Tears filled her eyes. *Don't cry. Don't cry.*

Mazy took the letter back from her and folded it up. "You really want this, don't you?"

Sloan took a deep, ragged breath. She wet her lips, her eyes focused on her lap. A swirl of emotions took root in the pit of her stomach—embarrassment, hurt, and even a hint of anger. She did want this more than anything. She wanted a different life than the head shop or Ashwater could offer. "Yes, I do."

"Then it's settled. You're going to Edgewood this fall."

"You don't know that." Sloan fell back on Evie's bed. She wished it would swallow her up.

"Yes, I do. That admission committee is going to be begging you to go there once we're done with them." Mazy got up and paced. "We'll start on Monday by sending a couple emails and make some phone calls. We need to make sure they have all your current test scores, grades, and academic extracurricular activities."

"Extracurricular activities?" Sloan raised herself up on her elbows. Last she checked, she wasn't part of anything extracurricular except Snowboarding Club.

"Yes. We need to let them know you forgot to mention that you are the secretary of student relations for student government."

Sloan raised her eyebrows. "The what?"

"Yes. Secretary of student relations. Job duties included welcoming new students and disseminating information to students. All things you already do."

"And when did I get this title?"

Mazy pursed her lips. "I'll get the paperwork done tomorrow and get it on record Monday."

Huh. Perks of being close with the class president.

"I'm not done." Mazy glanced at Sloan. "You still with me?"

"I guess?"

Watching Mazy strategize in front of her was like

watching a dog with a bone. She was all teeth, and the bone didn't stand a chance. She rattled off some more ideas, and Sloan nodded. After what seemed like the longest tirade Sloan had ever heard, Mazy exhaled. "That pretty much covers it. What do you think?"

"I think you should run for President of the United States."

Mazy smiled demurely. "It's not off the table. But seriously, what do you think?"

Sloan stood, tears still in her eyes but for a very different reason. She hugged Mazy. "I think you're a force, Mazy, and I don't know how to thank you for being such a great friend."

Mazy hugged her back. "They didn't realize who they were dealing with. That's all."

"No, they didn't." Sloan smiled.

"Did I miss something?" Evie asked, from the door.

The girls separated. "You did," Mazy said, smiling. "Sloan's going to Edgewood in the fall."

Sloan stared at Mazy. That was fast.

"Awesome. Congrats." Evie pulled the towel off her head and sat at her vanity.

"It is great. Right, Sloan?" Mazy asked, eyebrows raised.

Sloan didn't have the confidence Mazy did, but she was grateful for her help. If Mazy wanted her to stay positive, that was what she'd do. "Edgewood, here I come."

"Now go put on that hot red number so we can get to Purgatory early. There's going to be a huge line."

Mazy leaned down behind Evie to fluff her hair and pucker her lips in the mirror.

Sloan grabbed her bag. Mazy was right—there would be a long line, and she wanted to be front and center when Lotus took the stage. Butterflies took flight in her belly, replacing the stagnant hollowness from the letter.

This concert was going to be epic. She only wished Derrick could be there too.

15

OPPORTUNITY KNOCKS

Derrick

When his internship hours were over, Derrick headed to the diner to take Luke's shift for him. He had a lot on his mind. Between watching an android autopsy and Dr. Rice's disappearance, his mind was spinning. He was actually surprised at how well he handled the former. After the initial shock and cutting, his mind settled. There was so much they could gain from the procedure. It would take time, but Raj and Jasmine were spot on—seeing how the systems worked up close would help them transition from android-prosthetics to human-prosthetics.

Dr. Rice, on the other hand, remained a problem. She was gone, and he was tired of carrying the syringe around. He resolved to tell Payton about the syringe on Monday. His gut told him he could trust her. She was obviously good at keeping to her word, since she was asked to not tell him where Dr. Rice was, and he thought she genuinely liked him.

Sadly, that wasn't all he was juggling in his brain. He was super bummed he couldn't go see Lotus with Sloan. He liked the band just as much as the next person, but that wasn't what made his heart ache. That was solely his desire to be near Sloan.

He clocked in and got to work, drowning his sorrows with customers' Friday night specials and banana splits. He shared the shift with Celia, who didn't seem to mind not going to see Lotus. After the dinner crowd left, business slowed to a crawl. He sat down on a stool at the counter to count his tips.

"Friday nights are the best for tips. Am I right?" Celia took a seat next to him.

"Definitely." Derrick did his best to smile. Most people tipped better because it was either payday or the start to the weekend.

"So I've been meaning to ask you about your internship. Do you like working for Bio-Core? I know they're affiliated with Arcadia too."

"Uh, yeah, sure."

"Yeah?" She leaned closer, her eyes flashing.

"Why—"

"Oh, sorry." She leaned back, smiling. He could see why his brother liked her so much. She had a light about her. An optimism. "I'm thinking about Arcadia for my first PT job. I just passed my licensing exam."

"That's awesome. Congrats." He had forgotten she was only working at Dixon's temporarily since she was there so much. He wondered how she found the time go to school, work practically full time as a waitress, and still coach the high school cheerleading team.

"Thanks. You're actually the first person I told."

"Really? Well, I think you'll be an excellent therapist. You're really good with people."

"I hope so. You know, people don't realize how important physical therapy is for people like..." She inhaled sharply and looked down at the counter, a shadow cast across her face.

Ah. That was why she wanted to work at Arcadia.

Her dad was a patient there. Derrick didn't know all the details, but her dad had suffered some kind of trauma that left him comatose. No one really knew much about the details, but Celia was in high school at the time.

He put his hand on her shoulder. He hadn't lost anyone in the way she had, but the hurt was palpable. "You're going to be great. Maybe you should talk to Gage about a recommendation. He put a good word in for me."

"That's a good idea. Thanks." She glanced at the door to the kitchen. "Don't say anything to Eric—er, I mean your dad—yet. I don't want to stress him out until I know for sure I've got another job."

Derrick had mixed feelings about how close his dad and Celia were. He hoped it was more of a father-figure thing. Otherwise...ew. The thought turned his stomach. "No problem."

"Thanks." She hopped off the stool.

He did his best to smile and stared back down at the dollar bills in front of him. He was scheduled to close. That meant filling salt and pepper shakers and ketchup bottles. "If You Were Here" by Thompson Twins played on one of the table jukeboxes. There were a ton of eighties songs on them. He checked his smartwatch and sighed. The concert was underway by now, and his brother was probably dancing with Sloan. He hoped she was having a good time.

"You thinking about Sloan?" Celia's eyebrow arched.

"Huh?" He laughed nervously and ran his hand through his hair. Was it that obvious?

She sat back down and pursed her lips. "He'll understand, you know. Just because they're best friends doesn't mean you can't like her."

"Are we talking about the same person? My brother, Luke?" He shook his head. "I doubt he'd understand."

"Do you really think you're the first guy to fall for his brother's best friend? They make rom-coms about this all the time."

"Yeah, well, this is real life and he's my twin. Besides, I don't really know if Sloan is that interested anyway."

She laughed. "Please. If she were any more into you, she'd be inside you."

Derrick frowned. "Uh…"

"Wait. Sorry. That came out wrong." She blushed. "What I mean is, she likes you too. If you'd be honest with yourself, you know it's true."

Maybe she was right. He did get a vibe that he and Sloan were on the same page. Still, he hated the thought of there being any weirdness between him and Luke before he left for college. "Well, it doesn't matter now. Besides, I've got a lot of salt shakers to think about."

"Yes, it does."

"Huh?"

Celia grabbed a small stack of bills in front of him. "I'll take this as payment for finishing out your shift. You've got a concert to go to." She checked her watch. "My guess is that they will be finishing their first set in about half an hour. That gives you plenty of time to get there for the end of their second set. You might even get there in time for a dance with Sloan."

Derrick was speechless. His mind raced at the thought of seeing Sloan. "But I don't have a car."

"You can take mine." She reached into her apron and tossed her keys to him.

"But then you won't have a car to get home."

"Your dad can give me a ride."

He glanced down at his Dixon's Diner T-shirt. He wasn't dressed for a concert. He opened his mouth to protest again.

"You have extra shirts in your locker in the back." Celia, seemingly done with the conversation, looked down at her nails. "I need a manicure."

"How did you—"

"You better get going. You're wasting time."

He stood, his heart rate whipping up into a frenzy. Was this really happening? "I, uh—"

"Derrick." She stared up at him, her large, hazel eyes wide. "Go."

"Okay." He felt awkward and excited at the same time. She was doing him a huge favor. Not sure how to leave, he hugged her. "Thank you so much. I promise I'll make it up to you."

"All right, all right. I'll hold you to it." She patted his back. "Now get out of here."

He ran to the back to retrieve a fresh shirt and his backpack. Come to think of it, he had a Lotus T-shirt in his locker. He grabbed it, dodging his dad, who was in the walk-in freezer, and bee-lined it to Celia's car.

"I Will Follow" by U2 played on her radio. He chuckled to himself. Perfect.

Sloan

It was an incredible second set. They'd just finished dancing to a cover of "Blister in the Sun" by The Violent Femmes before the band took a break. She'd danced so much her legs felt like jelly. She beamed up at Luke, who hadn't left her side since the concert started. She missed Derrick, but Luke was the best wingman a girl could ask for.

"This is awesome," she yelled, her ears still ringing from the loud music.

"I know." Luke smiled and draped his arm around her shoulders. He wore his black Lotus T-shirt from last year's tour.

She squeezed his hand. This was how it was between them. Comfortable. Safe. She'd always wanted a sibling, but her parents had enough trouble conceiving her. They got her Buck instead. He was a good boy, but he didn't listen very well. A knot formed in her stomach. She'd been so worried about getting into Edgewood that she hadn't thought about losing Luke. "I'm going to miss you next year."

"I'll be an hour away." He pursed his lips. "Besides, you can come and visit me. The tailgating is supposed to be sick."

She wiped her damp forehead with her arm. "I know. Just, it won't be the same."

"I'm not dying, you know."

"Duh." She elbowed him in the ribs playfully. "I have to pee."

She looked around for Evie, Iris, or Mazy. Evie and Iris were in deep conversation with their boys. Mazy was nowhere to be seen. "Have you seen Mazy?"

"Isn't that her up there?" Luke pointed at an upper deck.

Sloan followed his line of sight. Sure enough, Mazy was perched at the railing, surrounded by a bunch of kids from school, who appeared to be hanging on her every word. She smiled. Holding court, as usual. She looked past the bar and located the sign for the restrooms. A line had formed for the women's room, and she was already thinking about crossing her legs while she waited.

"Don't move. I don't want to lose this spot. I'll be right back," she said.

"Do you want me to—"

"No. There's a huge line. Plenty of bathroom buddy options."

"Girls are weird."

"Yep. Now, stay."

Sloan pushed her way through the sea of bodies on the dance floor toward the restrooms. Her bladder felt like it was going to burst.

You shouldn't have had an entire bottle of Coke on the way here.

She got in line behind a girl with legs that went on for days who wore a white tube top and high-waisted denim shorts. Sloan smiled at her, antsy and swaying. She really had to go.

The girl harrumphed. "Welcome to hell."

"Thanks, I can't say I'm happy to be here."

"You having a good time?"

"Yeah. That last set was amazing. I love their original stuff, but I'd be lying if I didn't have a soft spot for their alternative covers."

"I know, and they always play new covers each concert."

"I take it you've seen them before."

"Yup. This is my twentieth concert this tour."

"Wow." Sloan nodded. "Are you like a roadie?"

"Well—" She tilted her head and smiled. "Yeah, kinda."

Huh. A roadie with benefits. Sloan wondered which of the band members she was hooking up with. "Cool. I'm Sloan."

"Maya."

Sloan hopped from side to side in her hold-the-pee dance. Why was the women's room always so long and the men's room had no wait?

"Hey, want to try the guy's side?" Maya asked.

"Do you read minds?" Sloan smiled.

Maya laughed. She had the whitest teeth, and her smile made her whole face light up. "Come on, let's go."

Sloan took a deep breath, steeled her bladder, and followed. There was no turning back now. The door to the men's room swung open, and a guy walked out.

Maya pushed against the door and peered in. "Anyone home?"

"Hey," a couple of male voices said in unison.

Maya pushed the door open wide so Sloan could see. There were four guys at urinals. "Do you guys mind? The women's room line is so long."

Two of the guys at urinals pinched off their flow and zipped up. The other two looked Maya and Sloan up and down and continued their business. One of them said, "Go for it."

A giggle rose in Sloan's throat as the two shy guys pushed past her without washing their hands. "Aren't you forgetting something?"

But they were gone, practically taking off in a run.

There were two stalls open on opposite sides of the bathroom. The girls split up, Sloan taking the one furthest away. There was something disturbing about using the men's room. Like, it was dirty and smelly compared to the women's room. But the way Sloan's bladder felt made it more of a necessity than a choice.

After what felt like forever and a day, Sloan finally emptied her bladder, sighing in relief. Before she could open the stall door, two feet appeared in front of her door, and they weren't Maya's. A chill ran down her spine. Was it Steel?

"Maya?" she asked warily.

"Still here," Maya replied from a distance.

"Sloan?" a male voice asked.

She exhaled the breath she was holding, recognizing the voice. It was Will. She opened the door. "What are you doing?"

"What am I doing? You're the one in the men's room."

"It was my idea." Maya was putting some lip gloss on at the mirror. "Feel better?"

"Yes." Sloan joined her and washed her hands. She glanced at Will. "How did you know I was in there?"

"I didn't until I heard you. I had to go and, clearly, I couldn't use the urinals." Will pointed at Maya.

Maya rolled her eyes. "I doubt you've got something I haven't seen before."

Will muttered something under his breath. "I'm a private person."

A boy from school opened the door, took one look at the girls ,and bolted.

"I think we'd better get out of here," Sloan said, drying her hands.

"Good idea," Will added.

The girls left. Outside Maya asked, "You know that kid?"

"Yeah. He's new at my school."

"So weird. I went to school with someone who looked exactly like him. But that was like five years ago." Maya shrugged. "Anyway, nice meeting you.

I've got to go. They're going back up for their next set, and I'm needed backstage."

"Oh, right." Sloan smiled. "Nice meeting you too."

Maya disappeared down a hallway, and Sloan turned back to the crowd. She would have to fight her way back to where Luke was. She had a fleeting thought about crowd surfing her way there, but she was wearing a dress. She wrapped her hair around her fist and lifted it off her back, trying to cool off before she jumped back into the sea of warm bodies.

Someone touched her shoulder.

She whirled around, prepared to find Steel behind her. "Jesus. Quit creeping up on me."

"Sorry." Will shoved his hands in his pockets, the laser lights flashing in his dark eyes. "You are still standing in front of the men's room, you know?"

"Oh, right." She glanced around nervously. She'd better get her paranoia in check. But that was what she got for assaulting a lunatic. "Sorry for jumping down your throat. I'm a little on edge."

"Why?"

"It's not a big deal. I had a run in with some jerk the other day. He's probably looking for revenge because I kneed him in the balls."

"Dude." Will took a step back, his eyes wide. "That's not cool."

Sloan fought the smile creeping up on her lips. It's not as if she went around busting balls for fun. "Trust me, he deserved it."

"I don't think anyone deserves…"

She narrowed her eyes.

"Okay, okay." He held up his hands defensively. "If you say so."

"I do." She turned back toward the stage. "So what do you think of the band?"

"They're really good. Some other kid said they'll do some more covers for their next set."

"Yeah. Should be tight."

"Where's Luke?"

Sloan pointed back at the crowd. "That way. We've got a good spot. You can join us if you want."

"Nah, I don't like crowds."

"Okay, suit yourself." Sloan waved and pushed her way through the crowd back to Luke.

"Took you long enough," Luke said. "They're about to start up again."

"And I even skipped the women's room and used the men's to save time."

Luke shook his head. "Gross."

The band members walked back on stage and grabbed their instruments. Sloan recognized the opening notes of "Jane Says" by Jane's Addiction.

"I love this song," Sloan said.

"I know." He grabbed her hand and spun her around as she swayed her hips to the music.

The rest of their friends joined them in their little bubble on the dance floor, everyone grooving to the music.

Sloan raised her arms above her head and sang along. She had a feeling this was going to be a night to remember.

16

ALTERNATIVE KISS

Derrick

Purgatory, with its neon lights illuminating the darkened sky, was adjacent to the only restaurant in the neighboring town of Limbo. Besides Purgatory, there wasn't much to see in Limbo. Honestly, it always gave Derrick the creeps.

But nothing was going to stop him from being here. Not tonight.

He pulled Celia's car into the only spot he could find on the edge of the parking lot. The place was packed. He got out of the car and looked down at his backpack on the passenger seat. He glanced around and frowned. This part of the lot was barely lit. The perfect place to break into cars. He looked down the aisle at the entrance to the club as "Head Like a Hole" by Nine Inch Nails reverberated off the cars into the night air.

Derrick shut the door and locked it. Sloan was

worth the risk. As he walked toward the club, his stomach did a few flips. He wiped his moist hands on his jeans. He couldn't wait to see her.

He approached a bald bouncer with a Louts T-shirt similar to his sitting on a stool next to the door. He had a cigarette between his fingers and was pulling long drags. Nope—the distinct skunky smell wafted toward him. That was a joint.

Derrick handed him his ID.

The bouncer gave him an odd, second look, but Derrick was used to that. "Didn't you already go in?"

Derrick frowned. Then realized he was probably talking about Luke. "That's my twin brother."

"Ah. With the hot girl in the red dress." The bouncer handed him back his ID and drew an X on his hand to indicate he was under twenty-one. "Don't forget to pay the lady inside."

"Thanks." Derrick walked toward the door, but something about the way he described his brother and the girl he assumed was Sloan, bothered him. He turned back to the bouncer. "They're just friends."

The bouncer shrugged. "Who?"

"My brother and the girl in the red dress."

"Okay?"

"It's just…you made it sound like they were together or something."

"I did? Well, I see a lot of people, especially twins apparently." The bouncer rolled his eyes. "I was just saying they looked tight."

Derrick rocked back and forth, feeling more unsure by the second. "When you say tight…"

The bouncer stood. "Dude, are you going in or not?"

Derrick backed up. "I'm going. Sorry."

The place was packed. Multicolored lights moved around the club, illuminating the crowd. A balcony extended around the perimeter, but most people were on the dance floor or at the bar. The band was so close to the crowd the people in the front row could almost touch the band members. That was the nice thing about Purgatory—all their concerts were intimate and close. Derrick bobbed his head to the music.

A woman with black-and-white hair sitting in a booth said, "It's ten."

Derrick handed her a ten. There was probably only thirty minutes left until the concert was over, but he didn't care. He glanced up and saw Mazy on the balcony with some other kids from school. She was leaning over the railing, swaying back and forth to the music.

Where was Sloan?

He didn't see her in the sea of people in front of the band. If he had to guess, that was where she'd be. He glanced toward the bar and smiled.

There you are.

Sloan was indeed wearing a red dress, her straight, dark hair cascading down her back. She faced away from him, ordering a drink. The bartender walked away, and Sloan turned back to the band. She cupped her hands around her mouth and screamed.

He strode over to her just as the bartender set

down her drink. He swooped in and grabbed the glass before she could and drained it. Yuk!

"Luke," she said. "Get your own."

He set the empty glass down, his lips puckered. "Since when do you drink tonic water?"

"I don't. It was supposed to be water." Her expression softened from daggers to silk. "Derrick. How did you—"

"Celia took the rest of my shift." He turned toward the bartender. "This was tonic water, dude. Can we please have two plain waters?"

"Sorry," the bartender said, frowning. "It's busy, you know."

"I'm so glad you're here," Sloan said. The next thing he knew, her arms were around his neck in an embrace. She smelled musky, and her skin was dewy.

He was tempted to kiss her shoulder but held back.

"Me too." He pulled away and held her hand. "You look amazing, by the way."

"Thanks." She blushed and looked down at his T-shirt. "You look, um, like your brother?"

"We *are* twins."

"It's the shirt. You're both wearing the same shirt."

Of course we are. That's why the bouncer was confused when he saw him. "Where is he, anyway?"

Sloan looked around. "I'm not sure. Last I saw him, he was headed to the bathroom. Everyone else is dancing, I think."

"Do you want to dance?" he asked.

Her lips parted, and he couldn't help but stare at their fullness. She squeezed his hand. "Lead the way."

Lotus was playing "Just Can't Get Enough" by Depeche Mode. He pulled her close and pushed through the crowd. Along the way, he saw Adam and Evie dancing along with Gage and Iris.

"'Sup, Derrick?" Adam asked.

Gage nodded at him, Iris clinging to his arm.

Derrick nodded and continued to the back corner of the dance floor. He turned to face Sloan, spinning her around. She swayed her hips to the beat. Ever since Adam had come to Ashwater, Derrick had grown to like dancing. But he liked anything that was competitive in nature. This, on the other hand, was about being with Sloan, and he wanted to be even closer.

"What else did they play?" Derrick asked, swaying to the beat.

Sloan spun around and put her arms in the air. "The first set was their newest album, and their second and third have been mostly eighties alternative. Adam's been in heaven."

"Cool." He grabbed her hand and leaned close. "Hey, I'm sorry I missed most of the concert."

Sloan smiled. "That's okay. You're here now."

The song ended, and the lead singer said, "Okay, time to get blue."

The bass player played the telltale notes to "Letter to Elise" by The Cure. Derrick grinned at Sloan. "He wasn't kidding."

"I know, but I love this song."

"So I guess we'll be depressed together?" Derrick raised his eyebrows and reached for Sloan's waist.

She wrapped her arms around his neck. "I don't know. I think the song is more about change." She turned and whispered in his ear, "And change can be good."

He held her close, as they swayed in unison. They were surrounded by people, but Derrick felt alone with her. It was as if they'd carved out their own private bubble and the rest of the world melted away. He'd wanted to be here with her like this for so long. She felt so right in his arms, like she belonged there. He ran his hand up and down the small of her back. Her hair smelled like coconut and summer.

"I opened the letter," Sloan whispered. She was talking about the letter from Edgewood.

"And?"

She looked up at him, her adorable face crinkled up. "I was deferred."

"Oh no. That sucks. Are you okay?"

"Yeah. I mean, at first I wasn't. But then Mazy said she was going to do lots of stuff to help me, and I think it'll be okay."

Derrick laughed and pulled her against him again. "If Mazy's involved, you're good."

He rested his head against hers. God, she was intoxicating. He'd had feelings for her for such a long time, but because of Luke, he'd never told her. Being around her for the past year was agonizing. In fact, if Will and his friend hadn't been on the disc golf course, he'd probably still be.

Derrick pulled back and tilted her chin toward him

as the song hit its guitar solo. Her eyes were glassy from the smoke machines.

He glanced down at her mouth, her lips parting, inviting. "I want to kiss you."

"It's about damn time." She grasped the back of his neck and pressed her lips against his.

Her lips were warm and supple against his. She deepened the kiss, drawing him even closer. His head was swimming, intoxicated by her. She moaned against his mouth, and it was the most sensual thing he'd ever experienced.

Sure, he'd kissed other girls and even gotten to second and third base.

But it was nothing like this. This was Sloan—the girl he'd been in love with for a long time. He wanted to tell her. He needed to.

"What the actual fuck?" a familiar voice yelled, cutting through their intimate moment like a needle scratching a vinyl record.

Derrick's heart sank into his stomach. Luke.

Luke's mouth was open, and his eyes searched for some shred of evidence that this was some kind of mistake. He'd seen that look before. It was the same look he had when he found out their parents had flushed his goldfish, Harry. Derrick had taken Harry out of the tank, not realizing he would die. He felt terrible then. Now, was much worse.

He stepped away from Sloan.

"Uh, hey—" Derrick tried to smile.

Luke ignored him and glared at Sloan. "What are you doing? He's my brother."

Sloan shifted nervously. "I, uh, it was nothing."

She stared down at the floor.

Seriously? Now it was Derrick's turn to stare at Sloan. He was about to tell her that he loved her, and the kiss was nothing?

Luke shook his head at Derrick. "Of all the girls out there, you gotta go after my best friend?"

Derrick opened his mouth to respond but noticed who was standing next to his brother. It was Steel, grinning like the Cheshire Cat. He narrowed his eyes. "What are you doing with this asshole?"

Luke stepped forward, putting Steel behind him. "He's the one who told me about you two. Don't change the subject."

"This is my fault," Sloan interjected. "Don't be mad at Derrick." She reached for Luke's arm.

He pulled away from her. "I'm not just mad at Derrick. You're pretty high up on the list too."

Sloan reached for him again. "Please, let's just talk."

"No, I can't deal with this." He put up his hands. "I'm out of here." He took off into the crowd.

"Luke—" Sloan said, clearly wanting to go after him.

Derrick grasped her arm. "Let him go. He needs to cool off. Besides we have—" He turned to where Steel was standing. He was gone. "Where'd Steel go?"

"I don't know." Sloan got on her tiptoes and looked around the crowd. "He's gone."

The lead singer announced their last song and started playing. Derrick rubbed his temples. His vision was cloudy, and he couldn't think straight. He wasn't sure if it was from stress, but he felt really weird. "I need some fresh air."

Sloan grabbed his hand. "Okay, let's go."

Derrick followed her out of the club and into the night air. He breathed deeply, trying to clear the fog in his head. The combination of smoke and Luke finding out about them was wreaking havoc on his brain.

Not to mention that Sloan said the kiss was nothing.

"Are you okay?" Sloan asked.

"Yeah." He shook his head. "I think I need to go home. Do you need a ride?"

She frowned. "I think you are the one that needs a ride home. How'd you get here?"

"Celia let me borrow her car."

"Keys." She held out her hand.

His first instinct was to tell her no, but he was in no condition to drive. He handed her the keys and pointed toward the edge of the parking lot. As they walked toward the car, he couldn't shake the feeling that they were being watched. He glanced around a few times, but turning his head made his headache worse. He let it go. He was paranoid because of how he was feeling—that was probably all it was.

Ugh. Tonight was a disaster.

17

EPI-OOPS

Sloan

S hit. Shit. Double shit. *Nothing?* The kiss meant nothing?

Of all the things Sloan could have said, that was what she picked? She groaned inwardly and glanced at Derrick. His cheeks were flushed and his eyes cast down at the ground. This was all her fault.

They walked in silence to Celia's car. Lots of other kids were leaving too. Although it wasn't in her nature to leave a concert early, Derrick was clearly not feeling well. Besides, when Lotus finished, the parking lot would be a mad house. Now was the time to beat the traffic.

They drove down the mountain road toward Ashwater in silence. A few times, she glanced over at him, wondering what to say. He looked sad and tired. She scolded herself over and over again for being so insensitive. Not to mention he was the one who was going to have to go home and deal with Luke, not her.

As soon as she saw the sign for Eden's Pass, she veered over and took it.

"Where are you going?" he asked, sitting up straighter.

"Quick detour." She peered over at him. "I'm not a serial killer. I promise."

He relaxed back into his seat, but the troubled look on his face remained. She was no doubt the cause of it. She pulled into the disc golf parking lot. Memories of playing here with Luke and Derrick flooded back.

She sighed inwardly. She'd really made a mess of things.

Sloan turned off the car and faced him. "I'm an ass. I didn't mean what I said to Luke. You know how things always come out wrong for me."

Derrick cleared his throat, his eyes focused on the dash. "Yeah, I know. The problem is you never say things you don't think are true. Luke comes first with you."

She opened her mouth to respond but quickly shut it. He had a point. If push came to shove and she had to pick Luke or Derrick, what would she do? She didn't like how the hypothetical ultimatum made her feel. She never wanted to lose Luke. They were like yin and yang as far as best friends were concerned. He'd always been there for her. Maybe that was why she'd said what she did. She'd rarely seen that kind of hurt in Luke's eyes like she did tonight. She wanted to take it away, and saying nothing was going on between her and Derrick seemed the way to do it.

Sloan watched Derrick. His brow was furrowed and lips tight. Her heart clenched.

She had been wrong.

And so had he.

"I don't think it's true." She grasped his hand. "I've wanted to kiss you since the first time you touched me here on this course. Sometimes I can't sleep at night because all I can think about are your fingers caressing my side. I made a mistake. I told Luke what I thought he wanted to hear to make him feel better. But I swear it was a lie. That kiss meant a lot to me." She squeezed his hand. "I like you, Derrick. Like, really like you."

"I think that's the longest you've ever spoken to me without saying something crass."

Sloan searched his eyes, which were unreadable. She frowned. Was he mocking her? An inappropriate swear word was on the tip of her tongue when he pressed a finger to her lips.

"Before you do that," He smiled. "I really like you too. I have for a while. Much longer than you, I think."

"Oh." She smiled. "For a second there, I thought I was going to have to kick you out of the car you borrowed."

He leaned over and cupped the back of her head, their eyes meeting closely for the second time tonight. "I'm so tired of pretending I don't have feelings for you."

Hearing him say out loud what she'd been feeling

for weeks was a relief. Their lips met for a brief kiss, and she whispered, "Me too."

"I know it sucks right now, but I'm glad Luke knows. It'll take some time, but he'll eventually be okay with it."

"He's so mad." She sighed and wrapped her arms around his middle, her head against his chest. He was warm and solid.

"I know. I could feel the anger rolling off him in waves." He stroked her hair.

Sloan pulled back as another thought occurred to her. "Speaking of anger...why was he with Steel?"

"I was wondering the same thing."

"I didn't tell you this at the time, but I heard Steel's voice in my head after I displaced his brovaries. He said—"

"I'm sorry, did you just say brovaries?"

"Yeah. Balls, sack, whatever. Anyway, he said that payback's a bitch. Maybe getting Luke to see us kiss was his revenge?"

"No, I don't think so. It doesn't make sense. Like, why was he fixated on us in the first place? He's got a vendetta against Gage, not us." He reached for his backpack, which was on the passenger side floor, and set it on his lap. He opened it and peered inside. Satisfied with what he saw, he looked back at her.

"I've got a bad feeling." His eyes read just north of serious.

Her skin prickled. "About what?"

"You can't tell anyone what I'm about to tell you,

okay?" Derrick rubbed his forehead, now beaded with sweat.

"Hey, you don't look good. You haven't since we left the club." She felt his cheek with the back of her hand. It was damp and clammy.

"I have the worst headache. I think it must have been from the smoke." As soon as the words left is mouth, his hands trembled.

Her chest tingled, her heart skipping a beat. "Derrick, you're freaking me out. What's wrong?"

"I—" He gripped his backpack to his chest, which was now also shaking violently. His eyes rolled back into his head as his whole body convulsed.

"Oh my God, Derrick." Panic rose inside her, her pulse whipping up into a frenzy. She reached for him, not sure what to do. His whole body was rigid like a board. Was he having a seizure? She cupped his face. "Can you hear me? Derrick?"

He gurgled something inaudible, his lips tightening.

911. She should call 911. Where was her phone? Shit. Luke had it. Why did she wear a dress? "Where's your phone?"

She tried to move his backpack, thinking it would be in his pocket, but he wouldn't let go of it. "Derrick, please let go. I need to find your phone."

Finally, she pried the bag free from his steel grip, but the contents went everywhere. "Damn it."

She was having trouble breathing herself now. Every hair on her body now stood on end, and tears streamed down her cheeks. She didn't know what to do. She wasn't one to pray, but, "Please, God, let him be okay," left her lips.

Something caught her eye in the center console. It was a strange yet familiar looking cylinder with an orange tip. She picked it up. An EpiPen. People with serious allergies carried them. Luke didn't have any allergies that she knew of, but Derrick might. She turned over the syringe. It had a weird glow.

Before she could give it more thought, Derrick went still.

"Derrick? Oh my God!" Her hands shaking, she uncapped the safety at the top. "Please let this work."

Sloan drove the needle end straight into his thigh.

She held it there for a few seconds and then released it, dropping it back onto the center console.

"Please be okay." She leaned over him again, placing two fingers on the side of his throat. She'd learned CPR a few years ago but barely remembered the count and procedure.

Thank God. He had a pulse. She exhaled.

Next, she put her face by his mouth. She sighed in relief as his breath tickled the hairs on her cheek.

She took a few ragged breaths, trying to calm her nerves.

Phone. I need to call 911. Before she could search Derrick's pockets, the car door opened, causing her to jump.

"Well, this is an interesting turn of events." Will drew in a ragged breath, frustration etched on his face. "Only in Ashwater could something like this happen."

She stared up at him, slack-jawed. *How did he...? Interesting turn of events?* "What are you doing here?"

"I can see you have questions. But we have a more pressing problem at the moment." Will nodded to the passenger seat.

That snapped her back to reality. She turned and looked at Derrick. "I don't know what's wrong with him. I think he had an allergic reaction to something."

"Yeah, you could say that." He paused. "Is this Luke or Derrick?"

"Derrick." His eyes had grown very serious.

"Good." Will let out a breath.

"What do you mean, good?" Sloan turned back to Derrick and grabbed his hand. "Look at him. Does he look good to you?"

"I can't explain it all now, but it's good it's Derrick."

"You know what's wrong with him? Is he going to be okay?"

"Maybe."

"Maybe?" Sloan pushed Will back and got out of the car. She didn't trust him now. Not one bit. "What the hell does that mean?"

Will pulled out his phone, glancing down at the used EpiPen. "I assume you used that on him?"

"Yes."

He tapped his phone and put it up to his ear. "Yeah, it's me. I need an ambulance at Eden's Pass disc golf parking lot asap." He paused. "Right. Yes, I'll be here." He tapped his phone again and put it in his front pocket.

It's me? Like 911 knew him by voice alone? Sloan felt like her head was going to explode. Derrick was unconscious in the car, Will was stalking them, and damn it, she had to pee again. She shifted from side to side and eyed some public bathrooms nearby.

Will looked her up and down. "Go. I'll watch over him."

"Thanks, but I'll hold it."

"Suit yourself." He leaned against the car and crossed his arms.

Sloan pivoted and crossed her legs. She didn't care if she peed right here in front of him—there was no way she was leaving him alone with Derrick. "What did you mean it's good it was Derrick? And why are you stalking us?"

"There will be time to discuss later, but if it had been Luke, he'd be dead. At least with Derrick, there's a chance he could come out of this. It depends."

Something knotted up in the pit of her stomach, and it wasn't making her bladder feel much better. "Depends on what?"

"I'm guessing, you."

"Me? What the hell are you talking about?" She grabbed him by the shirt. "I swear to God, if you don't start making sense, I'm going to lose my shit."

Will looked up toward the road leading into the parking lot. "We'll have to talk later."

Sloan followed his line of sight. A few seconds later, she heard another vehicle approaching. An ambulance with their lights and sirens off pulled up next to them. That was odd. This seemed like one hell of an emergency to her.

Once the EMS team got out of their truck, she went back in the car and squeezed

Derrick's hand. "I'll be right back."

One of the EMS crew opened the passenger side door. "I got this, miss."

Sloan nodded and scooted back out of the car. She grabbed Will by the arm. "Let's go." "What are you doing? Where?"

"While they take care of Derrick, you're coming with me to the bathroom." She wasn't

going to let him out of her sight for a second.

"What is up with you and bathrooms today?" Will shook his head.

"Don't leave without me," Sloan said over her shoulder to the EMS workers as she bee-lined it to the restroom, Will firmly at her side.

She'd get to the bottom of this hot mess. All she cared about was that Derrick was going to be okay.

Sloan glared at Will. He seemed to know exactly what was wrong with Derrick and she intended to find out what he knew. She wanted real answers, none of this maybe crap. Who was he? What was up with that weird call to 911? Oh and why was he stalking them? Her head swam with questions. She swore under her breath. It was going to be a long night.

First things first—a girl's gotta go.

PART II

18

NOW WE WAIT

Derrick

Derrick felt light, like he was floating, yet his surroundings were pitch black. A shiver ran down his spine. He was not alone.

"Hello?" he asked into the void. His voice sounded strange, muffled.

No one answered, but the darkness around him dissipated. Tiny stars surrounded him. As they moved closer, they changed to a vibrant, pulsing green. More intrigued than frightened, he reached for one that floated just above his hand. "What are you?"

The light receded away from him as if it had a will of its own.

"Is this a dream? Where am I?" He didn't really expect an answer, but it was worth a shot.

As if in response, the lights surrounded him, cocooning him from the darkness. They moved closer and closer. He shut his eyes, the light too bright. His skin itched. His heart pounded, and panic took hold of his body as they pressed into him.

They were not stars in space. They were sentient, full of purpose, and they wanted in.

Sloan

Sloan awoke to the sun on her face and a dry mouth. She sat up.

Ouch. What the—

She grabbed her bicep, rubbed it gingerly, and glanced around, trying to sweep away the cobwebs and remember where she was and why she'd slept in a chair.

It was some kind of waiting room. A woman in a white lab coat walked through a nearby corridor. She didn't recognize the place, but it was definitely some kind of hospital. Sitting across from her, slouched down with her head in her hand, was Mazy. She wore a vaguely familiar dress.

Sloan glanced down at her own clothes. Red dress. Her breath caught as the night before came rushing back.

Purgatory. Lotus. Derrick.

She sat up. He'd had a seizure at Eden's Pass. Past that it was a blur. Was he okay?

"Mazy," she whispered.

Mazy's mouth twitched.

Sloan got up and shook Mazy's shoulder. "Wake up."

"I'm up." Mazy bolted upright, looking around wildly. "I'm up."

"Sorry." Sloan sat down next to her. "Where are we?"

"Arcadia," Mazy said, half-yawning. She took a deep breath and rubbed her sleepy eyes.

"Oh."

"He's in Room 203." She reached into her purse and grabbed Sloan's phone. "Here. You were already passed out over there when I got here last night. I called your mom and told her we were going to stay here with Derrick. What were you on?"

"I wasn't on anything." Sloan frowned. Passed out? On? She hadn't taken anything. On the other hand, she had no memory of how she had gotten here.

"Well, you must have been uber tired then." Mazy stretched.

She'd sort out her memory later. She was happy to have her phone back. But it also reminded her of what happened right before they left Purgatory. "How's Luke?"

"I have no idea. I haven't seen him."

"But he had my phone."

"Well, then, he did a shit job looking after it. It was sitting on the bar at Purgatory. You're lucky I found it." Mazy pursed her lips. "Come to think of it, it is odd how out of all those people I was the one to find it. Huh."

"It doesn't matter. Do you know how Derrick is?"

"The last I heard, he hadn't woken up. His mom stayed in his room."

Sloan stood and headed to the hallway. The place smelled of alcohol and latex, and the fluorescent lights above her head flickered. She hoped it wasn't doing that in Derrick's room, or he'd have another seizure. She went to Room 203 and knocked, opening the door.

Derrick's mom was asleep on a recliner. She opened her eyes. "Morning."

"Good morning, Mrs. Dixon."

Her heart clenched when she saw Derrick. He looked pained. That was the only way she could describe his face. Didn't most unconscious people look peaceful? Derrick didn't. His eyebrows were knitted together, and his mouth was turned down. His forehead was beaded with sweat. Her mind whirled as images of him convulsing flashed before her eyes. Then, there was nothing. No memory after that.

Mrs. Dixon got up and dabbed his forehead with a washcloth. "Will you sit with him for a bit? I'd like to check in with my husband. Luke didn't come home last night."

Something in the pit of Sloan's stomach twisted. "He didn't?"

"No." Mrs. Dixon sighed. "I know. As if things weren't bad enough."

"I'll stay." Sloan sat down next to Derrick. After Mrs. Dixon left, she looked at his hand, trembling slightly. She sat down and took it in her own. He was warm and clammy.

"I don't know if you can hear me, but I'm here." She stroked his hand with her thumb.

He didn't respond in any way that she could tell

except his shoulders relaxed some against his hospital bed.

She wasn't sure what to do. She'd never sat with someone who was unconscious before. "That was some concert, huh?"

What are you doing? He can't answer you.

"Do you—um…"

Again, he can't answer.

Sloan opened her favorite music app on her phone. "I'll just play some music. That's soothing, right?" She picked some Sam Smith. "Stay with Me" played, and she smiled. Appropriate.

Her mind drifted to the kiss she'd shared with him on the dance floor. She regretted lots of things from last night but not that. She'd wanted to kiss him so many times over the past few weeks, and last night, it'd finally happened. She stared at his lips, remembering how they felt on hers. The thought made her toes curl and her breath catch. She could have stayed in that moment forever. God, he was such a good kisser.

Then she remembered what happened next and sighed. Everything turned to shit. Luke got pissed at both of them, and now Derrick was lying in a hospital bed with some strange illness. Her hopes for something real with Derrick were going down the toilet fast.

The door opened. "How is he?"

Sloan stared up at Will. She remembered seeing him last night, but the rest was hazy. "He hasn't woken up. What are you doing here?"

Will sat down in the recliner Mrs. Dixon had slept on. "I heard what happened. Just wanted to see if there was any change."

"No. Nothing. Did you see him at Purgatory? Was he acting strange at all?"

"No, not that I could tell."

She rubbed her temples. "You'd think I'd be accustomed to weird shit happening. I've lived in Ashwater my whole life. But this? This is really strange."

The side of Will's mouth turned up. "So far the strangest thing I've witnessed is a girl using the men's room."

She narrowed her eyes at him. "This is no time to joke."

"Fine. What's so strange about Ashwater?"

Sloan opened her mouth and promptly shut it. Now was not the time to out her android friends. "It's nothing." She glanced down at Derrick. "I just really need him to wake up."

Will got up and stood next to her. He put his hand on her shoulder.

She jumped at first, his familiarity unnerving.

He didn't waver. "I've seen the connection you two have. If there's anyone that could get him through this, it's you."

Her shoulder tingled, and he spoke as if he'd seen something like this before. She wasn't sure why, but it was strangely comforting. She didn't want to question it. "Do you think he can hear me?"

"I don't know. But it doesn't hurt to try, does it?"

Sloan nodded and squeezed Derrick's hand. "Thanks."

A FEW HOURS PASSED, and she stayed by Derrick's side. She told him about her plans for dealing with the deferment letter to Edgewood and how Mazy would be giving her all kinds of positions with student government to make her look good to the admissions committee. She told him that she could really use his advice about it. She talked to him about his internship at Bio-Core. She didn't have a clue about what he was doing there, but she knew he loved it. She talked to him about Adam and Dance Paradise. He needed Derrick to help program some new songs for the game. She even lied and told him that Luke forgave them and was okay with them dating. She was a terrible liar, but it was worth a shot.

Nothing.

Not a blink or a squeeze of the hand. Not even a twitch. She considered kissing him. Hey, didn't it work for Prince Charming or whichever dude it was that kissed the girl in the glass case?

She sighed. She was tired. Sloan laid her head on the bed next to his hand and closed her eyes. Just a few minutes of sleep.

As she drifted off, she thought, *Come back to me. I need you.*

Derrick

When he opened his eyes, the stars were gone, along with the dark void. There was a low, incessant buzzing inside his head. He turned around a few times to acclimate to his surroundings.

He knew this place.

Derrick was standing on the bank of the lake at the summit of Eden's Pass. He peered into the crystal blue water at his reflection. It looked as tired and cold as he felt. He rubbed his arms and looked up at the waterfall cascading down over rocks jutting into the lake. The sky was dim, twilight with stars above his head.

A rustling behind him caused him to turn. At first he thought it was an animal, but a boy stepped into the clearing.

Will.

Well, sort of. His eyes were different. They glowed green like the fireflies that floated through the air around him.

"Will?" Derrick asked.

"Yeah." Will approached and reached out his hand. "How do you feel?"

Derrick took a step back, his hands trembling. "What's wrong with your eyes?"

"Nothing." Will looked down. When he looked back up, his eyes returned to their normal dark color. "I never intended it to go this way. They don't want to hurt you, you know?"

"They?" Goosebumps formed on Derrick's forearms. He wanted to go back to the darkness. At least there he could close his eyes and shut out the lights.

Will glanced around, a sense of urgency in his eyes. "Try to relax."

Another voice came from somewhere above, familiar and comforting—*I need you.*

Derrick knew it immediately. "Sloan?"

"Yes." Will's body began to flicker and fade.

"Wait—"

"Let...them...in." Then he was gone. Dissipated like a cloud of smoke.

Let them in? What did that mean? Derrick walked toward the spot Will had stood, only to find mountain air. He looked up at the sky. "Sloan?"

She didn't respond, her presence gone too. His chest tightened, a lump forming at the back of his throat. He was alone. "What am I supposed to do?"

Then, as if answering him, fireflies surrounded him.

He caught one in his hand, cupping it gently. He peered down. It wasn't an insect with a glowing abdomen at all. It was a spark of green light. Like an ember from a fire. Yet, it moved and buzzed in his hand like it had a mind of its own. "What are you?"

The spark glowed brighter, and Derrick had an overwhelming sense of peace as the cold receded from his hand, arching outward. His shoulders relaxed, and he welcomed the comfort.

Slowly at first, more sparks surrounded him, warming him.

It wasn't like in the void. This time, he wasn't afraid. His body lifted off the ground, enveloped in the sparks' brightness, warming his skin then his muscles then his bones. His body vibrated like a live wire as they raised him up into the night air. Higher and higher he rose, the bright lights cocooning him until together, they jettisoned off in the night sky like a shooting star.

Before he succumbed fully to the beings, he thought of Sloan. *I need you too.*

19

A FAVOR

Sloan

I t wasn't Mrs. Dixon or Mazy who woke Sloan. It was Mac Grayson. She glanced up at Derrick. He was still out of it, but his face had softened. Maybe her nearness had helped.

Mac cleared his throat again. "A moment?"

Great. Time to get interrogated. She followed Mac out of the room. Mazy was waiting outside as well, but she'd changed from the evening before. Heaven forbid she look disheveled. Evie and Adam were there too.

"She's exhausted, Dad. Why do you have to do this now?" Evie crossed her arms. She was sporting a high ponytail, denim overall shorts, and her Docs. There was something about her small frame that made her even more formidable. Like no one else besides her could talk to her dad that way.

"You three go visit with your friend," Mac said to the others. "I need to speak to Sloan alone."

"Fine." Evie smiled at Sloan. "Derrick's going to be okay. I know it."

Mazy nudged Sloan's hand and smiled before following Adam and Evie into Derrick's room. Just before the door closed, Adam played "Wind Beneath my Wings" by Bette Midler on Evie's phone.

Evie swatted Adam's arm. "Stop it."

Sloan grinned, fighting a giggle.

Mac pointed to the area where Sloan had slept the night before, and they sat down. He pulled out a small black tablet and pen. "All right. Walk me through last night."

"Uh, sure." Sloan took a deep breath. There were blanks. Big ones. She recounted everything she remembered right up to Derrick's seizure.

"Wait, so you were at Eden's Pass in the disc golf parking lot in Celia Black's car? You were driving. Is that right?"

"Yes."

"Then what?"

"I, um, called 911." She wasn't sure why, but telling him she couldn't remember anything after that point didn't seem like a good idea. She was in the driver's seat, and even though she knew she hadn't smoked or had any alcohol, he might not believe her. She rubbed her damp palms on her dress. She really needed to change.

Mac tilted his head. "You called 911?"

"Yeah."

"Huh. Mazy told me she found your phone back at Purgatory."

Right. Her heartbeat quickened. Of course he'd already talked to everyone else. "Oh, I must have used Derrick's phone."

"Really? Do you remember what time that was?" Mac's expression was steely, his eyes prodding.

"Uh, no." Sloan glanced around. Even if she could remember what happened, she likely wouldn't have noted the time.

"Was the dispatcher a man or a woman?"

"Woman?" Sloan swallowed hard. Seriously? Like a question? This lie was getting out of hand.

Mac sat back in his chair, assessing. "You don't sound so sure."

Sloan pulled on her hair, fidgeting.

"Do you want to know why you aren't sure?"

Her stomach roiled. "Okay?"

Mac leaned forward again. "Because there is no record of a 911 call."

Wait, what? If she hadn't called 911, then how—

"I can see you're confused. Trust me, you're not alone. Last night, an ambulance dropped you and Derrick off here. The attending staff downstairs can't remember the paramedics who dropped you off. They also left without a formal report." Mac scratched at some stubble on his cheek. "And here's the weirdest part—why would they have taken him here instead of the medical center? None of it makes any sense. Which is why I need information from you. What can you tell me about the trip from Eden's

Pass to here? Did you get the names of either of the paramedics?"

She had thought it odd that Derrick was taken here and not the regular hospital. But that thought only occurred to her this morning when she woke up. She sighed. It was time to come clean. "Sheriff Grayson, please don't take this the wrong way, but I don't remember anything after Derrick had his seizure."

Mac raised his eyebrows at her. "Seriously?"

"I swear, I didn't take any drugs or drink any alcohol."

"Of course you don't." He rubbed his forehead. "I swear, this town is going to be the death of me. If it's not a group of people simultaneously getting sick, it's mass memory loss. What's next? Aliens?"

Mac was referring to the fashion show this past winter in which Gage had spewed his mental mojo on most of the town, including her, and they'd all collapsed. No one had been seriously hurt, but Sloan had woken up with a massive headache.

After a moment, he looked back up and shrugged. "I believe you. The staff downstairs doesn't remember a thing either."

Sloan exhaled slowly. He believed her. "So, now what?"

"Now I have to get back to work. I'll know more when Derrick's toxicology report comes back. There are some similarities to the other overdoses I've been seeing."

"Oh no. Most of them didn't make it, did they?"

Sloan's heart whipped up its pace. What if Derrick never woke up?

"That's true. But from what Derrick's attending physician has told me, his vitals are much stronger."

Mac thanked Sloan for her time and asked her to give him a call if she did miraculously remember anything. Sloan opened Derrick's door and peeked inside. The others were sitting and talking. Evie had a pencil in her hand and a sketchpad resting on her knees. She was drawing Derrick while he slept. Sloan frowned. Sketching the unconscious? Okay. Weird.

"Do you guys mind staying with him while I go home and change? I'm gross." Sloan asked.

"Sure. This is going to take a while anyway." Evie didn't look up from her work.

Sloan eyed Adam and Mazy. She mouthed, *What is she doing?* to Mazy.

Mazy shrugged. "It's how she copes with stress."

"Okay. I'll be back in a little while." She went over to Derrick and squeezed his hand.

Mazy caught her eye before she left and tilted her head curiously. Then, as if surmising something in that perfect brain of hers, she smiled.

AFTER A QUICK SHOWER and a bite to eat, Sloan stopped by Relics to fill her parents in on what had happened to Derrick. What she didn't expect to find was Luke waiting for her. Truth be told, she was more than happy to see him since his mom had said he hadn't come home last night.

Her mom left them alone to talk. Instead of her normal familiarity with him, she waited for him to make the first move. His expression was unreadable, and he still wore the same clothes from the night before.

"So, last night happened." Luke had his hands in his pockets.

"Did you see your brother yet?" Sloan didn't want to talk about the kiss.

"I'm headed there next. Mom said he's still unconscious."

"So you talked to your mom. Good. She was really worried."

"Yeah." He rocked back and forth on his heels.

She tugged on her hair. This was unbearably awkward.

"I heard that you were with him when it happened." He frowned. "What exactly did happen?"

Sloan sighed and rubbed her arm where it was sore, as if the act could somehow conjure up her memories from the night before. "He had some kind of seizure at Eden's Pass. I stopped there on the way home."

"Wait," Luke interjected. "You were driving? Why?"

"Derrick wasn't feeling good. It was probably because—" She stopped, realizing she was going to bring up the kiss. "Anyway, after the seizure happened, I can't remember a thing. I remember being freaked out about Derrick, and then hours later, I woke up in a chair outside his room at Arcadia."

Luke frowned as he worked through what she'd told him. "Were you on something?"

"No." She'd have thought the same thing if she didn't know any better. She'd wondered herself because she was woozy when she woke up. Speaking of last night…"Where were you all night?"

"I, uh…" he started. He pursed his lips as if gauging how much to say.

What was that all about? They always told each other everything. Her mind wandered to Derrick. Well, almost everything. "Luke," she pressed, "why didn't you go home?"

"I didn't feel like it. That's all."

"Look, I'm not exactly the model kid, but your mom was seriously worried. And after what happened to Derrick, that wasn't cool."

"How was I supposed to know Derrick was going to overdose on something?" Luke narrowed his eyes at her in defiance.

Overdose? The word struck a chord in her mind. Similarities to the other cases. That was what Sheriff Grayson had said. She squeezed her eyes shut. Why couldn't she remember anything? It was super frustrating.

She gave up and stared at Luke. "Derrick would never take drugs like that, and you know it."

"Yeah and he would never kiss my best friend either."

Sloan inhaled sharply. And there is was—the judgment she was waiting for. "Just go see your brother. I don't want to talk about it with you."

"Well, I can't exactly talk about it with him, now can I? Do you know how that makes me feel? I was so angry the last time I saw him. Now he's unconscious in a hospital bed."

"That's fair. But you don't need to be an asshole to me. It's not like we were sneaking around behind your back or anything. It just happened." Well, that wasn't entirely true. They'd had a couple of private moments together.

"Look. I don't want to fight with you. Especially now. I stopped by to ask a favor."

"A favor?"

"I really need your help." Luke stepped closer to her, his eyes imploring.

He meant it. They'd been best friends for a long time, and she knew when he needed her. Besides, she really wanted to put the hard feelings behind them. "Sure. What do you need?"

"Come with me."

"Okay…" Sloan didn't watch a lot of superhero stuff, but her Spidey sense was tingling. She followed Luke outside and around the back of the store. She didn't mind helping Luke, but she wanted to get back to Derrick ASAP.

She lifted her head up toward the sky. The day had grown warm, and the sun felt good on her face. A light breeze with the scent of pine caught some wisps of her hair.

Sloan closed her eyes and breathed in. *Please let Derrick be okay.*

Luke's jeep was parked next to the building. Her

lips parted. There was a pair of legs curled up in the backseat. She glanced at Luke, who wouldn't meet her gaze. Instead, he had his hands shoved in his pockets, eyes cast on the old asphalt by his feet.

Sloan approached the vehicle and saw the owner of the legs. Her chest clenched. "Jesus Christ." She whirled around, eyes wide. "What the hell is he doing in the back of your jeep?"

Luke's cheeks reddened. "I know. Things got kinda crazy last night."

"Kinda?" Sloan ran her hand through her hair. "You've got a crazy person in the back of your jeep."

A loud yawn made her turn around again. "I'm not crazy." Steel sat up and stretched. He made a smacking noise with his mouth. "I need food."

"You need a hell of a lot more than that," Sloan said. "You'd better start explaining, Luke."

"I don't know. We kinda hung out."

"Hung out?" This was all too much. She grabbed Luke by the arm and dragged him away so she could speak privately. "I know you are hurting because of what's going on between me and Derrick, but this is not okay. He's a bad guy. We have to text Gage."

Sloan pulled her phone from her back pocket.

But Luke grabbed it from her. "No. We're not doing that. Look, I didn't plan to hang out with him last night. It just sort of happened. After I saw you with Derrick, I was pissed. Steel convinced me to go with Shannon and some other girls to a party at Edge-wood. I figured, why not? I didn't exactly want to go home and see Derrick. Then Steel and I ended up bonding over some beer pong."

"You were drinking and driving?" Sloan asked. This story was getting worse and worse.

"No. Steel drank for me."

"Well, isn't he just the best guy in the world." Sloan rolled her eyes.

"Hey, he was pretty cool actually. It's not the same, I know, but he has issues with his brother too."

"Issues? Dude, he tried to kill Gage." She couldn't believe her ears. Was he really trying to defend Steel's behavior?

"Technically, that's not true. Gage tried to kill him first."

Sloan's mouth formed an O. "Who are you? Because the Luke I know would never be like this."

Before Luke could respond, Steel approached them, grinning. "Who's up for pancakes?"

Sloan whirled on Steel, who immediately covered his crotch, remembering the last time he'd goaded her.

"Is that a no?" Steel asked.

She put her head in her hands. "Oh my God. Please tell me this isn't happening."

"Let me handle this," Luke said to Steel.

"You got it, bro," Steel said.

Bro? Enough. She crossed her arms and glared at Luke. "What is it you need from me?"

"Steel needs a place to crash. Can he stay at your cabin?" Luke asked.

Sloan groaned. She would do anything for Luke,

but this? This was too much. "Why? Why do you have to help him?"

"I don't know. I just do. He was cool last night when I was feeling really shitty. I want to return the favor. He can't stay with me obviously, and you have a cabin that no one is using."

"I thought you had money now," Sloan asked Steel. "Why do you need a place to stay?"

"I need to fly under the radar, if you know what I mean." Steel winked.

"No, I don't." She looked back at Luke. "He is manipulating you. This is not a good idea."

"I swear I'll be a model tenant. No shitting the bed," Steel said.

"You disgust me, and that's saying a lot," Sloan replied.

Luke grasped her arm. "Please? I know what I'm doing. Plus, I think you owe me for not being honest."

Sloan pursed her lips. Low blow. If this was what it would take to make things right, she may as well sell her soul to the devil. "I hate you, Luke Dixon."

Luke arched an eyebrow the way he always did when he was about to get his way. "Is that a yes?"

She groaned so loudly it almost turned into a scream. "For how long?"

"Two nights, maybe three," Steel said.

"Fine. I know I'm going to regret this." She glared at Steel. "110 Aspen Lane. The code is 4120, and don't do anything to mess up the place."

Steel smiled. "I swear, I'll be a good boy. Do you have food there?"

Sloan turned back to Luke, ignoring Steel's question. If she wasn't already weary from sleeping in a chair all night, she was now. She reached for her phone back. "Can we please go see Derrick now?"

"Just one more thing," Luke said. "You can't tell anyone about Steel, especially Gage."

"Of course not. Because when all of this blows up in our faces, they can steer clear," she replied sarcastically. "Anything else, your highness? My first born?"

"No, I think that's it." Luke sighed. There was a lot weighing on him. Sloan could see it in his eyes, and it wasn't just about her and his brother. "Let's go see Derrick."

Steel walked back toward the jeep. "Can you guys give me a—"

"No," Sloan and Luke said in unison.

Steel held up his hands in surrender. "That's cool. I'll find a ride back to my bike."

20

AWAKE

Derrick

Derrick exhaled as he woke, and he'd never felt better in his whole life. The second he opened his eyes, it was like the world had become more vibrant, crisp. The white sheets covering his bottom half gleamed, and the walls were the color of the sky in July. But that wasn't all. His mind was on fire—new connections and neural pathways were developing and evolving. He could feel it happening, like learning something new but times a thousand. He sighed with pleasure as his brain released dopamine. He sat up and touched his temple. He didn't know what was happening, but he wanted more.

"It's normal," Payton said, sitting next to his bed.

He inhaled sharply and pulled at the sheet covering him. "Where am I?"

"Good. You can talk." She smiled. "You're at Arcadia."

"Of course I can talk. How...what happened?" His voice sounded strange, strangled. Like he hadn't used it for a while.

"Do you want the long or short version?" She poured him a cup of water.

Derrick took the cup and swallowed some water, the coolness soothing his scratchy throat. "Thanks."

"I was hoping they would have taken care of the effects of the drug they found in your system by the time you woke up, but I guess they work at their own pace. Honestly, the fact that you woke up at all is a testament to your strength."

Drug? The only drug he'd ever tried was marijuana, and Sloan had assured him nothing would happen. He frowned. "I didn't take any drugs."

"I had a feeling it wasn't voluntary." She sat back down. "What's the last thing you remember?"

He leaned back against the pillow, his mind racing.

Sloan. He met up with her at Purgatory, and they danced. He smiled as he recalled what happened next. He pressed his lips together, remembering the kiss with crystal clarity. The smile left his lips as he remembered Luke seeing them together and storming off.

The next bit was hazy. Somehow he ended up in Celia's car with Sloan. She was driving and stopped at Eden's Pass. That's when the pain started.

Derrick closed his eyes, concentrating. He was missing something, an important detail.

"How long have I been here?" he asked.

"Today is your third day."

"Three days?" He ran his hand through his hair. Yep, it had definitely been three days.

"My mom must be going nuts."

"You got that right. Your mom is a force." Payton smiled. "Don't worry though. We had one of our kind speak with her to calm her down. She's okay now."

"What do you mean by 'one of our kind'?"

She got up and locked her door.

"Um, what are you doing?" He sat up, his muscles tense.

"This isn't usually my thing, but since we have rapport, I offered. I'm pulling the Bio-Core confidentiality card—I need your absolute assurance that you will tell no one what I'm about to tell you. Can I trust you?"

On one hand, she was right. He had signed a confidentiality agreement when he started at Bio-Core. On the other hand, she'd kept information from him about Dr. Rice. He wasn't sure who her allegiances were to.

He weighed his options. Oh wait, he didn't really have any.

She had all the answers, and he had none. But were her answers going to be the truth?

"You can trust me, but why should I trust you?" he asked.

"That's fair." Payton tugged at her white lab coat as if deciding on how to best approach the previous mistrust between them. "All I can tell you is that I am loyal to a fault with my family." She smiled. "By some amazing twist of fate, you are now part of my family. I'll always be honest with you from here on out."

"Family? We're not related."

"Please just let me explain." She pressed her hands together, imploring him. Her eyes read sincere.

"Fine. You have my word I won't say anything."

Payton sat back down and leaned toward him. "Do you believe in evolution?"

He followed suit and leaned in. He wasn't sure where this was going, but he was certainly intrigued. "Yes."

"What if I were to tell you that humans were evolving into something different?"

"Different? How?"

She removed her glasses and set them on the table. When she looked back up, there were bright green sparkles in her eyes.

Derrick grabbed the railing next to his bed, his breath catching. "What the hell?"

"I assure you that what you're seeing in my eyes has nothing to do with hell." She grinned.

His heart was beating so fast he thought it might burst. His knuckles were white as he gripped the railing. There was something familiar about her eyes.

His dreams. Will. Dr. Rice. The syringe. The specks were the same.

He cleared his throat. "How?"

Payton blinked a few times and put her glasses back on, her eyes returning to their normal dark irises. "They're an alien lifeform. We call them chondria. Our relationship is symbiotic. They are what allow me to excel in my field. They fuel my brain in ways I don't think I'll ever understand." She leaned back in her chair. "When I was seventeen, I was approached by someone like me. He told me about chondria and that I was compatible with them. I was given a choice to join with them and become a host. I agreed."

Aliens. Freaking aliens!

Derrick let go of the railing and stared down at his hospital bed, his mind awhirl as he grappled with what she was telling him. He was no stranger to the unusual. Ashwater already had androids that lived with humans and people were supposedly abducted by aliens. If only people knew the alien part was true. Never in his wildest dreams did he think something like this was possible.

He looked back up at her, more curious than ever. "How does it...feel?"

Payton tilted her head and chuckled. He glanced around. Why was that funny?

After an awkward silence, she said, "Oh. I told you this isn't usually my thing. Um, they feel good. I guess that's one way to put it. I don't really feel them except when they gravitate to my eyes or concentrate on a specific part of my body. They help me heal faster and correct any deficiencies in my body. Paper cuts are a thing of the past."

"Why are you wearing glasses then?"

She fluffed her hair and smiled. "Because I look good in glasses."

"Are they sentient?"

"They are, but they don't communicate the way we

do. It's more like feelings." She arched her eyebrow. "You really don't—"

Before they could continue, there was a knock.

Payton got up and opened the door. It was Sloan, and she looked beautiful. Her hair was down and she wore a white tank top that made her tan skin shimmer. But it was the way her lips parted that set his body on fire as he remembered their first kiss.

Behind her was Adam, Evie, Luke, Mazy, Gage, and Iris. "Alive and Kicking" by Simple Minds played on someone's phone.

Evie elbowed Adam, who muttered, "Deal with it."

"You're awake." Sloan launched herself into Derrick's arms.

"Yep." He hugged her tightly, breathing in the tropical scent in her freshly washed damp hair. He glanced up at Adam. "Yes, I'm still alive."

Evie laughed. "You should have heard what he played when we visited you the first time. Your outlook wasn't so good."

Sloan released him and sat in a chair next to him, her hand maintaining contact with his arm, her eyes never leaving his. The concern on her face was palpable.

"I'm okay." He squeezed her hand.

"Well, I'm going to give you some time with your friends." Payton stood. "Just don't overdo it, and I'll come back later to continue our conversation."

Derrick nodded. Yeah, he still had a million questions and didn't know what chondria had to do with him.

Payton patted his arm and left.

"She's pretty," Sloan said.

Derrick smiled. "Don't be jealous. We're just colleagues."

"Who said anything about you?" Sloan arched an eyebrow, and the left side of her mouth turned up.

Everyone laughed while Derrick frowned. "Ha ha."

"I'm mostly kidding." Sloan squeezed his arm.

Derrick rolled his eyes.

Luke moved closer to the bed, his hands in his pockets. "I'm glad you're okay."

The last time they were together, Luke was super pissed about him and Sloan. But Derrick had been here three days. Was Luke okay with everything now? "Thanks. Um, could I have a minute with my brother?"

"Sure. Come on, guys," Gage corralled everyone out the door.

Sloan smiled and got up too. On her way out, she said to Luke, "Remember, he just woke up."

"I know," Luke said.

After the door shut, Luke walked over to the machine reading Derrick's vitals. "You're really doing okay?"

"Physically, yeah. But I still feel like shit about what happened between us. I never meant for it to happen, I swear."

Luke slumped down in the chair. "I'm not gonna lie, I hate that it's Sloan. Anyone else, dude. Anyone."

"I know. I'm sorry. I tried really hard to not like

her, but she's…" Derrick couldn't find the right words. She wasn't just pretty—she was funny and warm and always told it like it was. Not to mention she was an incredible snowboarder and good at sports, gaming, and like a million other things.

"Amazing," Luke said plainly. "It's the reason she's my best friend."

Derrick smiled. "Yeah."

"Well, in case you're wondering, I forgive you. You two can do whatever it is you plan on doing." Luke leaned forward and balled his hand into a fist. "But if you hurt her, I'll be forced to kick your ass."

Derrick smiled. So it took an overdose to get his brother to forgive him. "I won't, and thanks."

Luke stood and tapped him on the shoulder. "I'm going to go find Mom. She's going to be so happy you're awake." He turned to leave and paused. "Also, Evie's been drawing weird pictures of you while you were asleep. You might want to ask her for those." Luke shivered.

"Oh, God. That's weird." Derrick didn't think he wanted any of the pictures. But he made a mental note to tell her to throw them away.

Once Luke left, Derrick chatted with his friends and parents for a while. He was happy to be with them but distracted too. He wanted to continue his conversation with Payton in the worst way. Sloan noticed and asked if they should leave to let him rest. He was feeling a little worn down from his mom's incessant questions about his wellbeing.

After they left, his mind wandered to his conversation with Payton. What did aliens have to do with what happened to him? Did they have something to do with what was going on in his head?

As if on cue, there was a knock on the door. Derrick's eyes itched. He rubbed at them, but that made them tingle more. It was an odd feeling. Not really painful, just weird.

The door opened, and Will walked in, his eyes lit up like Payton's.

Derrick inhaled sharply. "What's going on? What are you doing here?"

Will smiled. "Time to bust you out of here."

21

FRUITFUL

Sloan

She regretted her decision to go with Luke the second he pulled into the gravel driveway of her family's cabin. Steel's bike was parked in front of the garage. Next to it was an overflowing trash bin.

"What is he thinking? That will attract bears and who knows what else." Sloan got out and slammed the car door shut. She stomped over to the trash bin and picked up a bag of Funions, an egg carton, a ton of apple cores and orange peels and… She stopped. "Ew. I am not touching that."

Luke joined her, peering over her shoulder. "Is that—"

"Yes. Yes, it is." Sloan took a deep breath. She wasn't the squeamish type, but there were some things not even she wanted to see outside her family's cabin.

"Whoa. That dude gets around." Luke tossed it in the bin. "There. Gone."

She glanced up at the windows and pushed Luke. "After you. You're my shield to all the gross things I'm sure Steel has done to defile my family's cabin. Thanks for this gift, by the way."

"I'm sure it's fine." Luke's mouth turned up in a smirk.

She narrowed her eyes at him. He knew it wasn't going to be *fine*.

When they reached the door, they heard music blasting from inside.

Sloan frowned. "Is he listening to Madonna?"

"I think so." Luke shook his head. "This can't be good."

Luke pushed the door open as "Material Girl" by Madonna washed over them. The cabin had an open concept with the kitchen and living areas combined into one. The living room was empty, but there was a haze of steam and a heavy scent of soap wafting from the hallway.

Steel was showering.

Luke and Sloan walked inside. The kitchen was relatively neat except for a pile of dirty plates in the sink.

"Not too bad, right?" Luke asked.

"Not nearly as bad as I thought it might be." Sloan moved into the living room.

The shower turned off, and a guy's voice belted out the chorus.

Luke stared at Sloan and mouthed, *Oh my God.*

She covered her mouth and did her best not to laugh. He actually had a decent voice, even though his choice of music was…interesting.

A door opened, and more steam poured out from the hallway. Then Steel appeared, wearing nothing but a white towel, water beaded on his skin. He ran a hand through his damp, jet black hair. Sloan's eyes went to the tattoo on his arm and chest, a large snake wrapped around his arm and shoulder, its head positioned on his upper chest, fangs out, ready to strike. She arched an eyebrow. She had to admit, it was a sick tat.

Steel smiled when he saw them and smacked his hands together. "Sweet. Company. I've been lonely."

Sloan rolled her eyes, thinking about the trash bin's contents. "Not that lonely."

"Dude. What are you listening to?" Luke asked.

"Don't hate on my tunes. Madonna's tight."

She couldn't stop staring at the snake. With each breath he took, the snake undulated. It was making her uncomfortable and not in a way she liked. "That's some tattoo."

"Thanks." Steel glanced down at it. He took a step toward her, his eyes strangely playful.

She took a step back.

"You can touch it if you want. Don't worry. It doesn't bite…often."

"No thanks. I'm good." She didn't know what it was, but there was something seriously damaged inside him. One minute, he's singing Madonna, and the next he's threatening to bite her.

"Okay, well, what do I owe you for this visit?" Steel said.

"Just checking in on you," Luke said.

"Oh." Steel glanced around, his hands fidgeting. If Sloan wasn't mistaken, she'd say he was confused. "That's, um, cool, I guess. I'm just going to go get changed." He turned to leave but paused and turned back around. He pointed at the sofa. "Uh, don't sit there." He pointed to a chair. "Or there. Maybe just stand."

Sloan's eyes widened. She wasn't one to be at a loss for words, but she seriously had nothing.

Luke, on the other hand, had no problem. "Bro, that is so wrong."

"I'll take care of it," Steel said. "I promise. I know a guy."

"Be right back." The song changed to "Like a Virgin" by Madonna, and Steel swayed his hips. He left Sloan and Luke in the desecrated living room as he danced his way back down the hallway, singing.

Sloan shook her head. "This is so gross, Luke. I really hate you for this. My parents and I watch movies on that couch." She pointed to the chair. "And that's Buck's seat."

"I know. I'm sorry. I'll make it up to you somehow."

She turned the music off. She couldn't take it anymore. While they waited for Steel, she went over to the fridge and opened it.

The entire fridge was filled with fruit. Apples, oranges, watermelon, cantaloupe, nectarines, plums, kiwi, grapes, raspberries, strawberries. She shut it, shaking her head. Well, it could have been worse. There could have been body parts in there.

Steel came back wearing black shorts and a white T-shirt, the snake still faintly visible beneath. She hadn't really spent any time with Steel, but he and Gage did look a lot alike, apart from the black hair and snake.

Oh, and Steel's killer tendency.

"Why do you have so much fruit?" Sloan asked.

Steel gave her a sideways glance. "Because it's good." He nodded at Luke. "What do you want?"

Luke peered inside the fridge. "I'll take an apple."

Steel grabbed an apple and tossed it to him. "What about you, Miss Unreadable? You want some kiwi? It's already peeled."

Sloan did like kiwi, but now was no time to be exchanging niceties over fruit with Steel. She crossed her arms. "No. Look, you've been here for three days now. When are you leaving?"

Steel pouted. "Oh, Sloan. Don't get your boy shorts in a bunch. We're even now. I've forgiven you for your kick to my boys. Believe me, you really dodged a bullet." He put his arm around her. "We're friends now."

"Yuck." She pushed his arm away. "We most certainly are not friends. I let you stay here for Luke, not you."

Steel frowned. "Okay, okay, I get it. It's time for me to move on. It's just that there are people looking for me I'd really like to avoid. Can you give me a couple more days?"

"Who's looking for you?" Luke asked.

The genuine concern on Luke's face made Sloan groan. Who was this person, and what did they do with her best friend?

Steel opened his mouth to reply, but a glance at Sloan made him change his mind about what he was going to say. "Don't worry about it. It's better you don't know."

"Oh. Okay." Luke looked at Sloan, his eyes imploring. "Just a few more days?"

Sloan got a very bad feeling in the pit of her stomach. Steel was bad enough. From the way he was talking, it sounded like there were criminal types after him. Steel was right about one thing—it was better they didn't know what trouble he was in. But now he was asking for more. If she agreed, they could get the hell out of here. If she said no, Luke would pout and who knew what Steel would do. She doubted it would involve more Madonna.

"Fine." She put her hands on her hips. "But I want you out by the end of this weekend. That gives you four days."

"Thank you," Steel replied.

"Don't thank me. Thank Luke. And I expect you to remove all traces that you were here including all that fruit and have this place professionally cleaned when you leave."

"Absolutely. You have my word."

"Because that's worth anything," Sloan said under

her breath. She hoped he meant it, but she wasn't holding her breath.

Crunch.

Sloan glared at Luke as he munched on his apple, the sound cutting through the awkward silence.

Luke shrugged his shoulders in response. "What?"

Steel smiled. "So, do you guys want to hang out for a while?"

Sloan crossed her arms and left. The last thing she wanted to do was spend one more minute with Steel or his snake. If Luke wasn't hot on her heels, this deal was off.

Derrick

Derrick gripped the passenger handle of the car to steady himself. Will was hellbent on speeding. His eyes stopped itching, but his mind had gone from functioning to overdrive. Something inside him had changed. He didn't know how, but he could feel his mind map out connections to information. It wasn't long until the information he'd gathered from Payton, his dreams, and Will gave him the answers he sought. The truth formed in his mind as plain as day—he was a host for chondria like Payton and Will. The only blank spot was how.

"Where are we going?" Derrick asked.

Will glanced over at him and smiled. "By the look on your face, you've realized that you're like me now." He gripped the steering wheel emphatically. "I knew it would be your brain."

He couldn't deny his mind was on fire. It was as if he had answers to questions before he even asked them, but he still wanted confirmation. "What do you mean by 'my brain'?"

"Your special ability. All hosts have one. Some of the brightest scientists are hosts."

Interesting. "What's yours?"

"I'm a tracker. I find things. The most important of which is potential hosts."

Derrick looked at the familiar road ahead of them, fishing for confirmation again. "You still haven't answered my first question."

"Which was?" Will raised his eyebrows.

"Where are we going?" Derrick narrowed his eyes. He'd just asked him.

"Bro..." Will glanced from Derrick to the road, frowning. "I'm not a geek host like you. We're going to your lab at Bio-Core to test out your special ability."

Derrick smiled. Wow. He was firing on all cylinders now. His skin prickled with excitement. He felt amazing and couldn't wait to test out his ability. There was just one more thing he needed to understand. "How did this happen to me?"

"Your girlfriend injected you with a strain of chondria." He arched an eyebrow. "She probably saved your life."

Girlfriend? Will was talking about Sloan. Derrick inhaled sharply, his cheeks warming. He liked the sound of that. But why would she inject him? As soon as the question formed in his mind, so too did the answer—the strange feeling at Purgatory, losing control at Eden's Pass. The syringe in his bag. She injected him thinking it was an EpiPen and he was having an allergic reaction.

Well, in this case, it sort of was. They'd expelled the drug and healed the damage to his body.

What else can I do now?

Will laughed. *I love the brainy ones. You guys figure stuff out so fast.*

"You heard me?" Derrick raised his eyebrows.

"All hosts can think to others. Sometimes it takes a while to get the hang of it. Not you."

"Does that include non-hosts?"

"Technically yes, but only with extreme caution. We keep our identities secret."

Gage and Steel had that ability too. Were they hosts? Before he could ask, Derrick thought of something else. Luke. They could always sense what the other was feeling or thinking. His breath caught. "What about my brother? Is he a potential host too?"

"I'm afraid not. You'd think so because you're twins but no. It's a difficult dilemma for us, and we don't understand why." Will sighed. "Don't get any bright ideas. Chondria will kill anyone who isn't compatible. I've seen it firsthand. It's why most potential hosts who have a twin decide not to go through with it. Our aging slows down so we can't stay in the same place for long. I'm sorry."

The revelation hit Derrick in the gut like a ton of bricks. That was why they kept their identities secret. He couldn't tell his brother or anyone for that matter. Hosting was more like a curse. "Well that sucks."

"I know, and there's more. But for right now, let's focus on the positive." Will swerved into the parking lot of Bio-Core, tires squealing.

"You're a menace on the road." Derrick pressed his hand to the dash as his stomach flipped. His chondria had been fighting his nausea ever since they'd left Arcadia. For that, he was thankful.

Will chuckled as he pulled into a spot and parked. "You ready to test out that kickass brain of yours?"

"If it means getting out of this car, then yes."

TWO HOURS LATER, Derrick had changed his mind about being a host. It was the best thing that had ever happened to him. He was working faster than he thought possible, solving issues he'd only scratched the surface of before. He was elbow deep in android tissue, his aversion to post-mortem dissection gone. Raj and Jasmine were right—the answer to all their problems was right under their noses.

Will was right at home at Bio-Core. No surprise there. After all, Will had told him many brilliant scientists were hosts. He even had his own ID badge. After he grew either bored or disgusted watching Derrick sort through the android cadaver, he left. He said something about checking in with someone and some paperwork he had to fill out.

Derrick was barely listening though. His mind was on fire, and he wanted to direct that intensity toward his team's research.

Raj and Jasmine weren't due to come in for another

hour or so, and Derrick wanted to have something to show them when they did. The prototype they'd been working on was now functioning as they'd hoped it would, but he knew he could enhance it even more. Streamline the processing. Make it so that the user would have full use and sensation like it was their own hand or foot. Complete connectivity to the central nervous system. Just like Adam and Iris.

His fingers couldn't move fast enough on his keyboard as his mind rattled off code. His heart raced, and his body felt like a live wire as everything besides the computer in front of him faded into nothing.

He was on a mission.

22

INTERRUPTION

Sloan

T he only thing on Sloan's mind was Derrick. He'd been working nonstop at Bio-Core since he'd left the hospital. He'd even gotten a pass from Principal Kelly to skip classes. She knew he was passionate about his internship, but she needed to see him. They hadn't talked about anything that happened, and it was eating her up inside. Had he decided they shouldn't date?

As she walked through the front doors of the massive facility, she was struck by how legitimate the front end of Bio-Core was. Visitors strolled around the large atrium entry, marveling at the massive fountain that erupted from the floor at the center of the room. If they only knew what lay in the bowels of this place.

She shivered. The sooner she found Derrick, the better.

Sloan approached a woman at a counter. The

woman's hair was pulled tight into a low bun, and she had at least three layers of makeup caked on.

"Excuse me," Sloan said, "could you tell me where to find Derrick Dixon?"

The woman glanced up at her and frowned, her annoyance with Sloan's request obvious. "Sure."

"Thanks." *Well, excuse me.* Someone isn't very good at customer service.

She gave Sloan a visitor pass and pointed her toward the elevators, giving her directions. What the woman didn't know was that this wasn't Sloan's first time in this freakshow palace. She pressed the button and waited for the elevator. The doors opened, and two men, one blond and the other dark-haired, came out in a heated argument. She backed up, but neither noticed she was there or that their conversation was now public.

"You've had enough chances, and so has he," the blond said, pointing at the dark-haired man. He was exasperated. That much was obvious.

"I assure you, it won't happen again." The dark-haired man's voice was steady and confident.

"Enough. The decision has been made." He strode toward the back of the atrium where the drug and medical division was located.

The dark-haired man groaned and swore under his breath.

Sloan tried to quietly enter the elevator undetected, but the dark-haired man saw her.

He put his hand on the frame of the elevator so the

doors couldn't close. "How long have you been standing there?"

"Um, not long." She didn't like the malice in his eyes or the familiarity—like he was ready to eat her for lunch. She pressed a button. *Move your hand, buddy.*

He tilted his head, and for a split second, Sloan thought he might get back in the elevator with her. He leaned toward her and said, "Well, okay."

He moved his hand and walked away.

The doors shut, and Sloan drew in a ragged breath. Her shoulders shook, as if cold from his sinister stare. She didn't know what she'd just witnessed, but that dude was creepy as hell. Why did Derrick have to work here?

She made her way down to Derrick's lab. She wasn't sure if she was supposed to knock or walk inside. The lady upstairs just told her the number of the lab. She raised her fist a few times and finally knocked. She heard footsteps, and then the door opened. A tall woman with a white lab coat answered the door. She looked to be in her late twenties. She smelled like vanilla, and her hair reminded Sloan of fusilli. Yum.

"Can I help you?" the woman asked.

"I'm looking for Derrick Dixon." Sloan tugged on her visitor badge. How was it that Derrick got to work with such attractive women? First Payton, now this woman. She couldn't let it go. "Also, does anyone *un*attractive work here?"

The woman laughed. "Yeah, he does."

She pointed to a man sitting with Derrick at a

console. Sloan's breath caught at the sight of Derrick. He was super focused and pounding on keys with a ferocity she'd not seen before. Ouch. Those poor keys. Neither the man nor Derrick looked up at them.

"I'm Jasmine." She extended her hand.

Sloan shook it. "Nice to meet you."

"Derrick?" Sloan asked.

He looked up, his eyes readjusting as if snapping out of a trance. Then he smiled, and Sloan's heart melted. "Hey, you came to visit me."

You bet your sweet ass I did. "Yeah. I hadn't heard from you, so I thought I'd stop by."

The man working next to him stood. "Hello, I'm Raj."

"Sloan."

An awkward silence followed. Sloan glanced around, not sure what to do. She was hoping to talk to Derrick alone.

"Hey, Raj, let's take a break and give them some privacy," Jasmine said, catching on.

Raj said, "But we're on to something—"

Jasmine cleared her throat.

"Oh, right," he said, frowning. "Well, we'll get back to it soon enough."

Sloan shoved her hands into her sweatshirt pockets and stared at Derrick. He looked surprisingly well rested, given all the hours Luke said he was putting in here. After Jasmine and Raj left, she asked, "Are you okay?"

Derrick smiled. "I'm sorry. We've just had a major breakthrough, and it's been hectic."

"I get it." Did she though? Hadn't they had a breakthrough of their own? She looked down at her feet. She'd been ghosted before and this was pretty much what it felt like. "I'm sorry to bother you."

He reached for her hand and pulled her in for an embrace.

She laid her head on his shoulder and sighed. "Are you having second thoughts about us?"

Derrick pulled back and rubbed her arms. "No. Oh my God, no. I'm sorry. I really just got caught up in my work."

"I had to ask."

"Come on," he said, grabbing her hand. "I want to show you what I'm working on."

"Okay." Her heart lightened. She wanted to see what he was up to here, and hopefully he'd have time to work on her too.

Excitement rolled off of him as he tugged her to a large glass case in the center of the room with what looked like a white, sinewy human arm. Red and blue wires wove in and out of the arm. Derrick went to a control panel in front of the arm and pressed a few buttons. The arm moved, flexing the hand and fingers.

"This is going to revolutionize prosthetics. One of the biggest issues is the connectivity to the nervous system. Use is one thing, but sensation is another. We're developing an implant that will allow a person to feel sensations in the prosthesis like it is their own biological limb."

Sloan walked over to the arm. "Wow, that's amazing. Where does the implant go?"

"That's the tricky part. The implant must be imbedded in the cerebellum. It's behind the brain stem. Raj said the surgery is complicated, and...well, we've got our work cut out for us."

"I'm sure you'll get there." She turned back around. "So, when will you have some time off?"

"I've got some time right now." He reached for her waist and pulled her close.

She inhaled sharply, her skin tingling under his touch. *Yes, please.*

Derrick pressed his lips to hers, and she welcomed the warmth by putting her arms around his neck and pulling him closer. His lips were soft and supple, and his technique was stellar—each caress of his tongue sent tiny shockwaves through her body. A split second of reality hit her as she wondered if there were cameras watching them. He sucked on her bottom lip, and the thought dissipated.

He trailed some kisses down her cheek to her neck, and they reverberated all the way to her toes. She sighed. She was happy that she came to visit.

"No!" Someone yelled.

Sloan jumped away from Derrick, her heart racing.

Payton, the woman she'd met in Derrick's hospital room, stood in the doorway to the lab, eyes wide. "What are you doing?"

Derrick frowned. "Kissing my girlfriend?"

Sloan smiled and drew her freshly kissed bottom lip into her mouth. *Girlfriend?* If Payton wasn't so distraught, she'd fist pump.

"Um, I need to speak with you about something work related," Payton said.

"Can't it wait?" he asked.

"No, it can't." Payton stepped away from the door and stared at the floor, waiting for Sloan to leave.

Well, that was rude. Payton had quickly devolved from a hottie to a nottie.

"I guess that's my cue to leave?" Sloan asked.

"I'm sorry. I will make it up to you tonight. Meet at Jack's?" Derrick said.

"Sounds great. Text me." She kissed him chastely on the lips and headed to the door, staring down her adversary, her lips a thin line. "Payton."

Payton's eyes never left the floor. "Sloan."

Sloan didn't know what was going on, but it had nothing to do with work and everything to do with her. She closed the door to the lab and considered eavesdropping. She sighed.

No need. She trusted Derrick.

As she made her way upstairs and out of Crazy-Core, she made a mental note to keep an eye on Payton.

Derrick

"You can't date her," Payton said.

Derrick ran his hand through his hair. He hadn't slept in a long time, but he didn't remember Payton being in charge of his love life. "Who are you to decide that?"

She put her hands on her hips and sighed. "Didn't Will explain that part to you?"

"What part? I've been working. He told me to focus on the positive of being a host. So that's what I'm doing. Now if you don't mind…"

"Damn it, Derrick, I'm trying to tell you something important. If you sleep with Sloan, you'll kill her."

The breath left his lungs. "I'm sorry, did you just say I could kill Sloan?"

"That's exactly what I said. She's human, and you're a host. You experienced bonding by blood. The other way to bond is intercourse."

"Oh my God." He sat down at his desk chair and rubbed his forehead. A headache was coming on. Thankfully, he didn't need aspirin anymore now that he had chondria. "Why is this happening? We just got together."

"I'm sorry. I know I can be blunt, and I assumed Will told you about this." She sat down next to him. "I know you really like her, and what's not like? She's adorable. But it's just not possible long term."

"So…What? I have to be alone?" The gift was feeling like a curse again.

"No. Not at all." She smiled. "I'm not alone. I mean, it took some time, but eventually, I met my girl-friend. Hosts have gatherings from time to time. You'll meet all kinds of people. You'll see."

"This sucks." Derrick shook his head. "How am I going to explain this to Sloan?"

"Well, there's only so much you can say."

"You don't understand. I have to tell her. I trust her completely."

"Derrick, that's so not a good idea."

"Well, that's too bad because I'm going to tell her anyway."

"You're exasperating, you know that?" Payton stood and crossed her arms. "Must run in our family."

"Our family?"

She smiled, her chondria reaching her irises. "Yeah, turns out, the chondria you were injected with were mine. We're asked to donate our chondria from time to time for research. That's why I said we were family now. You can trust me."

Instinctually, Derrick's chondria gravitated to his eyes too, with the same itch he felt before, his chondria drawn to Payton as they sensed their kin nearby. While he was still new to being a host, he was learning that this was one of their ways of communicating. He and Payton were connected, and he could trust her with his life. "I do trust you."

"So you'll listen to me then about not telling Sloan?"

"Nope."

She groaned. "Will is not going to like this one bit. Where is he, by the way? He always stays close with a new host."

"Earlier this week, he said something about checking in and paperwork." Derrick scrunched up his face, trying to recollect if he'd seen him since. "I think he stopped by a few times since, but I don't remember him telling me anything else. The last three days have been intense with work."

Payton's expression changed, her eyes softening. "You have to take breaks, Derrick. I know it feels really good right now, but even with chondria, you're going to crash. When's the last time you ate or slept?"

While he could rattle off all kinds of important mathematical equations and lines of code, he didn't know the answer to her question. "I don't know."

She stood. "Come on. We'll figure out a solution to your girl problems over some burgers."

His stomach growled. Burgers did sound good. His eyes tingled as chondria surfaced in the irises of his eyes. They did that when he had an intense response to something or someone. They were in his eyes when he was kissing Sloan. If Payton hadn't interrupted, Sloan would have seen them.

Payton smiled. "I'll take that as a yes."

Derrick grabbed his bag. "Only if we go to my family's diner. My dad makes the best burgers."

"Lead the way."

23

BURGERS AND SPIES

Derrick

D errick hadn't been to the diner since his last shift, the night of Purgatory. Dixon's had always felt like home to him. Now, walking through the front door, it felt foreign. His lab was his home now. Late afternoon, or—as Luke and Derrick called it—the slump, was the perfect time to grab some food and not have to wait. Celia was working and his mom was at the cash register. He introduced Payton to his mom. She insisted Celia wait on them since he'd brought a guest.

They grabbed a booth, and Derrick handed Payton a menu.

"I love diner food." She scanned the menu with a sparkle in her eye.

He couldn't agree more.

Celia came over to the table, all smiles. "Good to see you. You feeling better?"

"Yeah," he said. "Hey, I'm sorry about leaving your car at Eden's Pass. Luke said they called you to go get it."

Celia shrugged. "Oh my gosh, don't worry about that. I'm just glad you're all right." She glanced at Payton, her eyebrows knitting together. "Um, how's Sloan?"

Derrick caught on to Celia's game right away, his cheeks warming. "She's good. This is one of my coworkers, Payton."

"Nice to meet you," Payton said. "Don't worry, Derrick and I don't play on the same team." She arched an eyebrow for emphasis.

Celia laughed. "I like her. What can I get you?"

After they ordered their burgers, Payton popped a few quarters in the mini jukebox and played "Take on Me" by A-ha.

"Not you too." Derrick laughed. "It's like the whole town has gone back in time or something."

"Or maybe I just like the eighties?"

"You and everyone else."

Peyton shrugged. "Now, about this girl problem. There are people who know about us, including a special branch of the FBI, which is what Will was probably referring to when he mentioned paper-work. He has to register new hosts. The keyword is 'host.' Sloan is not in that category. So, you could tell her, but I don't see the point. You can't be with her."

"Let me worry about what goes on between me and my girlfriend."

"Also, how will she react? Dr. G. already erased her memories of injecting you with the chondria."

"I'm sorry, what did you say?" A knot formed in his stomach. He didn't like the sound of this.

"That's standard practice when a situation like this happens. We have serum for it. Don't worry. There aren't any side effects."

Derrick closed his eyes and drew in a long, slow breath. This was his reality now—both wonderful and annoying. He was changed, and there was no going back. But he was also no stranger to the odd and unusual. He was a native of Ashwater, after all, where androids hung out in arcades and dress shops. He'd have to make the best of his new life.

"No one touches Sloan again," he said. "No more serums. And no more telling me what I can and can't do. I'm grateful for this gift—don't think I'm not. But I want Sloan to know she saved my life. She's important to me, and I'm going to tell her."

"I've been wondering ever since your first day at Bio-Core if you had it in you to survive there. There was no denying your intelligence and drive, but I wasn't sure you had the balls to back it up." Payton cracked a smile. "Clearly you do. Consider yourself warned, little bro. I won't stand in your way."

"Thanks. I appreciate that." His stomach growled.

She laughed. "That's one thing chondria can't fix."

IT WAS the best burger he'd ever tasted. He wasn't sure how that was possible since he'd eaten the same burgers for most of his life, but this one was perfect. Payton enjoyed hers as well. Although, she requested blue cheese on hers. Gross.

As they finished up their burgers, Garcia came over to their table.

"Payton," he said, his facial expression unreadable.

"Garcia." She didn't give an inch of her true sentiments either.

He smiled at Derrick. "How are things going? Are you feeling better?"

Derrick cleared his throat. "I'm okay."

"Oh, well, that's good. Your mother was so worried." He looked around and then asked, "How are things going at work?"

He's sure got an interest in you, Payton thought to Derrick.

Derrick knocked his knife off the table, and it clattered to the floor. Quickly, he reached down and grabbed the knife. Getting used to people thinking to him was going to take some time. The way she was smiling told him she'd done it on purpose.

He looked back up at Garcia. "Things are going well. I like the team of doctors I'm working with."

"Good. Well, if you need anything, you only have to ask." He opened his mouth as if he wanted to say more but then shut it. "Nice to see you, Payton. See you later, Derrick."

After he left, Payton leaned toward Derrick. "Well, well. Someone's taken a shine to you. What's that all about? Last I heard, Garcia only cared about one person—himself."

"He claims he's turned over a new leaf."

"Yeah, right." She rolled her eyes. "You didn't happen to see him that night at Purgatory, did you?"

"No." He frowned. What was she getting at?

"Well," Payton said, stabbing a french fry into a puddle of ketchup, "I have it on good authority that an arrest in the overdose cases is imminent and Garcia is the prime suspect."

"No." He shook his head. "That can't be right."

"How do you know?" She arched an eyebrow at him and whispered, "He's probably spying on us right now."

"For who? He doesn't work at Bio-Core anymore, and the last person he worked for, Mr. Strickland, is dead."

"I don't know, but he's very interested in you, caring even, and that doesn't jive with the Garcia I knew."

"He's different now." Derrick sighed as Garcia leaned on the counter in front of the cash register, talking to his mom.

"How so?"

"Because he's in love with my mom."

Payton's eyes widened. "You're joking, right?"

"I'm afraid not." He nodded toward the cash register. "Look for yourself."

She followed his view to the counter where Garcia grinned like a lovesick puppy as he fawned all over Derrick's mom.

Derrick's stomach turned over—she appeared to enjoy the attention.

"Huh," Payton said. "So is your mom into him too?"

He shrugged and stabbed some ice at the bottom of his cup with his straw. He didn't really have an opinion. His parents had been having problems for a while, mostly about money. He didn't want to discuss his parents' relationship with Payton—or anyone, for that matter. He glanced out the window and met a pair of violet eyes staring back at him from the parking lot.

Iris.

Derrick waved to her. What was she up to?

Instead of waving back, she blew a kiss at him then walked away.

His head flinched back. "That was weird."

"What?"

"My friend, Iris, was outside just now. She blew me a kiss."

"And why is that weird?" Payton offered.

"It's just not like her, and it's the second time she's done something weird like that."

"Well, there is a glare. Maybe she thought you were someone else?"

Derrick knew that couldn't be true. While she didn't have any of her internal weaponry anymore, her optical lens was perfect. "Maybe."

"Okay, I think I've had enough Ashwater gossip for one day. I haven't spent that much time in town, but it's definitely mysterious and dripping with melodrama. And that's saying something, given my own secret." She smiled. "I guess *our* secret now."

"Yeah, it's definitely an interesting town." He grabbed the check Celia set down on their table. "You want anything else?"

"No, I'm good. Thanks for dinner."

"No problem."

After parting ways with Payton, he walked toward Jack's and texted Sloan.

DERRICK: *Headed to Jack's now. Meet u there?*

A thumbs-up emoji appeared in response.

Dark clouds hovered over the buildings on Main Street. A storm was on the horizon, and he couldn't shake the feeling it wasn't the only thing sweeping through his hometown. A cool breeze grazed his bare forearms, causing the hairs to stand on end. Storms in spring were common and nothing to worry about, but his weather app was warning of back-to-back storms over the next day or so that could have damaging winds, hail, and potential for tornadoes.

He shivered as his chondria gravitated to his exposed arms to warm him. He thought about Iris's air kiss and Garcia flirting with his mom. Both gave him the creeps, but the unease in his stomach was about something else.

His mind and body had changed. He could hear things more clearly, see better. Smells and tastes were more vivid.

Most importantly, he could sense things now in a way he never thought possible. An overwhelming sense of foreboding was hitting him hard, and he had no idea why. Was this just another host thing he had to get used to? He glanced both ways up and down Main

Street and crossed the road, forcing the feeling from his mind. He replaced it with the dark-haired beauty he now called his girlfriend.

Sloan

Jack was flipping through a magazine at the front counter, and a red-haired Daisy was at the snack bar tending to the hot dog roller. Sloan hopped on a stool at the snack bar. The dogs looked like they belonged in a nursing home.

"Time of death?" Sloan asked Daisy.

Daisy pursed her lips. "I don't think they're ready for the bin yet. You hungry?"

"Pass. But I'll take a Coke."

"You got it." She grabbed a bottle of Coke from the fridge and set it in front of Sloan. "My adorable nephew is with Adam in the DP room."

Sloan flushed, something she didn't do often. "Oh, cool."

"Don't you 'oh, cool' me." Daisy smiled slyly. "He already told me you're dating. I must say, I'm thrilled. You two have been dancing around your feelings for a while now. It was almost as annoying as Luke's crush on that waitress."

Sloan smiled, butterflies taking flight in her stomach. It happened every time someone mentioned them being together. She put some money on the counter and grabbed her Coke. "I like the red, by the way. It's a power color."

Daisy fluffed her short, spiky locks. "Thanks. Have fun."

Adam and Derrick were dancing to "Dance Hall Days" by Wang Chung. They were such geeks. Adam was a better dancer, but Derrick still had some moves.

When the song finished, Sloan announced she was present by clapping. "Nice."

Derrick turned around, and the second his gaze caught hers, her heart fluttered. She couldn't put her finger on it, but there was something different about him since the accident—an aura. Like he was stronger, more confident, taller?

He walked over to her and reached for her hand. "Hey, glad you could make it. I missed you."

"I just saw you like a couple hours ago."

Derrick drew her in for a hug and whispered, "Too long."

She hugged him, resting her chin on his chest and breathed in his earthy scent—sandalwood. She made a mental note to ask for his sweatshirt when he took her home.

"I'm going to Evie's house," Adam said. "She wants to try out a new angle. You guys are welcome to play whatever you want."

They turned toward Adam. Sloan arched an eyebrow. "New angle?"

Adam smiled. "Yep. She's super excited."

Sloan stifled a laugh, and Derrick did the same.

"Are you talking about her drawing you?" Derrick asked.

"Yeah." Adam frowned, his eyebrows knitting together. "What else would I be talking about?"

Derrick nudged Sloan's side.

She giggled. "I'll never get tired of you, Adam."

"Thanks, I guess." Adam walked toward the door. "Just make sure you turn everything off when you're done."

"I got it," Derrick said.

"Can I pick a song?" Sloan asked, walking toward the control console.

He grabbed her hand, pulling her back. "Sure, but I want to talk to you first."

That sounded ominous. "Okay. About what?"

"What do you remember about my seizure?"

"Uh…" Sloan frowned. That whole time period was still a blur. "Not much. Why do you ask?"

He ran a hand through her hair. "Because I want you to know that you saved my life."

"I did? How?"

"When I found Dr. Rice behind the diner, she gave me a syringe from Bio-Core. I'd been carrying it around with me ever since. She asked me to keep it a secret. She said it could put people in danger. So I didn't tell anyone."

She put her hand on his chest. "Oh my God. That must have been awful keeping that secret. You didn't even tell Luke?"

"No. I didn't want anyone I care about to get hurt. Anyway, that night at Eden's Pass, you found the syringe in my bag and injected me with it." He brushed the backs of his fingers on her cheek, carrying sparks across her flesh. "It's what saved my life."

His words landed in her mind, but something was preventing her from connecting them with a memory. It was like she was listening to a story about someone else. She rubbed her temples. "Why don't I remember any of this?"

"Because Dr. G. erased your memories of it."

"Why?" Her heart whipped up a few beats, her skin prickling. Her arm did hurt when she woke up the morning after.

"Because of what was inside the syringe. What's inside me now."

She parted her lips. Inside him? What was he talking about? "Dude, you're freaking me out."

"It's okay." He pulled her close and pressed her head to his shoulder. "You're safe with me."

Sloan shuddered against him, her mind moving in a million directions. She took a few deep breaths and listened to his heartbeat, steady and calming. The question was on her lips—she just had to ask. "What's inside you?"

Derrick pulled back. His eyes glowed a peculiar green.

She reached her hand up and touched his temple. "Your eyes."

He cupped her hand with his own and smiled. "It's called chondria."

"Does it hurt?"

"No. They feel a little weird, I guess."

"They?"

"They're alien symbiotes."

"Shut up." She raised her eyebrows.

"Only in Ashwater, right?" He had a point. Add alien symbiotes to the list. Not that most people who lived here didn't already think aliens existed. Just not so tiny.

"So, you're saying I injected you with them?"

"You did."

Sloan closed her eyes and tried to will herself to remember. When nothing came to her, she opened her eyes and groaned. "So frustrating. Will I ever get that memory back?"

"I don't know, but I don't want you to worry about me or anything like this ever happening to you again."

"I have so many questions."

Derrick smiled. "Ask away."

After a while, Sloan was more at ease. Derrick explained what he knew about chondria and how they interacted with his body, enhancing him. He also explained that most humans were not compatible with them. That part was a bummer. She'd easily have signed up to host and not just because of Derrick. It sounded freaking awesome.

"So that's basically all I know. Can you keep this between us?" he asked.

"Of course. But—"

"You're thinking about Luke. I'll tell him, just not right now." He cupped the back of her head and kissed her.

She reached around his waist and interlaced her

fingers, holding him to her. "Okay. Now, how about we play some DP?"

"You think you can beat me? I'm like a real super-hero now." He grinned.

Sloan released him and headed toward the console. "We'll see about that. I won't argue that those aliens help your brain solve stuff I can't even fathom, but I highly doubt they enhance your ability to freestyle better than me."

He held out his hands in challenge. "Bring it on."

She selected "Alive" by Love and Rockets. "Appropriate, right?"

Derrick smiled and nodded.

They got to their places on the dance floor, and Sloan was struck by how easy it was for her to stay calm in the face of the unknown. She didn't rattle easily, and she'd always believed that was her strength. So what that her boyfriend was a host for alien symbiotes? They were about to play a game created by an android, and this was Ashwater after all.

24

BREAKTHROUGH

Derrick

The next day, Derrick had a breakthrough at Bio-Core. He'd finally cracked the code on connecting the nervous system to their developed prosthetics and prosthetic tissue. The technology was like nothing else in the world. Now their only problem was finding a way to test it. The implant needed to be in the cerebellum. The surgery alone had an extremely low chance of successful implementation. Raj's surgery on their 3-D model worked brilliantly...after ten attempts. It would be next to impossible to recommend the implant for human trials. They needed better odds than one in ten.

Raj patted Derrick on the back. "Don't think of it as a failure. It's more like a challenge. We'll get there."

"I guess." He sighed. He'd worked so hard on the implant. He knew that piece of the puzzle was a perfect fit.

The phone by the door rang, and Jasmine picked it up. She glanced at Derrick. "Yes, sir." She hung up the phone. "Max would like to see you."

"Okay." Derrick headed out of the lab.

Was he in trouble? He'd kept his newfound secret from everyone except Sloan. Was Max a host too? He made his way to the top floor of Bio-Core.

Dana was at her desk smiling. "Good to see you, Derrick. You can go in."

"Thanks, Dana." He smiled back. He could see why Gage's grandfather had chosen her. She was so nice. He wondered how she was getting on with the new CEO.

When he opened the door, Max wasn't seated at his desk as Derrick expected. He was by the windows overlooking the town.

"Max?" Derrick said.

"Come here," he said, not turning from the windows.

Derrick joined him at the windows. Ashwater looked tiny from up here. But he could still easily make out Main Street, Jack's Arcade with its neon lights, and Dixon's. Surrounding mountains cloaked the town and its secrets from the outside world. On the horizon, heavy, dark clouds filled the sky. His skin prickled. The storm would be here soon.

"To grow up in such a beautiful place is a gift," Max said. "I envy you."

"I can't complain. I've always felt at home here," Derrick replied.

"I grew up in Chicago. Foster care."

Derrick glanced at Max, whose expression looked pained. "That must have been hard."

Max smiled, extinguishing any sorrow his memories may have conjured up. "It wasn't as bad as people think. I was one of the lucky ones. My foster mom is the reason I'm strong now. Well, her and my black belt in Tae Kwon Do."

Derrick laughed and nodded at a display case with a katana sword. "I bet."

"But seriously, there are things in life that no book or class can teach you. You know what I mean?"

"I do, actually. It was the reason I wanted to work here instead of go to MIT."

"See? That's what I'm talking about. You've got the drive for it. You were the right choice."

Derrick cleared his throat. If he only knew how he'd changed. "Thank you."

"Sometimes in life, you get thrown a curveball. Like me taking this CEO position. It's not an easy job. The responsibility for the security of a company like this is overwhelming. Difficult decisions have to be made." He paused, as if one of those choices was on his mind now. "Some people don't have the stomach for it." Max was focused on something out the window, deep in thought.

Derrick inhaled sharply, and his stomach dropped. "Excuse me, but are you firing me?"

Max laughed as he came out of his trance and patted Derrick on the shoulder. "No, you've been doing very well here. Blowing the competing teams out of the water from what I understand." He leaned close. "I'm going to fire them."

Was he serious? Derrick's eyes grew large.

"I heard that you made some progress on the implant." Max headed over to his desk. "How's that going?"

Derrick's chest tightened, and he was thankful his chondria were there to calm his breathing. His gut told him to be on guard. Max had been nothing but nice to him so far, but that didn't mean he was in the clear. There was a point to this meeting. He cleared his throat and sat down. "It's going very well. We have a prototype that is promising. Jasmine and Raj are working on the procedure."

"Good. I'm glad to hear it." Max leaned forward, his steely blue eyes intent on Derrick's. "And how are you feeling?"

"Um, good." Derrick wet his lips.

"Glad to hear it. Such a terrible thing for someone as bright as you to be drugged like that. I'm sure the person responsible will pay for their mistake."

Derrick didn't have a clue who'd drugged him. It wasn't Garcia. That much, he was sure of. Max was unreadable, but it seemed that he knew more than Derrick did. And mistake? That was an odd choice of phrasing. He thought about asking Max what he meant by it, but something in his gut told him to let it go. His only goal was to get the hell out of here and not get fired. After all, he still didn't know if Max was serious about firing some of the other teams of doctors. He hoped not.

"Yes, I hope they're caught too." Derrick rubbed his now sweaty palms on his pants and stood. "Is there anything else?"

Max eyed him closely. A thought seemed to linger, but he decided against it. Instead, he turned his attention to his computer. "That's all. Thank you for the update. Glad you are feeling better."

Derrick turned and did his best not to run. What did he mean by someone as bright as him? Last he checked, all involuntary drugging was illegal. A chill ran down his spine that even his chondria couldn't soothe. All the other overdoses were random. Derrick wasn't sure if it was a slip of the tongue or if Max intended for him to know, but he definitely had more intel than the police.

Sloan

Sloan had spent the better part of the day putting up signs for the upcoming graduation party and not spilling the beans about Derrick turning into an alien host. Dark clouds, like inkblots from psychology class, hung over the school. She rubbed her bare arms, wishing she'd brought a sweatshirt.

Mazy opened the front door to the school. "Okay, you've got all of them posted out here. We just need the gym and the girls' locker room."

Sloan sighed and nodded. Getting into Edgewood was requiring a lot of work. Her new extracurricular titles basically meant she was Mazy's personal assistant. "I'll start in the locker room."

The final bell had rung, and girls who had gym class during eighth period rushed out of the locker room, creating a bottleneck at the door. Sloan fought her way in.

Apart from a few stragglers, the place was empty. The lights were off in the gym teacher's office, and the fluorescent lights overhead flickered dimly. She started at the back and worked her way forward, taping flyers up at each interval of lockers. There was a picture of what Mazy called 'fabulous prizes' on the front and dollar signs all around it. Mazy had done a good job fundraising for the door prizes, and there were some decent things kids could win. Sloan had her eye on a lift ticket for the next ski season.

A door swung shut somewhere toward the front of the locker room, and the quiet chatter from the few girls finishing up ceased. Sloan continued taping up the flyers, one after the other. It was very dull work. Between two lockers, a girl with sandy blond hair passed by.

"Iris?" she asked.

The girl didn't respond. It sure looked like Iris. Sloan rounded the corner of the lockers, but the girl was gone. Huh. Maybe she was delirious from all of Mazy's hard labor. She turned back around, and the air left her lungs like she'd been punched in the stomach.

Iris was standing behind her.

Sloan covered her heart, trying to slow its pace. "You scared the hell out of me."

"Oh, sorry." Iris peered down at the stack of papers in Sloan's arms. "What are you doing?"

"I'm putting up flyers for the graduation party. You and Gage going?"

"Sure." Iris's lip twitched as if Sloan had said something amusing. She reached for the tape. She smelled sweet, different. "Here, let me help you."

"Are you wearing a new perfume or something?" Sloan asked.

"Yes. It's Dior Poison. Do you like it?"

"Uh, yeah, sure." Sloan focused on the remaining spots for the flyers as Iris handed her tape.

Iris cleared her throat. "So, I have to deliver a bunch of donated clothes from Dalia's to Arcadia later, and they have to be sorted through. Would you be willing to help me out?"

So that was why she was here. Was Sloan wearing a Free Help sign on her back today?

"I was planning on hanging out with Derrick tonight," Sloan said.

"Oh." Iris frowned, her bottom lip jutting out. "I guess I'll have to do it myself."

Sloan pursed her lips and studied Iris. This was new. She didn't remember Iris ever giving a guilt trip before. It wasn't in her programming, android or otherwise. What was worse was that it was working. Sloan could add the good deed to her list of community service projects for Edgewood. Plus, Mazy would kill her if she didn't take advantage of the opportunity.

"Okay, I'll help," Sloan said. "When—"

"Fantastic." Iris's face lit up, and she tossed Sloan the tape. "Meet me in the lobby of Arcadia at seven."

Before Sloan could reply, Iris was gone. She stared after her. And people said Sloan was rude?

25

AN ARREST

Derrick

The wind was picking up. Derrick rubbed his arms, signaling his chondria there to warm him. He had his hand on the door to Jack's when a commotion across the street caught his attention.

There was a squad car, and Sheriff Grayson's truck parked out front of his family's diner. Both vehicles had their lights on. The door to the diner opened, and Sheriff Grayson led out Garcia in handcuffs.

Garcia was none too happy about it either, yelling and fighting against the restraints. "You've got the wrong person. I would never do this."

Derrick's mom, dad, and Luke were right behind them. His mom's brow was furrowed, a scowl on her lips. His dad and Luke looked more confused than anything. Luke spotted Derrick, said something to their parents, and jogged toward him.

The door to Jack's opened, and Jack, Daisy, Adam, and Evie came outside.

"What's going on?" Jack asked.

"As if Ashwater needed any more drama," Daisy added.

"I'm not sure. But from the looks of it, Sheriff Grayson arrested Mr. Garcia," Derrick said.

"Why am I not surprised?" Evie crossed her arms.

Adam started playing "Beverly Hills Cop Theme Song" by Geek Music on his phone and made a few pop-locking moves with his arms to the synth beat.

Jack laughed, but Daisy wasn't amused.

"Adam—" she said, eyeing him.

Adam frowned and stopped the music.

Luke reached them, his eyes wide. "Dude. Sheriff Grayson arrested Mr. Garcia for the illegal drugs." His eyes met Derrick's. "Mom is super pissed."

Derrick watched Garcia being put into the back of a squad car. Something was off about this. "What evidence do they have?"

"I don't know, but Garcia completely denied it. Then Mom smacked him. He looked like he was going to cry."

"Good for your mom," Evie said. "That man deserves everything he gets."

Across the street, Garcia stared up at Derrick's mom, his eyes pleading. She responded by turning around and going back inside the diner. Derrick's dad followed her.

He didn't know what to think. On one hand, Garcia had done plenty of shady shit over the past year and definitely had connections at Bio-Core, which was where the experimental drugs had to be coming from. Also, Sheriff Grayson wasn't one to make an arrest based on hearsay. He had to have concrete evidence.

Still, Derrick's gut told him Garcia was innocent. Garcia would never jeopardize his relationship with his mom. Which also meant he wouldn't hurt her kids.

"Guys, I don't think he did this," Derrick said.

"You can't be serious." Evie glared at him.

Derrick pursed his lips. "Yeah, something doesn't seem right about it. He's been super cool lately."

Luke nodded. "I can't argue with that. He even offered to help me with schoolwork and stuff. But you can't deny he had access to Bio-Core."

"Okay, let's not jump to any conclusions." Jack fluffed his shaggy hair. "Speaking as someone who was accused of the same crime not too long ago, the police don't always have the right person in custody."

"Truth." Daisy sidled up to Jack, hugging his soft middle and making the tie-dye rings on his T-shirt bunch up.

Derrick's phone buzzed.

SLOAN: Hey, sorry. Gotta cancel tonight. I'm helping Iris with something at Arcadia.

Derrick frowned. Now that they were out in the open, it seemed like they never had any time together.

DERRICK: Ok, np. Talk later?

SLOAN: 🌚

Derrick put his phone back in his pocket. "So, I guess we should go see how Mom is?"

"Yep." Luke glanced at the others. "See you guys later."

On their way across the street, Derrick heard Will's voice in his head, *Meet me at the diner.*

He paused mid-stride and looked around. Was Will watching him? He closed his eyes and sensed where Will was. He was still learning all the nuances of how to communicate with other hosts, but he'd grasped the basics.

Will was close, a few miles away.

Um, yeah, I'm actually on my way there now.

"What are you doing?" Luke asked.

"What? Oh, nothing." Derrick did his best to smile, but something in his stomach twisted. He wasn't going to be able to keep pretending like this for long with Luke. They were twins, and Luke already sensed something was up.

"You've been acting so weird ever since the incident. I think you should get checked out again. There's something off." Luke eyed him closely, shaking his head.

"I'm fine. Better than fine actually. Let's just worry about Mom, okay?"

"Whatever. It's your body." Luke shrugged and ran the rest of the way over to the diner.

Inside, their mom was pacing, her eyes ablaze, arms folded across her waist. The customers, those who stayed for the arrest, looked terrified. Their dad, who was balancing his diner duties with calming his wife seemed confused.

"Athena, what is going on?" Derrick's dad set

down a large tray of empty plates. "This feels like an overreaction, even for you."

"Overreaction?" Her eyes flashed. "That man has been working for us for months, and now we find out he's been drugging kids—including our son? Do you have any idea how deceived I feel? I can't believe this. I…"

She spotted Derrick and Luke before she could continue her tirade. In general, their mom was an unstoppable force when she was riled up about something. Derrick had been on the receiving end of her rants many times. It was no fun. She strode over and hugged him so tightly he thought she might actually break a rib.

"Mom—" he squeaked.

"I'm so sorry. I was the one who let him work here. It's my fault he did this to you."

Derrick struggled under her embrace. "It's okay."

She released him and touched his cheek, her brow furrowed. "What's wrong? Something's wrong. Do you not feel well?"

"I'm fine. You were just squeezing too tight."

"Oh." She brushed back his hair from his forehead like she'd done thousands of times before. "I worry."

"Mom, I don't think Garcia did this," Derrick said.

"What are you talking about? Mac arrested him."

He frowned. Whoever was responsible was connected at Bio-Core. Which also meant they could have planted evidence just as easily as they got the drugs. No, this was all wrong. What he wouldn't do to find out what Sheriff Grayson had on Garcia.

"I don't know why, but I don't think he'd do that to...us." Derrick didn't want to say what he was really thinking—Garcia wouldn't do anything to jeopardize his relationship with *you*. Something else in his uber-sharp mind bothered him. Something about how he was drugged that night at Purgatory.

Before he could attend the thought further, Will walked inside, shivering.

"Hey, guys. The wind is really picking up out there." Will looked around at all the shocked faces. "Did I miss something?"

"Well, Mr. Garcia was arrested and charged with distributing the experimental drug that's been causing all the overdoses," Luke said.

"Oh. Damn," Will said.

"Grab a table," Derrick said. He turned back to his mom. "I think you should go home. Dad, Luke, and I can handle things here. Don't jump to any conclusions. Jack just reminded us Garcia isn't the first person arrested for this crime."

A glimmer of hope or something else flickered in his mom's eyes. She patted his arm. "You're right. I'm a hot mess. I'll head home." She glanced up at his dad. "I'm taking the truck. You can ride home with the boys."

After she left, Luke got back to waiting on tables. Today was Celia's day off, which meant their mom usually helped out with the counter. Derrick grabbed an apron from the back and told Luke and his dad he'd get started in a couple minutes.

Derrick grabbed a seat across from Will in the

dining room, out of earshot of anyone. "Make it fast. I've got to work."

"I just wanted to check in on you. Sorry it took me so long. There's a lot of paperwork and stuff when we get someone new. How are you doing?"

"Okay, I guess. I had a major breakthrough at work."

"And how's Sloan?"

Derrick frowned. What was up with this guy? Sloan had mentioned that he was super nosy about them, but this was weird. "Not that it's any of your business, but I'm not too happy about the fact that I can't be with her because I'm a host. Thanks for omitting that, by the way."

"Excuse me?" Will's eyebrows knitted together.

"Payton explained it to me, and it blows."

Will leaned back and closed his eyes. Under his breath, he murmured, "Can nothing go right in this freaking town?"

A regular seated at the other side of the dining room cleared his throat.

"Are you working?" he asked Derrick.

Derrick wasn't sure what was going on in Will's head, but he had a job to get to. "I have to go."

"Wait—"

"I don't have time." Derrick got up and headed across the dining room.

Sloan

Sloan rubbed her arms as the wind whipped her

long, dark hair across her face. She looked up at the dark sky. It was going to pour any minute. She hurried inside the front entrance of Arcadia Mental Facility. The lobby was empty except for a man at the front desk, busy on the phone.

She glanced around. The lobby looked eerily like a scene out of one of those murder mystery films. The walls were covered in floral wallpaper, and those candle chandeliers hung from the tall ceiling. Most of the furniture looked old and had clawed, wooden feet. Loot grandma's house much?

Where was Iris? She pulled out her phone to check the time. It was five after seven.

Sloan was just about to text Iris when the man behind the counter hung up his phone and stood. "Can I help you?"

"Hi, I'm supposed to be meeting my friend here to hand out donated clothes to patients. Her name is Iris."

The man looked down at a clipboard. "I don't see anything about that on my list." He glanced back up, smirking. "But that's nothing new. We sent all non-essential personnel home because of the storm. Why don't you have a seat and I'll go find out what you're supposed to do."

"Thanks."

She went over to an oversized plush chair and sat down, wriggling around to find a comfortable position. It was one of those looks-comfy-but-it's-really-like-sitting-on-a-rock chairs. Loud thunder cracked outside. She jumped, a yelp escaping her lips. The lights in the lobby flickered. She eyed them up like they were sentient.

"Stay freaking on." She didn't want to actually *be* in a murder mystery.

Sloan texted Iris: Where are you?

The bar at the top of her chat screen was at a crawl, the text not going through. She had terrible service here. Sloan put the phone up to ear, but her call wouldn't go through. She'd never been here before so she didn't know if her service was just bad here or if it was the storm. She hoped Iris was okay and not caught in the storm. Something crashing to the floor caused her to stand, her hands trembling.

"Hello?" she asked to no one in particular.

Where was everyone? She put her phone in her back pocket, went up to the counter, and peered over it. Perfect. Landline. Another loud crack sounded outside, much closer, and the lights flickered again.

This time, they went out. Sloan's breath caught in her throat.

Auxiliary lights turned on at the baseboards. She exhaled. *Thank you, thank you, thank you.*

"Excuse me, sir?" she called toward the door where the man left earlier.

No answer.

She turned around and picked at one of her nails. Maybe she should just go. She headed toward the door when the rain started. Sheets of water pelted the windows with such velocity she thought the rain might break the panes and wash away the vintage lobby. She didn't mind getting soaked, but there was no way she could drive in this. Before she turned back around to face her shitty predicament, the silhouette of a man behind her reflected in the window.

Sloan gasped and whirled around. The lobby was empty.

"Hello?" she said.

No answer.

She ground her teeth. *Damn you, Edgewood. Why did you have to waitlist me?* She was in this creepy mental hospital with no lights in the middle of a storm because of them.

Her gran's words resounded in her head, *No pain, no gain.*

Sloan huffed. There had to be people around here somewhere. She headed to the stairs and opened the door. As she traversed the steps, a familiar scent wafted in the air, enveloping her in its sweetness.

Iris?

Derrick

Dixon's closed early due to the storm. The last two customers made a dash for their cars right before the rain really started coming down. A few minutes later, tiny drops of hail pelted the windows of the diner. Derrick pulled his apron over his head and rolled it up. He shivered. Storms never bothered him, but something about being surrounded by all this glass made him feel vulnerable. He headed to the back to help his dad finish cleaning up and wait out the worst part of the storm. He hoped Sloan got to Arcadia before it started.

While Luke loaded the dishwasher, their dad cleaned the grill and nodded at some condiments. "Hey, put those back in the fridge."

"Sure." Derrick got to work.

The backdoor was ajar, the outer half-screen door holding the weather at bay while allowing fresh air in at the top. A gust swirled through the kitchen, cooling Derrick's skin and dampening the heat from the grill. His dad never left for the night unless the grill was completely cooled.

The front door opened and closed, causing all three of them to jump.

His dad asked, "Did you lock the front door?"

"Sorry." Derrick headed back out to the front.

Gage and Iris were there, soaked through. Iris's eye makeup ran down her cheeks, making her look ghoulish. Gage had transformed from Ashwater High's best dressed to drowned rat.

Derrick grabbed some towels from behind the counter and locked the door behind them. "What are you guys doing out in this?"

"The road to my house is flooded so we had to turn around. It was here or Jack's. Iris was hungry for real food, so you won."

Derrick frowned. "Uh, we're closed."

"What about french fries?" Iris asked, her eyebrows raised.

He tried not to laugh. She was a sorry sight. His dad was going to be annoyed with him, but he couldn't kick them out in this weather either. "Hang on."

Derrick went back to the kitchen and asked him to turn the fryers back on. He'd have to stay later and take care of them. When he came back out, Gage and Iris had taken a seat at the counter, Iris's makeup debacle fixed. How did girls do that so fast?

"You're in luck," Derrick said. "Limited menu though. No grill."

They ordered some chicken tenders and fries to split. Easy enough. As Derrick dropped the food in the fryers and set the timer, something niggled at the back of his mind. Wasn't Sloan supposed to be meeting Iris at Arcadia? Was Arcadia an excuse for her? Maybe knowing he was a host was too much for her. His mind raced, creating all kinds of elaborate and terrible reasons why she didn't want to see him. He shook a basket with fries. *Hurry up.*

Once the food was cooked, he raced back out front and set their food down. "Why isn't Sloan with you guys?"

Iris and Gage glanced at each other.

"What do you mean?" Gage asked.

"Sloan said she was helping you deliver a clothing donation from Dalia's at Arcadia," Derrick said to Iris.

"I'm not aware of any clothing donation." Iris shrugged and popped a few fries in her mouth.

"But—" Derrick's mind whirred, as his chondria assisted him in his analysis of the situation. Why would Sloan lie? They were all close friends, and he would find out from Iris that they never met up.

"What's going on?" Gage asked.

"Sloan texted me and said she couldn't hang out because she was helping Iris." He reached into his pocket and retrieved his phone. He pulled up his text conversation with Sloan and showed it to them.

Iris shook her head. "I didn't ask Sloan to do that."

Derrick studied Iris. She had been acting strange

lately. What if she was having a glitch again? "Are you sure?"

Iris glanced between Derrick and Gage. "I swear. I can't find a shred of truth to this in my memory files."

"You have been acting strangely lately," Derrick said. "Could it be another glitch or something?"

Iris's mouth formed an O and "A Little Respect" by Erasure played on the jukebox next to her. "I don't know what you're talking about. I have not been strange, and I'm not glitching." She grasped Gage's arm. "You believe me, right?"

Gage put his arm around her and kissed her damp hair. "Of course I do." He looked back at Derrick. "Do you think Sloan was lying?"

"No. I mean, I guess she could have. But why? We're good."

Derrick glanced back at Iris, whose eyes darted back and forth, either from nerves or searching her files. Something was going on with her. He was sure of it. "Iris, do you remember the night I offered you a ride home a while ago?"

"No." She shifted on her stool.

"You were sitting on a bench in front of Dalia's."

Iris looked from Derrick to Gage, fear creeping up on her face. "I, uh, don't. I swear." She looked down at her hands. When she looked back, she said, "My memory files are not damaged, and I have no memory of that event."

"Enough." Gage reached for Iris's hand. "You're upsetting her."

Derrick opened his mouth to protest but closed it.

Gage was right. Iris was looking rather disturbed. "I'm sorry," Derrick said. "I'm just trying to get to the bottom of what happened."

"I'm sorry I don't remember you offering me a ride," she said, her eyes glassy.

Gage put his arm around her. "It's fine. As a precaution, we'll get you checked out to make sure everything is okay."

"Okay." Iris looked down at her lap and swallowed hard.

The door to the kitchen swung open, and Luke burst through, his eyes wide. "Guys, there's a tornado warning."

Then Derrick heard Will's voice inside his head. *Sloan's in trouble. Meet me outside now.*

He cringed as the voice echoed in his head like a howl in a cave.

"What's wrong?" Luke asked him.

Before he could respond, sirens wailed in the distance.

Sloan

The hair on Sloan's scalp prickled. The hallway was deserted except for a few people in scrubs rushing in and out of rooms with clipboards. The auxiliary lights were still on, providing light at her feet and dimmer lights above her head. She didn't know what part of the hospital this was, but it was calm compared to the storm outside. She crept down the hall, hoping to catch one of the fast-moving scrubs.

As she passed an open door, a hand grasped her forearm, causing her to jump. It was an elderly woman with tufted white hair and hazy blue eyes. The woman moaned and pointed to her mouth. Sloan tried to wriggle free from her grasp, but she wasn't letting go. The woman moaned louder and pointed to her mouth again, her grip pleading her urgency.

"I don't know what you want," Sloan said. She glanced down the hallway, hoping to catch a scrub's eyes.

More moaning and mouth pointing.

"Are you hungry?" Sloan asked. Not that she had any food on her.

The woman shook her head vehemently.

Finally, a scrub came to Sloan's rescue. She had a badge that read Anita. "What's going on here?"

"This woman is very agitated," Sloan said.

"Mrs. Jeffreys, I was going to get to you in just a minute." Anita released the old woman's grip on Sloan's arm which has left quite a mark from her death grip.

The woman pointed to her mouth again and moaned.

Anita glanced at Sloan, her eyes narrowed. "You are on the wrong floor, miss. You better get going."

On the wrong floor? She didn't even know why Sloan was there. "But—"

Anita led the woman back into her room and shut the door in Sloan's face.

Sloan stood there for a minute, slack-jawed. *Note to self—never come here again.*

She turned around and slammed into another scrub coming from the other direction almost knocking her to the ground. "Hey—"

"Watch where you're going," he growled and continued on his way without a second glance.

"Seriously? I'm fine," she said to his back. "Don't worry about me."

He extended his middle finger without turning around.

You're joking, right? Were there hospital wards for the rude and unpleasant? She headed back to the stairs.

ON THE THIRD FLOOR, Sloan found some doors labeled with doctors' names and not numbers. Good. Hopefully that meant no more grabby patients. She came to a door with Payton Glass's name and sighed in relief. She knocked a few times, but no one answered. Duh. Payton had probably left before the storm. Sloan tried the door handle, and the door swung inward. The office was decorated with photographed landscapes from around the world. There were twin refrigerators on one side and a desk in front of a window. The room was empty, but there was a pungent scent that told her otherwise—Chinese food.

"Hello? Payton?" Sloan said.

A sound coming from the floor on the other side of the desk made her skin itch. She peered over and stifled a scream.

Payton was laying on the floor.

Her neck was positioned weird, and it was…glowing. It reminded her of Derrick's eyes.

"Oh my God." Sloan knelt down and put her ear to Payton's mouth.

Payton exhaled a labored breath, but her neck was clearly broken.

Sloan couldn't move her. She took her hand instead. "Payton, it's Sloan Simms. I'm Derrick's, uh, friend. Can you hear me?"

A gurgle came from Payton's mouth as she focused her eyes on Sloan's. "Not safe."

"I gathered. Your neck…" Before she could finish, there were footsteps outside Payton's office.

Payton squeezed Sloan's hand. Her eyes told Sloan to be quiet.

Sloan held her breath, willing whoever it was to go away. A moment passed, and the footfalls moved on. She exhaled and looked back at Payton, who now had tears streaming down her cheeks.

"It's okay. They left. Who did this to you?" Sloan asked.

"I was wrong about you. He wants you. You have to get…" Payton squeezed her eyes shut, pain etched on her face. A distinct crack set her neck back in place. She gasped, and her head lolled to the side as the glow receded.

"Wants me?" Sloan whispered, squeezing Payton's limp hand. "Who?"

Payton didn't respond. What was she talking about, and who did this to her?

Sloan reached for the phone on the desk and put it

to her ear. No dial tone. She tapped the hook switch a few times. Nothing.

Okay, okay. Don't panic. She pulled out her phone again. She didn't have any bars.

Sloan... An eerie voice in her head made her jolt upright, looking around. *Come out. Come out...*

Sloan covered the sob threatening to give her away. She couldn't place the voice, but she'd heard it before. This was serious scary pants stuff, and she cursed Iris a few times—and Edgewood for good measure.

Don't lose it. Think.

She looked around the office for something she could use as a weapon. A stapler? No. She crouched over to the fridges and opened one. It was filled with test tubes of clear liquid labeled with water locations around Ashwater. Useless. Unless her stalker was thirsty. She turned around and searched the office again. Her heart pounded.

Finally, she found something. Propped up in the corner of the office was a tennis racket. She crept over and picked it up, swinging it a few times. She gripped it firmly. Sloan didn't know what she was facing, but Luke always said she had a killer swing. She hoped he was right.

27

RUN

Derrick

Derrick bolted out of the diner as fast as his legs could carry him. Faint words of concern from his brother and Gage wafted behind him. The rain pelted his body, soaking him through instantly. He didn't care.

Sloan was in trouble.

Will was waiting for him in the parking lot, his eyes glowing and serious. Derrick's stomach was rock hard. This was bad. He got in the car, and they sped off down Main. Adam was in the back seat.

"What are you doing here?" Derrick asked.

"I'm backup," Adam replied, making Will laugh.

Derrick glanced at Will. "Do you know…"

"Yes, I know how Adam is different, and he knows what we are for now. He's agreed to erase the memory files about us afterward. Trust me, we're going to need him."

"What's going on with Sloan?" Derrick's heart racing.

Will pressed on the gas and blew through a red light as rain bombarded the window so hard it seemed like it would break the windshield.

"Slow down." Derrick grabbed the handle on the door. "I'd like to get to wherever we're going in one piece."

Will swerved around some downed tree branches. "Right. Time to fill you in. I wasn't in Ashwater for you. Well, at least not at first."

"What does that mean?" Derrick replied.

"I'm only allowed to track and recruit one host at a time. Ashwater has always been a hotbed for potential hosts. Until we understand why, we limit our visits here. There would be too much suspicion otherwise. Originally, I had my sights set on someone else, but after I was here for a while, I realized I could potentially get a twofer. No tracker has ever done that before."

"A twofer?" Adam asked from the backseat, leaning forward.

"It means two for the price of one," Derrick said to Adam. To Will, he asked, "I assume one was me?"

"Yes, and I marked the other one that same night at Purgatory."

"What do you mean by marked?" Derrick asked.

"It's how I let other trackers know I've initiated contact with a potential host." Will held up a small, dark stone. "I'm supposed to give the potential host this too, but she didn't have any pockets in that dress."

"She?" Derrick asked.

Will arched a brow. "Red dress?"

"Are you talking about Sloan?" Derrick's chondria gravitated to his irises as excitement rose in his chest.

"Bingo." Will swerved around a slow car.

Derrick nodded slowly, contrasting his body jerking with the movement of the car. "That's why you were obsessed with us."

"Um, is obsessed the right word?" Will frowned.

"What would you call it?"

Will shook his head. "Whatever."

Derrick thought about his last conversation with Sloan at Jack's. "She wants to be a host."

"That's good to hear. Her life might depend on it."

"What does that mean?" Derrick asked.

"Only hosts can see a tracker's mark and only if they're looking for it. Somehow, she crossed paths with a host who wants to disrupt what I initiated."

"Who are you talking about?" Derrick shifted nervously in his seat.

Will took a turn at breakneck speed, causing everyone to slide to the side as the tires squealed.

"For now, all you need to know is he's dangerous and his ideas for our future are very different from most hosts. He's done terrible, cruel things. If we don't get to Sloan before he does…" He glanced at Derrick, his eyes serious.

Derrick's chest tightened, and his heart rate quickened. He couldn't bear the thought of anything happening to her. *Hang on, Sloan, I'm coming.* He gripped the door handle. "Can't you go any faster?"

Will pressed on the gas. "I can."

Sloan

Sloan wasn't keen on waiting this out. There was another door in Payton's office. Maybe it led to another area where she could find some stairs and get out of here. She tiptoed over to the door and tried the handle. Locked. She sighed and went back to Payton's still body. She reached into her lab coat pockets and fished out a set of keys.

One by one, she tried them in the door until she found the right one. On the other side of the door was a lab with more refrigerators and another door that led back to the hallway. With her tennis racket in one hand, she put the keys in her pocket and searched the room. Inside one of the fridges were more test tubes. But these had a dark liquid with what looked like glowing embers of green, blue, and purple.

She inhaled sharply as her memory of the night she saved Derrick came flooding back. It was the same as what was in the EpiPen she used to save him.

Sloan reached for one of the vials, mesmerized. The sound of someone trying the door in Payton's office startled her, and she dropped the test tube. It shattered on the floor. *Shit.*

She closed the fridge and backed up.

There you are, the voice said in her head. It sent chills down her spine.

Every pore on her face tingled as adrenaline rushed through her body. The door to Payton's office opened, and she headed for the opposite door that led back into the hallway, racket at the ready. She glanced up and down the hallway and took off running back toward the stairs.

It didn't take long for her to sense him chasing her. Her heart pounded in her ears as she slammed the door to the stairs shut and sprinted down the steps.

Above her, the door opened, and a second set of footfalls landed on the stairs behind her.

She couldn't look back. She took two steps at a time and burst back onto the second floor, hoping to run back into the scrub who'd given her the middle finger. She'd take rude over dead any day.

The hallway was empty. She ran as fast as she could, willing herself to bump into someone. Finally, she saw Anita coming out of a room.

"Help!" Sloan rushed to her, breathless.

Anita turned toward her. She crossed her arms and narrowed her eyes. "What are you still doing here?"

"There's someone chasing me." Sloan finally had the courage to look behind her, certain whoever it was would be there. But the hallway was empty.

"Look, I don't have time for this crap. I have a real job to do. If you aren't gone in the next ten seconds, I'm calling security."

Sloan grabbed Anita's arm. "Yes, that's a great idea. Call them." She looked back down the hallway, tightening her grip on the tennis racket. "Hurry, please."

Anita pulled her arm away and looked down at the racket.

"Maybe you do belong on this floor. Come on." She led Sloan to an empty nurse's station and picked up a phone. She pursed her lips as she waited for someone to answer.

Sloan held her breath and kept glancing back down the hallway. "Come on, come on."

"Huh. That's weird." Anita hung up the phone. "No one's answering."

"I told you, something is wrong."

"I think you're being dramatic." Before Anita could add anything else, the scrub that gave her the middle finger grabbed her from behind, covering her mouth. With his other hand, he injected her with a syringe.

His eyes glowed a vibrant purple.

Sloan screamed and backed away as he lowered Anita to the floor. Her heart pounded so hard she thought it might burst from her chest.

She headed back down the hall and stopped. Her pursuer from earlier had reappeared.

The lights were dim, so she couldn't make out his face, but he was tall and muscular. His eyes had the same violet glow as Anita's attacker. He and Middle Finger were hosts like Derrick and Will. But a lot scarier.

"Don't come any closer." She held up the racket, ready to strike.

The man took a few steps toward her and smiled as his face came into the light. "You've got some tenacity. I'll give you that."

Sloan recognized him as the man outside the elevator at Bio-Core. She didn't have a clue what he was planning, but she didn't want any part of it. She turned to make sure Middle Finger was staying put as she was basically sandwiched between the two of them. He was a good distance away so she focused back on her main threat.

"What do you want?" she asked.

"What do I want?" The man rubbed his chin, grinning. "I want lots of things. But to start with, I'd like you."

She pointed her racket at him. "Well you're ancient, and I'm taken, so if you come near me, I'll knock you on your ponytail-wearing ass."

He laughed. "I like you. You are going to fit right in." He looked over at the nurse's station. "It's okay. I can take care of her myself. You go make sure we aren't interrupted."

Middle Finger nodded and left through a door behind them.

"Stay away from me." She backed up, gripping the racket with both hands, as the man in the hall advanced.

The man sighed. "You should be thanking me. I'm saving you from the boring life Will Reed would have given you."

Sloan paused. "What are you talking about?"

The man stopped advancing and crossed his arms across his chest. "Check your right shoulder."

"Nice try." She narrowed her eyes and raised the racket again.

"My kind calls it a tracker's mark. You have one on your right shoulder. If you'd look, you'd see I'm correct. It's how I knew you were a potential host that day I saw you outside the elevators at Bio-Core. Only other hosts and the person marked can see it."

She pointed the racket at him. "I think I'd know if I had some mark on my shoulder."

"One would think." The man rolled his eyes and took a step forward.

"You stay where you are. I'm warning you. I've got a killer swing."

"Oh, for God's sake." He strode over to her.

Sloan raised the racket and swung as hard as she could at his outstretched arms. He yelped and swore under his breath. She pulled back and swung again, this time connecting with his shoulder. He groaned from the impact but still managed to knock the racket from her hands.

He had his arms around her so fast, she'd barely taken a breath. She struggled against him, but he held her still. His cologne was so overpowering she wanted to gag.

"Look." He pulled her shirt off her shoulder and motioned her to look at her reflection in a window in the hall.

"Don't you touch me, you pig," she yelled in his face.

He sighed, his grip keeping her still. "Look."

She looked at her reflection and stopped struggling. Sure enough, there was a glowing handprint, the fingertips grazing the apex of her shoulder. "What the hell is that?"

"I just told you." The man released her but stayed close. "Has anyone ever told you how annoying you are?"

Sloan ignored him and touched her shoulder where the mark was. "I can't believe this."

"Me either." He reached into his blazer and pulled out a syringe with a dark fluid and bright purple sparkles.

"What are you doing?" She backed up against the glass, her hands trembling.

"It won't hurt...much." He grabbed her arm. Before he could make contact, a flash of red light hit the syringe, and it exploded into a million pieces. At the same time, "Somebody Save Me" by Cinderella started playing at the nurse's station.

Adam, Derrick, and Will had emerged from the door where Middle Finger left.

"You disrespectful fool," the man growled. He grabbed Sloan's wrist and put her in front of him as a shield.

When Sloan met Derrick's eyes, he thought to her, *Don't worry. It's going to be okay.*

With Adam by their side, she had no doubt. Obviously, this asshole knew it too.

Will's eyes were ablaze with bright green lights. "Let her go, Malcolm."

Ah, so Will knew who he was. Malcolm's hands tightened on her arms as he backed down the hall, keeping her between himself and Adam's precise, deadly gaze.

"Time for me to go." He shoved her at Adam with so much force she lost her breath.

Sloan slammed into Adam's chest, and he caught her, slowing her momentum with the finesse of a professional dancer.

"Are you okay?" Adam asked.

She drew in a ragged breath, gasping for air. She righted herself and nodded. "Thanks."

"Come on," Will said to Adam.

The two headed down the hall after Malcolm, while Derrick stayed behind with Sloan. He pulled her into his arms, his hand on her cheek, turning her face from side to side. "What did he do to you? Are you hurt?"

"No, I'm okay." She grazed his hand with her own. "I guess it was your turn to save me, huh?"

"I was so worried." Chondria were in his eyes, and it made her heart swell.

"I'm fine. Actually, I'm better than fine now that you're here." She put her arms around his neck and kissed the worry from his parted lips.

He whispered against her mouth, "I'm glad."

"Oh!" She pulled down her shirt, exposing the glowing mark on her shoulder. "You'll never guess what this means."

"You're a potential host?" Derrick asked, smiling.

She swatted at his chest. "How did you know?"

"Will told me. He was in Ashwater for you, not

me." He drew her back into his arms. "But thanks to your impulsive brain, we can both be hosts."

Sloan wasn't sure if it was adrenaline from earlier or the anticipation at becoming a host, but she giggled. "I can't wait."

Payton joined them, rubbing her neck. "Good. You're safe, then?"

The couple separated. Sloan had forgotten about Payton in all the chaos.

"Oh my God, you're up? How?" Sloan asked.

"Yep, all good. I'll tell you what, that Malcolm can be a pain in the neck." She laughed silently and covered her mouth. Tears came to her eyes. She motioned for them to give her a minute to collect herself, but the giggles kept coming.

It wasn't that funny. Had Payton hit her head too?

Derrick glanced at Sloan, confused.

"Malcolm attacked her. I think he broke her neck. I guess her chondria healed it," Sloan explained. She turned to Payton. "Are you sure you're okay?"

"Yes, I think so." She righted herself and turned her head from side to side, testing. "Look, I owe both of you an apology. If I hadn't told Derrick you weren't a potential host, this might not have happened. To be fair, it's really rare, even here in Ashwater."

"It's okay. You didn't know," Derrick said. "Will was originally here for Sloan. But after she injected me, he thought he might get both of us."

"That's why he didn't tell me or you about Sloan." Payton nodded slowly. "He's only allowed to register one new host at a time. He figured nature would take its course and…" Payton raised her eyebrows at Derrick. "Have you told her about the two ways to bond?"

"Uh." Derrick blushed. It was the most adorable thing Sloan had ever seen. Rare too.

Sloan grabbed at the front of his shirt playfully. "Yeah, Derrick. Tell me all about how you're going to bond me."

He grabbed her hand. "Stop."

Sloan made a tsk sound. "Later."

"Look, I should still have my neck checked out, but there's one more thing you should know. Malcolm did impart something else before he decided I was a flight risk. Of course I was a flight risk. I would rat him out a million times over. Like I'm so not that person he could trust to keep his evil secrets. I don't come off that way, do I? There isn't something about me that reads—hey, I like bad guys, is there?" Payton glanced up.

Sloan and Derrick stared at her.

"The night you were drugged," Payton said to Derrick, "you weren't the target."

Derrick stilled. Sloan looked up at him as his eyes darted back and forth, obviously working something out in his super smart brain. He put his arms around Sloan and drew her to him in a tight embrace. "Oh my God."

"What? What is it?" Sloan asked.

"Your drink at Purgatory. I took it before you could take a sip."

Her heart pounded as she also put together that

she was the target of the drugs. "Why? Who would do that?"

"It had to be Steel," Derrick said through his teeth. "He was there that night, and he's connected to Bio-Core." Anger rolled off him in waves, his arms tense.

"Hang on. You're saying he drugged me because I kneed him in the balls?" Sloan pursed her lips. Steel had sworn they were even at the cabin. Oddly, she believed him. Although, he did mention she'd dodged a bullet.

"Hang on. Steel is a minion. He does what he's told," Payton said.

Derrick nodded. "Okay, so if that's the case, who's doing the telling?"

Payton gasped and made eye contact with Derrick. They stood in silence for a moment, some telepathic obvious communication between them.

It was getting awkward, and Sloan didn't like being kept in the dark. "What? What have you two figured out?"

Derrick released Sloan and looked toward the hallway where Will and Adam took off, concentration etched on his face. He grasped her hand and squeezed. "Let's go talk to someone who will know why you were targeted."

"What about Malcolm?" Sloan's skin still crawled from where he'd touched her. There was no way she was going to run around town in the middle of a storm with that lunatic on the loose.

"Don't worry. Will and Adam will make sure he doesn't follow us."

"And you know all this how?"

Derrick tapped two fingers to his temple and smiled. "Come on. I'll fill you in on the way."

"Where are we going?" she asked.

"Bio-Core."

28

A MAN OF MEANS

Derrick

The rain had stopped, but the air was still dank and heavy. Derrick stared up at the intimidating building, the knot in his stomach tightening. Set at the base of the large mountain, the building itself still towered over them in the darkness like a metal fortress. On one hand, he loved the place. The technology and resources available made anything possible. But ambition was a double-edged sword, and tonight, it was after his girlfriend.

He squeezed Sloan's hand. "You ready?"

She cleared her throat, gazing up at the building. "Every time I go in this place, something crazy happens."

Fair point. "I can go by myself. But we'll need to wait for Adam and Will. I don't want you to be alone."

"No." She shook her head, tugging on his hand. "This is about me. I'm coming with you."

"Okay, beautiful." He kissed her forehead. "Let's go."

The lobby was deserted except for a security guard. Derrick nodded at him and held up his Bio-Core ID attached to a lanyard. The security guard waved, and Derrick and Sloan headed to the elevator.

"This is where Malcolm saw the mark." Sloan touched her shoulder and shivered.

Derrick nuzzled her hair and rubbed her shoulder. "Don't worry. It will fade."

They headed up to the top floor. Max was a self-proclaimed night owl who always worked late. Payton had told him as much. Derrick hoped tonight would be no exception. When they exited the elevator, he half expected to see Dana, but of course, she'd gone home. With Sloan's hand in his, he strode over to Max's office door.

"Let me do the talking," he said.

"But—"

Derrick put a finger to her lips. "Please?"

Sloan crossed her arms across her chest. "Knock."

He did as she asked. At first there was no answer or sound from within. Maybe he'd left. Derrick pulled out his phone and checked the time. It was nine o'clock. Payton said he usually stayed until eleven. He knocked again.

This time, someone stirred within. Footfalls toward the door made his heart beat a notch faster. The door opened.

Max had loosened his tie, his hair was disheveled, and was there such a thing as a nine o'clock shadow?

He glanced between him and Sloan. "Derrick. What are doing here?"

"Hi, Max. Can we come in?" Derrick asked.

"Uh, sure." Max turned around, inspecting his office like Derrick did when his mom wanted to come into his bedroom. He stepped aside and motioned them in then shut the door and indicated for them to take a seat. "What is it you want?"

"This is my girlfriend, Sloan Simms." Derrick watched Max's reaction carefully. If what he and Payton had worked out was true, Max already knew who she was.

"Pleased to meet you," Max said.

Sloan leaned forward in her seat. "Drugging people without their permission is a felony."

Derrick glared at Sloan. *What part about let me do the talking didn't you understand?*

"I would agree," Max replied, curtly. "Is there something you need, Derrick?" He crossed his arms and stared at him. His eyes were like daggers.

They were on thin ice, and if Derrick was wrong about this, he would likely be fired. But his gut and Payton's gut told him he was right. "I think what Sloan means is that they caught the person behind the drugs that have been causing the overdoses."

Max's shoulders relaxed slightly. "Ah, right. Garcia. You never can tell about a person. Well, except with him. He was a bad apple right from the start."

"Was he though?" Sloan asked. "Because I think it was this place that made him such a colossal douche."

Derrick closed his eyes. So much for subtlety.

"Miss Simms, I assure you Bio-Core is a top-notch facility that fosters success among its employees," Max said.

Derrick grabbed Sloan's hand. "I'm sorry, Max. Sloan is upset because we just learned she was the target when I was drugged. I drank the laced drink that was meant for her."

"Oh." Max looked down. "I see."

"Now, we're trying to figure out why she was targeted. As you said, Garcia was arrested for the crime. But the drug clearly came from Bio-Core's pharmaceutical division, and Garcia no longer works here."

"I'm not sure what you're getting at." Max stood. "Now, if you don't mind, I have work to do."

"We're just trying to figure out who would want to drug her." Derrick's chondria swarmed around his heart, calming its rapid beat. He stood too.

"Perhaps you should speak to Sheriff Grayson. I'm sure he can tell you more."

Derrick sighed. Max wasn't going to offer information, but he definitely knew more than he was letting on.

"Oh my God," Sloan said. "That's why you look familiar. You were with Malcolm downstairs the other day. You know, he attacked me tonight."

Max's eye twitched, and his hands balled into fists. "He did what?"

"At Arcadia tonight. He attacked her with a syringe." Derrick frowned. He thought Max and Malcolm were working together. Clearly, they weren't.

Although, Max seemed to be very aware of what Malcolm was capable of.

"Did he inject you?" Max leaned forward, his expression grave.

"No," Sloan said.

"That's good news." Max exhaled loudly, his normal cool demeanor returning.

A new theory formed in Derrick's chondria-laden mind, sending a chill down his spine. They needed to get out of there and now.

"I think we should get going." Derrick stood, pulling Sloan by his side.

Sloan resisted. Her eyes set with determination. "I'm not going anywhere until I get some answers."

A smile creeped up on Max's face. "I see why you like her."

We need to get out of here. He's dangerous, Derrick thought to her.

Sloan looked up at Derrick, eyes wide. "Um, you're right, let's get going."

"Just a moment." Max rounded the corner of his desk on her side. "Miss Simms, what do you know about vaccines?"

Sloan looked between Derrick and Max, unsure what to do. "Um, they protect people from diseases?"

Derrick pulled her closer.

"Yes, they are a necessity for a healthy population. Do you also have an understanding about clinical trials?"

"Yeah, I guess." Sloan pressed her back against Derrick.

"That's some of what we do here at Bio-Core. We test out cutting-edge vaccines and experimental compounds. In most cases, the side effects are minimal." He stopped in front of her. "But we've only ever had to deal with human diseases. Now, I'm afraid, we're in the midst of a natural selection process that is of a galactic nature. An evolutionary war is coming, and I'd like to be on the winning side of it. That is where you, or rather, someone like you, comes into the picture. Your DNA could be the thing that changes everything."

Derrick's theory was correct. Max was talking about hosts—the introduction of chondria to the human species. Sloan was targeted because she was a potential host. Some of the other victims likely were too. That was why Max was against Malcolm bonding Sloan. As a human, she was still viable for his study.

Regardless, Derrick wasn't going to let this mad scientist anywhere near Sloan. He placed his arms around her protectively. "She's not a willing test subject."

Before Max could reply, the door to the office opened. Derrick couldn't believe his eyes.

Dr. Rice stood in the doorway, her eyes ablaze with green chondria. Eyes narrowed, she said, "No, she's not, and neither was I."

Max's discomfiture told Derrick everything he needed to know. He'd been the one who'd attacked Dr. Rice. Derrick backed himself and Sloan out of his reach.

"Naomi, it's good to see you," Max said, the lie not even close to landing its mark.

"Yeah right," she replied. "Leave me for dead, much?"

Max shrugged. "You're being dramatic. You survived, didn't you?"

"Only because Will Reed had the decency to bond me after what you did."

"I heard. Too bad Malcolm got there late." Max arched an eyebrow, a menacing smile playing at his lips.

Derrick recalled his visit to Arcadia to see Dr. Rice. He'd run into Will in the parking lot, asking him to keep his visit there a secret. There was also the tall man who'd bumped into him coming out of the elevator. He didn't get a good look at the time, but that had to have been Malcolm.

Dr. Rice glanced at Derrick and as if able to read his mind, she thought, *You two need to get out of here.*

Derrick grabbed Sloan's hand and turned to leave.

But Max grabbed her arm. "Where do you think you're going?"

Sloan shook off his hand and pointed in his face. "If you touch me again, you'll lose a testicle."

"I can't let you leave." Max's eyes grew more serious.

Sloan's grip on Derrick's hand tightened, her eyes flinty. He knew what she could do to male anatomy.

But Max was no Steel. He had a blade he knew how to use five feet from them.

Derrick pulled her behind him. "You'll have to go through me first."

"Okay." Max lunged at Derrick, who parried to the side, pulling Sloan with him. Max groaned as he slammed against the chair Sloan had been sitting in.

Before Max could regain his balance, Derrick and Sloan headed for the door.

"You can run, but you can't hide," Max bellowed.

The two ran past Dr. Rice, and Derrick thought to her, *Be careful.*

Dr. Rice responded by shutting the door behind her.

Derrick and Sloan ran toward the elevator.

"That dude is crazy," Sloan said. "You should quit."

If he wasn't terrified for their safety, he would have responded with, "You think?" Instead, he pounded the down button with his palm. The doors opened. Inside were half a dozen Bio-Core security guards, human ones. Dr. Rice must have called them.

Relief washed over him. "Thank God."

The guards raised their weapons. "Stay where you are."

Derrick and Sloan raised their hands in unison.

"We haven't done anything wrong," Sloan said.

One of the guards got out of the elevator and pulled Derrick's hands behind his back. He cinched his wrists with a zip tie. Before they could get Sloan secured in the same manner, the other elevator opened.

Gage walked out with Iris in tow.

The next thing Derrick knew, the guards lowered their weapons. He'd forgotten how cool Gage's mental command was. Iris cut through the tie at his wrists.

"I am so glad to see you," Derrick said.

"Yeah, Adam sent me a text that you were coming here. Thought you might need our help," Gage said.

"Well, I'm not so happy to see her," Sloan said, stepping up to Iris. "Why the hell did you tell me to meet you at Arcadia? Are you like one of Malcolm's bots?"

Before Iris could reply, Gage stepped in between them. "Back up. She doesn't remember doing that."

"Doesn't remember? She's got a computer for a brain. She's lying," Sloan retorted, narrowing her eyes.

"Back off," Gage said. "She's going to be checked out ASAP."

Derrick reached for Sloan's arm. He didn't want Iris to freak out and hurt her. "It's true. She doesn't remember."

"I'm very sorry, Sloan," Iris said. "I'm afraid there's something wrong with my programming." Tears filled her violet eyes. She was obviously wrecked about it. Derrick hoped Sloan would see she meant no harm.

"Okay. Fine. It doesn't matter right now anyway. Can we please just get out of here?" Sloan asked.

The sound of heavy boots on steps resounded from the stairwells on either side of the floor.

Gage frowned. "Uh, you two better get moving." He pushed them toward the elevator he'd come came out of. He nodded at Iris. "Your turn, babe."

Droid guards. Gage couldn't touch them with his

mind control. Iris could handle them. They weren't nearly as cunning as her or Adam's lines.

"Steer clear of the lobby," Gage said as the doors to the stairwells opened and dozens of droid guards burst through.

"But how will we—" The doors to the elevator closed. "Get out?" Derrick asked.

Sloan wrung her hands and wiped them on her jeans. "My hands are all sweaty. What are we going to do?"

"We'll go to my lab." Derrick ran a hand through his hair. "No, they'll look for us there. We could go down. Underground. There are a ton of places to hide down there." He typed in his code to unlock the lower levels. He pressed one randomly and they headed down.

29

CLOSET SPACE

Sloan

Sloan slumped down on the floor, her head in her hands. She'd had just about enough for one day. Between the scare at Arcadia, the storm, and the lunatic in charge at Bio-Core, she didn't know how much longer she'd stay sane. They'd descended to one of the lower levels of the Bio-Core facility and found a small closet to hide in.

Derrick followed suit opposite her. The space was so small their knees touched.

"He's not going to leave me alone, is he?" Sloan asked, not looking up.

"No."

"I don't understand. Why me?"

"Do you remember when I told you that humans are rarely compatible with chondria?"

She looked up. "Yeah."

"I think Max is testing a drug to remedy the

compatibility issue. That's what he meant by an evolutionary war. Hosts versus non-hosts. I'm hypothesizing here, but it's likely that he's attempting to alter or mutate human genes in a way that could help non-hosts. A cure for non-hosts so that their body won't reject chondria."

"Except it doesn't work. Look what happened to Dr. Rice. You told me yourself that she was basically in a coma. And if I hadn't injected you with chondria, the same thing would have happened to you or worse."

He tilted his head as if deep in thought. "You're right. It's a risky process, and there haven't been any promising results. But that's not going to stop him from trying."

Sloan shivered and hugged her knees to her chest. "This sucks."

"I have an idea." He sat up and grasped her knees. "What if you're not a potential host?"

She frowned. "But I am."

"You're not getting my meaning." Derrick pulled her up from her sitting position so they were both on their knees facing each other. His irises were bright with chondria, like jade stars. Where was Adam when she needed him to play a sappy eighties' love song?

"Oh." She smiled demurely. "You mean if I become a host, he won't want my juju anymore."

He arched an eyebrow, but before he could respond, footsteps rushing in the passageway made her jump. He put a finger to her lips, his bright eyes wide. A few shadows of feet running past their hiding spot reflected on the metallic floor just beyond the door. Sloan held her breath for as long as she could until the sound ceased.

"What are we going to do?" she whispered. "We can't stay in here forever."

"I know. What if I go—"

"No. You can't leave me in here alone." Sloan glanced around, her mind going a mile a minute. If only they had a syringe filled with chondria. She could inject herself, and this nightmare would be over. *Wait a minute.* "Hey, so, we could take care of this problem right now if you're game."

Sloan raised her eyebrows at him.

Derrick looked around at the tiny closet. "You're joking. We can't possibly—"

Sloan rolled her eyes. She knew it was a long shot, but if she didn't care where the hell they were, why should he? She swatted his knee. "Oh, come on. While I appreciate that you want it to be all rose petals and stuff, none of that matters to me."

"Wait, are you being serious?"

"Hell yeah, I'm serious." She leaned toward him.

"I don't want my first time to be in a closet." His cheeks reddened, and he looked away. "I'm sorry."

"Oh," she said. He was a virgin? She'd assumed he wasn't because Luke wasn't and shared way more than she wanted to know. She backed away, unsure of what to do. This was super awkward.

"I'm guessing this is a surprise?"

"Yeah. Luke, um, well…"

"I know. But just because we're twins doesn't mean we do everything the same."

"Right. Of course." What was she thinking? So stupid.

"So, um, I assume that you're not?" he asked.

"Correct." Something in the pit of her stomach twisted. This was getting more uncomfortable by the minute. Could the floor please swallow her up?

He pulled her back over to him. She acquiesced, her legs situated across his lap. He tilted her chin and kissed her gently on the lips.

"I just wanted to be honest. That's important to me." He pushed her hair off her shoulder and smiled. "I think you're the most beautiful girl in the world, and I'd be crazy not to want to be with you."

No one had ever called her beautiful before. Sexy? Sure. Hot? Yep. Beautiful? Never. "You always know just what to say, don't you?"

"I try." He stroked her hair.

"So, then what's your plan?"

Derrick looked like Adam and Iris as his eyes darted back and forth, except Sloan knew he didn't have a CPU for a brain. After what seemed like an eternity, he smiled. "Okay, I know what we have to do. Unbutton your shirt."

Wait, what?

Derrick

Guards had located them, as he'd anticipated, and surrounded the small utility closet. Derrick's plan would work, so long as they didn't separate them. He hoisted Sloan in his arms and opened the door. In the corridor were no less than a dozen guards, a mix of droids and human.

A human guard raised his weapon at him. "Don't move."

Derrick stopped and glanced down at Sloan. Her head was nestled against his chest, eyes closed, cheeks flushed. He smiled inwardly, wondering if he were the reason for her rosiness. He looked back up at the guard, narrowing his eyes. "Tell your boss he's too late."

The guard stood there for a moment, unmoving. "We're to take her to Mr. Roberts."

He gripped her tightly. "She's not leaving my arms."

The guards looked at each other, as if one of them would have an answer to their dilemma. They hadn't expected Sloan to be unconscious.

"Okay." The guard in charge turned away and tapped on his comm device. "Sir, we have them. Yes, but she's—" A long pause. "Okay, right away." The guard turned back around and motioned for Derrick to go ahead of him. "Let's go. He wants her in the lab ASAP."

Derrick nodded and headed down the passage toward the elevators. So far so good. He wondered what happened to Gage, Iris, and Dr. Rice. Using his enhanced senses, he tried to locate Dr. Rice's mind. He wasn't skilled at this part of being a host, but she had to be close by. *Dr. Rice, if you can hear me, we could use some help.*

He waited for a response, but none came. Maybe

he hadn't done it right or she was no longer in the building. He hoisted Sloan higher in his arms and got into the elevator with the guards. This was going to take some finagling, but his enhanced mind was more than up for the challenge.

THE LAB WAS similar to Dr. Rice's but on a much grander scale. Massive storage freezers lined the walls, and at least a dozen work stations with high tech microscopes and robotic manipulators sat on counters. At the center of the room was a large desk. Max was seated at it, and in front of him lay a syringe.

Derrick tightened his grip on Sloan protectively. She stirred but didn't open her eyes.

Max stood, his expression changing from triumph to concern. "What happened to her?"

The guard who'd communicated with Max earlier stepped forward. "Sir, we found them hiding in a storage closet."

"Fine. Wait outside please," Max said to the guards, glaring at Derrick. After they left, he asked, "Why is she unconscious?"

"I bonded her." Derrick kept his voice even and his eyes on Max. "It takes a toll on your body. But you wouldn't know how that feels."

"How?" Max narrowed his eyes. "You don't have access to the specimens."

Derrick's lip twitched. "The old-fashioned way."

"Here?" Max shook his head. "In a closet?"

Derrick shrugged.

"This is why I don't take on high school interns. You're reckless." Max frowned, irritation rolling off him. "Why would you do this? The future of the human race is at stake."

Derrick glanced down at Sloan. Her dark hair cascaded over his arm, and her face was nestled against his chest. She was so beautiful. He'd do anything to protect her.

"Because I love her," he said simply.

He thought he saw a hint of a smile cross her lips.

Max groaned, glancing at the syringe. "Just so I wouldn't test this on her?"

Derrick nodded. "That's right."

"I don't think you realize how important this work is. Speciation has already happened. If we don't solve the compatibility issue, my kind will go extinct. And by my kind, I mean your friends, your parents, and your brother."

Derrick hadn't thought about his relationship with his family now that he was a host. Will said he had time so he didn't need to make any decisions right away. But the one thing he was sure of was that he would protect them with his life. "Do you really think testing experimental drugs on people without their consent is the way to do it?"

"You're not seeing the big picture. Hosts will eventually wipe out non-hosts. That's just the reality of the situation. If only a few people have to be sacrificed for billions, why wouldn't I?"

Max's assertion rolled around in Derrick's head. On one hand, what he said made statistical sense. If he did have the capability to solve the problem, the proportion of failed attempts compared to the population of the world was reasonable. But they were talking about human beings here. The error in Max's logic was that his assumptions about hosts were unfounded. Derrick couldn't really put it into words, but he was more empathetic of other people now than he was before. So far, that was all he'd sensed from the other hosts he'd met too. Well, besides Malcolm.

"You're wrong about hosts," Derrick said. "I'm new, and already my sense of compassion is stronger than ever. Hosts want to solve the compatibility issue just as much as you do. If anything, chondria make us more human."

Before Max could reply, an alarm sounded.

Derrick readjusted Sloan in his arms. His plan was working perfectly.

The guards came back into the lab. "Sir, the police are here and trying to access the lower levels. What are your orders?"

"Damn it." Max grabbed the syringe from the desk and placed it in the interior pocket of his suit jacket. "Escort these two out." Max walked over to Derrick and grabbed his arm. "This conversation isn't over."

"Yes, it is." Derrick held Sloan tightly to him.

Max hurried out of the lab.

He wasn't sure what Max intended to say to the police, but his only goal was to get above ground and the hell out of here. *Hang on, Sloan. We're almost clear.*

Flashing red lights blinded him momentarily when he entered the passageway. The siren was much louder too. He followed the guards to the elevators. One of the guards pressed the first floor button, and they headed up. They weren't safe yet, but any movement upward was progress.

The doors opened to the lobby, crawling with cops. Derrick had a split second of déjà vu. Not too long ago, he'd witnessed a similar scene when they'd rescued Adam from this place. Standing by the exit doors was Dr. Rice, Gage, and Iris. He took a deep breath and headed for them, separating himself from the Bio-Core guards.

"Thanks for calling the police," Derrick said to Gage.

"Sure. So, are you like me?" Gage asked, his eyes bright with hope.

Derrick had sent him the message from the bowels of the facility because they were best friends and Gage's telepathy was beyond strong. "I'm afraid not."

Gage nodded and looked down, his optimism gone. Being different had to be lonely.

My abilities are different from yours, Derrick thought to him. *I'll explain later.*

He looked back at Derrick, a smile returning.

"What happened to her?" Dr. Rice asked, deep concern in her eyes.

Derrick looked back to see where the guards were. They'd been cut off by a few police officers asking questions, but they were still eyeing him and Sloan.

"Outside," he said.

The group followed him out of the building. The storm had abated, leaving downed tree branches scattered around the parking lot. Mugginess hung in the air.

He sighed in relief. His plan worked.

Derrick leaned down and kissed Sloan. "All clear."

She opened her eyes and smiled up at him, not a hint of chondria in her irises. Although, he hoped she wanted to remedy that soon. "You were brilliant."

He dropped her to her able feet and rubbed his sore arms. "You're heavy."

"Then I guess it's a good thing you love me." She stretched her arms above her head.

"True."

Dr. Rice nodded at him, smiling. "Very nice. I was worried there for a moment."

Iris shook her head. "Would someone please tell me what is going on?"

"Absolutely," Sloan said. "But first, can we please get the hell out of here?"

"Not so fast," Sheriff Grayson said from behind them.

30

A STATION VISIT

Derrick

D errick and Sloan rode through town in the back of a police squad car. Gage and Iris were in another, headed to the Ashwater police station. The storm had taken its toll on the trees lining Main Street. Branches were split, and some of the smaller trees had been uprooted, lying on their sides like leafy corpses. Miraculously, the diner was unaffected, apart from some trash strewn about the parking lot. Gage had texted him that his house, up near the top of the mountain, had a few broken windows.

The last place Derrick felt like being was at a police station. But since Mac Grayson found them at the scene of an investigation once again, they'd earned their trip uptown. Besides, they were the only ones who knew Max Roberts and Steel were to blame for the illegal drugs and overdoses.

He swore under his breath. His parents were not

going to be happy picking him up. Now Luke will be the 'good one.'

The squad car pulled into a spot outside the station.

Sloan's phone buzzed. "Finally, this thing works when I'm busy?" She put the phone to her ear. "Luke? What's up?" She glanced at Derrick, her eyebrows knitted together, and she quickly turned toward the side window. "Uh, okay. But—" She paused. "Fine, just don't do anything. I gotta go."

"What did Luke want?" he asked.

"It's not important." The door opened, and Sloan got out.

Derrick narrowed his eyes. Sloan and Luke got into plenty of messes growing up. *What are you two up to?*

Inside, Gage and Iris sat on a bench, looking annoyed. Will and a tall man in a black suit that Derrick didn't recognize were also there. The Suit wore a stoic expression bordering on a scowl.

Will approached them. "Are you guys okay?"

"Yeah," Derrick said. "What happened with Malcolm?"

"Adam took care of him."

"Is he—" Sloan started.

Will shook his head and whispered, "No, we don't kill our kind—or any kind, for that matter."

"Oh." Sloan yawned and looked around.

Derrick put his arm around her, and she laid her head on his shoulder. He wanted nothing more than to take her home so she could get some rest. His chondria took care of his fatigue.

"So, you two…" Will arched an eyebrow.

Before he could say more, The Suit cleared his throat. Will glanced back at him and nodded.

"Another time," Will said to Derrick and Sloan.

Sheriff Grayson was at the center of the loud, bustling station, barking orders to his deputies. He looked tired and overwhelmed. Between the call to Bio-Core and calls from the storm, Ashwater's finest were stretched to the limit. When Mac spotted them, he waved them toward his office.

Will grabbed Derrick's arm. *Don't say anything about Malcolm to anyone. Adam wiped his memory files. So not him either.*

Understood, Derrick thought back.

Derrick squeezed Sloan's hand and whispered, "Nothing about Malcolm."

She nodded.

When they were all seated in the office, Sheriff Grayson said, "I've got my hands full tonight, so let's cut to the chase. What were you kids doing at Bio-Core in the middle of a storm?"

"Sheriff Grayson, you've got the wrong man under arrest. Mr. Garcia had nothing to do with the illegal drugs and overdoses. The man you're looking for is Bio-Core's CEO, Max Roberts." Derrick leaned forward. "And Steel Strickland is involved too. He was the one who drugged me at Purgatory."

"Or not." Sheriff Grayson leaned back in his chair and crossed his arms. "I can wait all night for the answer to my question."

Derrick frowned. *What? I thought we were cutting to the chase?*

"It's my fault." Sloan scooted forward in her seat. "I wanted to see where Derrick worked."

"In the middle of a storm?" Sheriff Grayson asked, unmoving.

"It was a little rain. What's the big deal?" Sloan shrugged.

"Okay." Sheriff Grayson shook his head. "The worst storm Ashwater has seen in over a decade and you're telling me that it was a little rain." He leaned forward and put his elbows on his desk. "Now, what's this about Max Roberts and Steel Strickland?"

"They are the ones behind the illegal drugs," Derrick said.

"I assume you have proof of this?" Sheriff Grayson raised his eyebrows.

"He admitted it to us tonight." Derrick glanced at Sloan, who nodded. "You have to arrest him."

"I'll take that as a no. Do you perhaps have a motive?"

"Um, I'm not sure," Derrick replied. The motive would expose him and Will as hosts.

Sheriff Grayson looked between him and Sloan. A moment passed, but it felt like an eternity. "Okay, look, I'm going to level with you. There is solid evidence Garcia was the one doing this. I'm not going to go after the CEO of Bio-Core with the word of two kids and no evidence."

"But it's the truth," Sloan said.

"Wait a minute," Derrick said. "Dr. Rice can back

this up. He was the one who attacked her." Come to think of it, where was she? She'd been with them outside the facility.

"All right." Sheriff Grayson picked up his desk phone. "Who brought Dr. Rice in?" He hung up and looked back at Derrick and Sloan. "She asked to make a stop at her lab at Bio-Core. She'll be in shortly. Now what about Steel Strickland? That's Gage's brother, right?"

Derrick opened his mouth to explain, but Sloan grazed his forearm.

"Let's just deal with one bad guy at a time, okay?" she said.

What was she doing? He wanted Steel out of their lives and behind bars as soon as possible. He could still be after her.

"I think that's smart," Sheriff Grayson said. "Is there anything else you two would like to share?"

"Nope. That's it." Sloan smiled. "Are we free to go?"

Derrick stared at her. Why was she so dismissive of Steel?

"Sure. I believe both your parents are here. They're taking care of your fines," Sheriff Grayson said.

"For what?" Sloan asked, defiantly.

"You violated the shelter in place order."

Derrick and Sloan frowned at each other. Their parents were going to be pissed.

Sloan

It was time to face the music. Sloan had a knot the size of a cantaloupe in her stomach. As she left Sheriff Grayson's office, a river of memories from her childhood came rushing back. Like the time she broke the most expensive bong in her parents' store. That was when she learned about the properties of glass. Or the time she coated their kitchen with green goo. How was she supposed to know hot liquids didn't work in a blender like cold ones?

Her mom appeared from the other side of the station. Her eyes were as serious as a heart attack. If she was mad, Dad would be livid. She glanced at Derrick.

"Good luck," he said, squeezing her hand.

"You too." She got up from the bench where they waited and went to her mom.

"I'm so mad at you," her mom said.

"I know." Sloan looked down at her feet.

Then her mom's arms were around her. "But I'm glad you're all right."

Sloan hugged her back. Tears pricked at her eyes as the weight of what she'd endured surfaced. She'd been set up, stalked, attacked, and hunted, and she couldn't breathe a word of it to her parents.

Instead she simply said, "I'm sorry."

"Come on. Let's go home. Your dad is waiting in the car." Sloan's mom turned them toward the door. "I'd keep your mouth zipped if I were you."

Sloan waved at Derrick. She hoped that he faired okay with his parents.

· · ·

ONCE SHE WAS HOME, she took a long, hot shower and curled up in her bed with Buck. He gave her a few licks on the cheek and settled down. As she stroked his fur, visions from the evening resurfaced.

There was one in particular she couldn't get out of her mind. It happened in a closet with a boy who loved her. Her heart swelled. The feeling was mutual. At the time, she was totally ready for him to bond her.

But he was so adamant that they wait. So confident that he could get them out without endangering her.

Her phone dinged twice, as two messages battled for her attention.

DERRICK: What did my brother say to you?

LUKE: Don't tell Derrick about Steel.

Oh crap. Sloan bit her lip. Her phone dinged some more.

DERRICK: ?

LUKE: 🙏

Sloan sighed and stared up at her ceiling. She had those glow-in-the-dark stars stuck up there. On one hand, Derrick was completely honest with her about everything. She should be too. But she owed Luke. He was still her best friend, and she'd lied to him.

This was a mess.

Luke confronted Steel about drugging Derrick at Purgatory. He said Steel was sorry and swore he was washing his hands of Bio-Core. She thought Steel was full of shit, but for some reason, Luke believed him and wanted to give him a second chance because of his difficult childhood.

Try more like fourth or fifth chance, and who didn't have a difficult childhood?

Well, Mazy probably didn't.

She groaned. This whole situation was making her head swim. So, she responded to them in the only way she knew how—she turned off her light and went to sleep.

31

GRADUATION

Sloan

Sloan didn't know how they did it, but they all made it to graduation in one piece. Even Gage, who she thought would have to take summer school, had caught up in time for graduation. She looked out across the lawn behind the school, her graduation gown draped over her arm.

Their class was small compared to others, but the school still set up a few hundred chairs for the graduating class and families. Mr. Garcia was there with a camera and tripod, deciding where to best set up. Since his release from custody after Dr. Rice testified it was Max Roberts who'd attacked her, he'd been nothing but a model teacher.

Too bad that weasel, Max, had left the country before he could be arrested.

"The Time of My Life" from *Dirty Dancing* wafted

toward her, making her smile. She didn't need to turn around to know Adam and Evie had joined her.

"Hilarious, Adam," Sloan said.

"He's definitely something." Evie sidled next to her. "So, are we allowed to sit together?"

"I think so." Sloan glanced at her friends. Evie had added sparkles to the corners of her charcoaled eyes, and Adam had gotten a haircut.

"Love your eyes, Evie," Sloan said. "Looking good, Adam."

"Thanks," Evie said. "You clean up nice too."

Adam smiled and bobbed his head to the music.

Up on stage, Mazy paced, her gaze serious as she mouthed her speech. Her gown was zipped up, and her cap perfectly sat on her head with bobby pins. She'd been practicing her speech in front of Sloan for the last two weeks. Sloan practically had the damn thing memorized too. But listening to Mazy's speech ten thousand times was a small price to pay.

It was because of Mazy that Sloan had finally gotten into Edgewood. A letter came a week ago that she'd been moved from deferred to accepted. She smiled. Things were looking up.

"You got this," she yelled to Mazy.

Mazy smiled and gave her a thumbs-up.

"Everything all set at Jack's?" Sloan asked Adam. "Mazy will lose her shit if anything goes wrong with the graduation party."

"Don't worry," Adam said. "Jack and Daisy have everything under control."

Before Sloan could reply, hands were around her waist, holding her tight.

Derrick.

"Hello, gorgeous," he said.

"Hi," she replied, leaning against him.

Luke, Gage, and Iris were with him. Gage tilted his head at Adam. "Senior year was definitely something, but I don't know if it was the time of our lives."

"It was the time of my life." Iris smiled up at him.

"Fair enough." He kissed her, his lips lingering afterwards.

These two...

"All right, keep it in your pants," Sloan said. "This is no time for a quickie in the bushes. Mazy needs us."

Everyone laughed.

"You and Mazy have gotten close, huh?" Gage asked Sloan.

"Yep. We're tight."

Gage nodded. "All right, let's do this."

Derrick

Mazy's graduation speech was on point. She would make an excellent motivational speaker or politician.

After they'd all received their diplomas, Sloan left with Mazy and Evie to change before heading over to Jack's, so Derrick rode with Gage. Luke said he had a stop to make too. Things had been tense between him and his brother, and it wasn't because of Sloan anymore. Now it was because his bleeding-heart brother had started a friendship with Steel. Luke swore that he had changed.

But it would take a lot more than Steel's word for Derrick to let his guard down. Steel was trouble. He just hoped Steel didn't take his brother down with him.

There was yet to be an announcement about a new CEO at Bio-Core after Max's departure, but Derrick was happy he could keep his internship. Now that he'd graduated, it looked promising that his position would turn into a full-time job. Rumors had spread that Raj was in league for the CEO position. He didn't know what that would mean for his team, but between him and Jasmine, they could handle it.

They'd gotten the procedure down to a fifty percent success rate—a flip of a coin. They were terrible odds, considering it meant success or death. What person would ever agree to that? But he had confidence in himself and his team that they would get there.

Gage found a spot in front of Jack's Arcade. Inside, the lights were brighter than usual. Honeycomb tissue-paper decorations and streamers hung from the ceiling and games. Banquet tables were set up with food from the diner. Daisy, wanting to contribute, also created a tower of tots with a cheese fountain. Jack had put on a polo and did his best to tuck his shirt into his jeans. He was at the door, greeting kids as they came inside. Adam was by the jukebox bobbing his head as "Forever Young" by Alphaville played. All in all, the place felt festive.

Derrick's chondria quickened inside his body as Will arrived. He'd learned that his and Payton's strain of chondria was a cousin to Will's. It made them family in a weird host way.

"Wow, the place looks great," Will said.

"Hey." Derrick grasped his hand and smiled. "You're still a year away from graduating, you know."

"Ha ha." Will smiled. "I just wanted to stop by and say hi. I won't encroach on your day."

"I don't think anyone will mind."

"I wanted to thank you for your discretion about everything. I know it's been a lot to handle."

"No worries. I understand why it's necessary." Derrick had another thought. One that had been on his mind for a while. "Don't you think it's odd that there are so many potential hosts in Ashwater?"

Will arched an eyebrow and grinned slyly. "Yes, we do. It's no coincidence that one of the leading biomedical facilities is located here. We had a long-standing relationship with Sam Strickland for a long time. Some of our best host scientists are connected to Bio-Core to investigate the anomaly. In fact, I believe you know one of them."

Derrick's lips parted as his enhanced brain connected the dots. "Oh, that's what Payton is doing. She's trying to figure out if there is an environmental connection to potential hosts in Ashwater."

Will nodded. "She's one of our best."

The door to Jack's opened, and Will waved. "Hey, Sloan."

Derrick's heart skipped a beat at the mention of her

name. He'd always had a physical response when she was near, but ever since becoming a host, it was magnified, like she was the center of his universe. He smiled at her. She wore a short, summery dress, and her long, dark hair was down. Mazy and Evie were behind her.

Sloan smiled back and said something to Mazy and Evie before heading over to him and Will. "Hey, guys."

"Hi." Derrick drew her into an embrace. He could feel every inch of the small of her back through the thin material. He liked this dress.

"Watch it, handsy." She arched an eyebrow, making him laugh. "Save some for later."

"Okay, I will." Derrick released her but kept his arm around her.

She turned to Will. "Hey, thanks for introducing me to your friend, Sophia. She's super cool."

"I thought you two might get along," Will said.

"Yeah, we really connected. Although, she's got a huge crush on you. You know that, right?"

Will shrugged. "Yeah. We're just friends."

"If you say so. But she's hot. That's all I'm saying." She made a pouty face at Derrick. "Not as hot as you though."

"I'm sure." Derrick squeezed her middle, reminding him of the first time he'd put his arm around her at the disc golf course.

"All right," Will said. "I'll leave you to your party. I've got a plane to catch."

"You're not going to spend your senior year here?" Derrick asked.

"Nope. I've got another year to go as a junior." Will smiled and straightened his suit jacket. "Later."

After he left, Derrick turned Sloan toward him. "Speaking of the future, what are you going to major in at Edgewood?"

A brilliant amethyst sparkle illuminated her brown eyes. "I'm thinking public relations. I have a way with people, don't you think?"

Derrick's pulse quickened. He kissed her gently then whispered, "Yes, you do."

EPILOGUE

Luke

A girl with blond hair. That was the last thing he remembered. Or had he imagined her? He couldn't move, let alone feel his arms and legs. Maybe he wasn't even conscious. Was this a dream? He inhaled a familiar scent but couldn't place it.

His brain was working for now, trying to figure out how he ended up like this. He'd stopped by the cabin to tell Steel his time at the cabin was over—Sloan was done. But Steel wasn't there. His things were, but he wasn't.

Then he saw her. Out the window. A girl with long hair the color of sand was standing by the tree line. Her back was to him, but she was familiar.

Then all hell broke loose.

There was an explosion, and everything around him collapsed.

He opened his eyes, trying to find the light, but

there was only black. His body, shrouded in it. He didn't know how long he'd been here or if he'd ever see light again.

Like a whisper in the wind, someone called his name. "Luke...where are you?"

Luke opened his mouth, but nothing came out. His mouth was so dry, it felt like his voice was stuck in his throat. He licked at his lips, but his tongue was like sandpaper. A small gurgle was all he could manage.

"Luke! Hang on."

He closed his eyes, his mind wanting to slip back into the void. Then something shifted above him. He knew he didn't have much longer in the state he was in. He heard what sounded like rocks being tossed and moved aside. Someone was digging him out.

Hang on a little while longer. They're close.

His chest felt lighter and lighter. Finally, bright light hit his eyes as the last piece of debris was lifted from his tomb.

A hand reached for him.

He tried to move his arm but couldn't.

"I got you," someone said, wrenching him free.

It was as if he were weightless in space. No pain, nothing.

His final thought before succumbing to the darkness his mind so desperately craved was that he recognized the familiar scent—oranges.

READ ON FOR WILL'S STORY...

*FIREFLIES TRILOGY, The adventure that
started it all. MELISSA KOBERLEIN*

I've been tracking humans my entire life. While each time is different, it's always the same rush.

Pennsylvania is unseasonably warm this April. I reach for an evergreen branch, the sharp needles pricking at my palm. It has been too long since I've been here. I close my eyes, breathing deeply the calming earthy scents of my home woods: pine, cedar, grass, algae on some rocks of a nearby stream, fresh water trickling down, and a distance away, violet wild flowers. Focused and determined, I open my eyes, smiling eagerly.

I'll find my quarry.

I reach down and press my palm to the ground. Images pass through my mind like frames in a movie. Two girls passed through here, one brunette, one blonde, both searching for something…another girl, a friend. They're local high school students about the same age as me, on a trail cleanup detail. The girl they're searching for has fallen into a ravine. She's afraid, but not seriously hurt.

Standing, I begin my hike, following the two girls in search of their friend. Five hundred feet up the trail, I catch up to them. Quickly, I hide behind a tree, my t-shirt scraping the bark.

It's her. The one I've been tracking. I've got to mark her to let the others know she's mine. Slowly, as if not by my own will, I step back onto the path to get a better look. She's navigating the trail as if she were born to hike, reassuring and leading the girl behind her. I feel an instant pull as my heart pounds from being this close to her. My instinct is to approach her now, but that would be foolish. I need to wait for the perfect time. Besides, she's focused on her lost friend. In fact, she's almost to the top of the ravine.

I consider yelling up to them, when she stops and turns toward me. Instinctively, I duck back behind the tree just in time, each breath coming fast and furious. I lean my head against the tree, closing my eyes, concentrating. She knows I'm here.

The brunette says, "What's up, Marley?"

"I thought I saw something," the blonde replies.

"I'm sure it's probably some other kids looking for Becca," the dark-haired girl says.

The blonde's name is Marley, and her senses are impeccable for a human.

They continue moving up the trail as I silently follow. I can't lose sight of her, not even for a second.

I want this one, and no one is going to take her from me.

ABOUT THE AUTHOR

Melissa Koberlein is a professor of communication and publishing in eastern Pennsylvania where she lives with her husband and their two daughters. She enjoys reading and writing about the spectacular, sci-fi, technology, and romance. Her passion for stories comes from an imaginative childhood where every day ended with a book. *Ashwater* is her newest young adult series. You can read her first series, *Fireflies*, available from Amazon and other retail outlets.

facebook.com/mekoberlein

twitter.com/melkoberlein

instagram.com/melkoberlein

ALSO BY MELISSA KOBERLEIN

"Raven's Sphere will make you happy, sad and laugh the entire book. This is a must read and a true page turner."

"A mix of Twilight and I am Number Four, the twist at the end was unpredictable, making it a good turn adding spice and intrigue to the plot." -Review from Writer's Digest